FLIGHT OF THE BAT

Flight of the Bat

By Donald Gordon

Author of *Star-Raker*

WILLIAM MORROW AND COMPANY
New York, 1964

They have sown the wind, and they shall reap the whirlwind.

Hosea VIII, 7

1

The man lay motionless in the snow. He was dressed entirely in white: white boots, white ski trousers, white anorak drawn up over his head. There was white anti-sunburn cream on his face. In his hands were white Zeiss Ikon binoculars, focused on the rocket site in the hollow of the hills.

He had been watching the rocket site for eight hours now, and he was exhausted and very cold.

The missile gantries and their host of ancillaries rose darkly out of the snow less than three miles from where the man lay hidden. In good visibility he could have seen them quite clearly. But visibility was not good. For it was dawn; over the Murmansk peninsula mist was being drawn skyward by the warmth of the rising sun, and in every direction coils of white were writhing up from the tundra like smoke from a forest fire. The man cursed softly. He shifted his binoculars a little, trying to focus first on the dishlike webs of the radar antennae, then on the tall umbilical servicing towers. But the mist eddied this way and that, in the cold air his breath condensed on the lens of the binoculars and his eyes watered with strain and kept slipping out of focus. This is no good, he thought. I'll rest five minutes, then look again. He put his binoculars down, shut his eyes and rested his face in the crook of his arm.

This is a crazy setup, he thought. In the 1960's a professional spy shouldn't be lurking in a snow hide; he should have his feet up in a centrally heated office, with the top-secret filing cabinets all neatly labeled in front of him. That, at any rate, was the way the Russians worked it—there wasn't a rocket site in the British Isles, it was said, or for that matter an R.A.F. station or a nuclear research establishment, which didn't have its Russian agent comfortably ensconced in some key position. It was very different, wasn't it, for those who spied for the West? They, as he knew all too well, were condemned to pose as tourists or to lurk like the heroes of some melodramatic film in snow hide or coniferous forest. *C'est magnifique,* he thought, *mais ce n'est pas la guerre.*

He sighed, polished his binoculars and raised them again to the gantries and domes of the rocket site.

The mist was dispersing a little now as the sun gained strength, and soon with every passing minute the man was able to see more clearly. He scanned his objective methodically, from left to right. First, the living quarters of the technicians and security guards. There were a lot of lights there; they glowed through the mist like daubs of phosphorescent butter, dancing, shimmering, congealing one with another, reflecting on the snow and making it difficult for him to judge whether there were more lights than was normal—but he thought there probably were. His binoculars moved on to the radar antennae. All was quiet there. The radar antennae lay lifeless, like monsters from an alien world, their skeleton ribs rising darkly out of the snow: in the foreground the web-shaped rondures seeming to invite the very stars to fall into their nets, in the background the questing prongs of the long-range detectors pointing inquir-

8

ingly into space. There's nothing, he thought, to interest me there.

It was a different story a little to the right. For there, among the gantries, railway tracks and servicing towers of the launching area, he could see signs of activity.

His interest quickened. So there *had* been something going on in the night. Maybe Intelligence had been right. Maybe he was on to something—something important. He wiped the condensation off his binoculars and focused them with the greatest care on the launching area.

It was difficult at first to see exactly what was going on. But with the sun gaining strength and the mist thinning out, the scene in front of him began to take gradual shape. He craned forward eagerly.

But when at last, after much straining of his eyes and much wiping of his binoculars, he was able to get the picture clear, he felt no elation: only a wave of almost pathological fear.

For there was no doubt about what was happening. Four intercontinental rockets were being prepared for firing.

And the Murmansk site, he knew, was never used for test or experiment.

The rockets meant business.

So the rumors had been true. He shut his eyes. He felt physically sick. I wonder, he thought, where those four are going to land. Oh, God, he thought, let it be anywhere on earth except the northwest coast of Scotland. He passed a hand over his eyes and wished that he weren't so cold and tired, that his binoculars were more powerful and wouldn't keep steaming up, that Intelligence had got someone *inside* the rocket base instead of having to rely on the cloak-and-dagger methods of another war and age. If only, he thought, I could get a better view of the rockets; if only I could see the casings; that would give me a clue as to when they'll be

9

fired. He found himself edging forward—as though the few extra inches would improve his view! He raised his binoculars again.

The mist was lifting rapidly now and overhead were patches of cobalt sky, in one of which Venus the morning star shone as palely delicate as a Christmas rose. The sun on his shoulders was warm. It's turning into a lovely morning, he thought. I wonder if it's a lovely morning in Wester Ross. If it is, Jeannie'll be up on the hills with one of the dogs, with the frosted bracken crisp under her feet and, far beneath her, tide rips swirling among the islands of the Hebrides like ink spilled into the sea, and I wish to God I were with her. He stiffened as the casing of the nearest rocket came suddenly into focus.

Through the last of the disappearing eddies of gray the metal casing shone strangely luminous, like frosted glass aglint in the sun. He caught his breath. For he knew what caused the luminosity. Hoarfrost. Hoarfrost formed by the condensation of air on a surface that was unbelievably cold. And why was the rocket casing so cold? Why else than because the rocket itself was being filled with liquid oxygen. And liquid oxygen, he knew, was put into a rocket only a matter of hours before it was fired.

So about eleven o'clock on a lovely morning in late October, the Russians were going to launch four intercontinental rockets. And not for a test.

Again the wave of fear swept over him. It came to him that he could well be watching the preparations that would lead to the end of the world: the last suicidal rites of the misnamed Homo sapiens. For several seconds he lay motionless, inert as a bird which watches the approach of a snake in horrified paralysis. Then the urgency of sending back a report got home to him, and he began very carefully to squirm back to the shelter of his snow hide. At the entrance

10

he paused; it occurred to him that he ought to make sure all four rockets were going to be fired. He scanned the gantries methodically, one by one.

The clink of metal came softly over the snow.

He froze. He knew that sound. It was the clink of a gun being cocked. Out of the corner of his eye he saw two shadows, pale and elongated in the path of the rising sun. Russian security guards, he thought. He could see the silhouette of the guns held lightly across their hips.

So this was the end of the road.

As in a dream, when events which seem to take many hours are compressed into a few seconds, so now the man's thoughts kaleidoscoped and concertina-ed in his last brief moment of life.

You fool, he thought; you poor, benighted fool. You knew you were bound to be caught in the end. Why didn't you give up years ago, when you married Jeannie? "Just one more trip, darling," you said, like a traveling salesman caught in the rat race. But it was one more after that, and then one more, and then one more again. And all your yesterdays were wasted in lonely vigils in rain-wet streets, in coding and decoding reports, in inconspicuous comings and goings between the trouble spots of the world. And now there would be no tomorrow. Oh, Jeannie, he thought, what will happen to you now? It's wrong, he told himself, to think of Jeannie. I ought to be thinking of mankind with a capital M, of all the millions of unsuspecting people whose lives will be snuffed out at midday when the Russian rockets land wherever they're going to land. And I ought to be thinking of how to get back a warning. But *how* can I get back a warning? If I make a dive for my gun, they'll kill me. If I could reach my transmitter, I might clamp down on the key; but the transmitter's back in the snow hide. He lay very

11

still. I don't stand a hope in hell, he thought, of getting at the transmitter. But I've got to try.

As one of the shadows moved closer, he started—he hoped realistically. He half scrambled to his feet.

"I am an officer of a light infantry regiment," he began in his best Finnish. "I am lost."

The guards were not impressed. One of them shook his head.

They don't believe me, he thought. There's only one hope. He flung himself backward into the snow hide, his fingers clawing desperately for the key of the transmitter.

The guns clattered briefly.

The bullets hit him across the chest, spinning him around and toppling him backward. For a second he saw the snow-covered hills, the morning star and the four intercontinental rockets spinning around and around like a Catherine wheel. Then a curtain of red fell over his eyes. But his fingers by now had found the key of the transmitter. They closed around it. Tightly. Then the key of the transmitter turned into Jeannie's hand, and he was glad, because for all he cared, mankind with a capital M could fry in the fires of nuclear fission so long as he and Jeannie were able to hold each other's hand. That was what mattered most. And squeezing her hand very tightly, he fell lifeless across the mouth of the snow hide.

After a while the younger of the guards approached the body. He rolled it over, and the first thing he noticed was the hand clenched around the transmitter. Quickly he bent down and pulled the transmitter away.

"Poor devil. He never stood a chance."

The other shrugged. "He was a spy," he said.

The young guard rolled the body over with his foot. "He was also a man."

12

A metallic clattering from the direction of the rocket site made them look up.

The gantries were moving back now on the eight-line railway tracks, leaving the rockets upright on their pedestals. And the rockets were things of unbelievable beauty. They speared the skyline in slim and graceful symmetry, and from their sides sparkling clouds of condensation were falling to the ground like bridal veils. The veils of condensation rose and fell, fell and rose, shimmering in the Arctic sun like trembling fountains of magnesium. Even as the guards watched, a small servicing tower with its "cherry picker" hoist moved up to each of the rockets in turn to make last-minute adjustments.

The older guard kept moistening his lips. "How much longer," he muttered, "before they fire?"

The younger guard looked at his watch. "Less than six hours," he said.

2

The earth rotated. And the morning star which had seen the Soviet rockets filled with oxygen two hours later shone pale over southern England.

Several Londoners that morning noticed the star as they went about their work. A gardener in St. James's Park, lifting dahlias, found that each time he straightened up and reached for his barrow it came swinging into his field of vision; a chauffeur driving along the Bayswater Road found that each time he pulled up at a succession of traffic lights it came to rest in the center of his windshield; and the Prime Minister, reading his morning batch of parliamentary papers, found that each time he looked out of his window the star gleamed at him reproachfully, reminding him that he had less than twenty-four hours in which to cram forty-eight hours of work.

The Prime Minister had a great many papers to read that morning. He was not pleased when his secretary brought in another and laid it beside him in the tray marked URGENT.

"A message for you personally," the secretary said. "Delivered by hand from the Russian Embassy."

The Prime Minister nodded. He finished the report he

14

was reading, then picked up the sheet of paper with its brief message typed neatly in the center. He had no presentiment of fear as he glanced at the message: no premonition of disaster. Why should he? The international situation—dominated by the cold war and the nuclear deterrent—was neither better nor worse than it had been for years; there had been, it was true, a vaguely disquieting report from Intelligence that morning to say that an agent with a wife named Jeannie had got himself shot while trying to pass a message about the Murmansk rocket site, but this the Prime Minister had told himself was no more than one of those little personal tragedies that the cold war was responsible for almost every day in almost every country; and certainly he was in no way prepared for the dozen lines of type which now stared up at him, threatening Armageddon.

My dear Prime Minister:

I am today sending you a communication of the very greatest importance for the future of the world, and I am sending it by rocket.

At 1 P.M. precisely, your time, a harmless rocket containing my communication will arrive in Hyde Park. Kindly give the message contained in this rocket your most careful study.

Similar communications are being delivered at the same time—and by the same method—to Washington, Paris and Bonn.

He read the note twice, from the courteously formal opening right through to the facsimile signature of the Chairman of the Council of Ministers of the U.S.S.R.

Then he sat very still for a long time.

To start with, his thoughts were confused and contradictory: anger (damned cheek, a Soviet rocket landing in the middle of London); impotence (we can't stop it landing; our anti-missile defenses just aren't good enough); relief

15

(at least the Russians can't be thinking of war—if they *were* thinking of war they'd not be sending us notes to put us on the *qui vive*); and bewilderment (but what's the point of it?). Then gradually, as his mind concentrated on the Soviet note to the exclusion of everything else, certain salient facts began to emerge, until at last he was able to see the heart of the matter with sudden and unexpected clarity.

That was his strength, the secret of his success, the key to his power. Most of the time he was happy to drift along with the prevailing current, like a nineteenth-century opportunist riding the tide of *laissez-faire;* but when he was faced with a crisis he measured up to it squarely, honestly and with a peculiar flair for dealing with it in the right (if not always the expected) way. And in times of crisis he kept his own counsel. It would be an oversimplification to say that he didn't trust his colleagues. On technical or specialized matters he sought their advice frequently, but on important issues he preferred his judgment to theirs. That was why, for all his popularity and surface bonhomie, he was a lonely man at heart. And that was why, now, he didn't call an emergency cabinet meeting, but preferred to play alone the hand he had been dealt and make only a handful of personal phone calls.

His first call was to the Home Secretary, to whom he gave brief instructions for the cordoning off of Hyde Park and the alerting of Civil Defense. His second was to the Marshal of the Royal Air Force, Sir Basil Timperley. His instructions were fuller this time: "Alert the anti-missile defenses; get your V-bombers airborne—and any hush-hush planes that can clear the danger area in time; arm the Thors; and do your damnedest to shoot the rocket down, by all means short of nuclear warheads . . ." He made two other calls, then replaced the receiver.

He had spoken with a great show of confidence. But at

16

the back of his mind was a seed of doubt: a seed too terrible for its existence even to be openly acknowledged. What if his judgment, this time, turned out to be at fault? What if this Russian rocket—in spite of the Chairman's assurance—was the real thing?

Yet what can I do? he thought. Eight million people can't clear London in a couple of hours. There's only one thing I *can* do: wait.

He leaned back in his chair and stared out of the window, half expecting to see the morning star. But the morning star was gone—snuffed out as though it had never been. Chilled by a sudden premonition, he shivered.

3

By the time Christabel Barlow was walking across the tarmac to the Bat, the morning star had vanished and the sun was shining weakly out of a mist-hazed sky.

The Bat, one of the first production models of Britain's latest low-level bomber, lay on the hard standing outside its test hangar at Farnborough. She wasn't a beautiful plane—her fuselage was too fat, and her wings too heavy and squat; nor did she fall in line with the conventional trend of aerodynamic design—the larger, slimmer, faster and higher chain of development which had characterized aircraft production since the war. She was in fact something of an oddity, a plane designed to give her maximum performance in the "heavy" air of sea level. But Christabel Barlow, who had worked on the Bat's instruments ever since the first prototype had landed at Farnborough nine months ago, had become exceedingly fond of her.

She clambered into the cockpit, carrying under her arm two small metal boxes which she was careful not to bump. She squirmed under the instrument panel, lay on her back in what she felt sure was a most unladylike position and set to work screwing one of her boxes into the dashboard above her.

18

It was cramped, finicky work. The screws kept falling out before she could tighten them, and rolling perversely under the pilot's seat. More than once Christabel Barlow used a six-letter word that nice girls of twenty-four shouldn't have heard of. But she retrieved the screws, blew the hair out of her eyes and kept on trying. She knew it was important that the box was installed just right.

It was a navigational aid * she was fixing to the instrument panel. The aid *looked* simple: just a box containing microfilms of a series of maps which unwound by remote control as the aircraft flew over the terrain in question and were then projected onto a miniature screen in the instrument panel, thus giving the pilot an accurate picture of the ground beneath and ahead of him. But the 8" x 10" box nevertheless represented one of the most important inventions of Farnborough's Instrument Department, where for the last two years Christabel had worked on research and development. And it *had* to be in position by midday. For the Bat was being test-flown that afternoon. By Squadron Leader Oakman.

Squadron Leader Oakman . . . Christabel's mind shifted from instrument to man: from work to play. For hadn't Squadron Leader Kenneth Oakman—the most eligible bachelor on the airfield—invited her that evening to the station dance? That, she reflected, as she tried for the fourth time to insert a screw into its elusive hole, was one of the nice things about working with the Royal Air Force. One met lots of interesting men.

* A full description of this device appears in Aircraft Engineering No. 392. A further refinement, specially applicable to the low-level bomber, is given in British Patent No. 871,926, which was formerly classified *Secret* by both British and U. S. governments but which has recently been released for open publication.

All her associations had been with the R.A.F. as far back as she could remember.

Her father had been an air marshal: a brilliant man, but far too outspoken and ahead of the times for his service career to be anything but a constant and bitter battle with the forces of the *ancien régime*—a battle in which he had several times avoided court-martial by a hairsbreadth. He had died four years ago, while one of his papers (castigating the service for its failure to replace aircraft with missiles) was being read by the Air Council, and the *ancien régime* had given him a slap-up funeral and heaved a sign of relief. The year he died his daughter took a first in science at Cambridge. She then worked for a year with Mecca Marine (mostly on radar), and was finally offered a first-class job in the Instrument Department of the Royal Aircraft Establishment at Farnborough. It wasn't an easy job, but she held it down; for she had inherited her father's brilliance. Unfortunately she'd also inherited most of his faults: intolerance, impatience and a positively unholy delight in tilting at sacred cows. It all showed in her face; the shock of unruly auburn hair, the mocking bright green eyes, the too-large mouth that could thin in a moment to an obstinate slit, the uptilted nose and the defiant chin. It was an attractive face—as men were quick to notice. It could almost, in an unusual sort of way, have been a beautiful face if only it hadn't been so wholly lacking in repose and marred so much of the time by an aura of discontent.

But the discontent was veiled now. The screw had found its hole and the little black box was held in place. She gave a sigh of relief—the moving map would be installed in time for its air test. And that, she reflected as she tightened up the screws, was another nice thing about working with the R.A.F.: one got plenty of opportunity for flying.

She'd done a great deal of flying in the last nine months,

for she had been a key member in the Bat's navigational tests. It saddened her to think that the Bat was nearly operational now, and that the tests would soon be over—though of course, she told herself, there'll be other tests on other planes . . . She straightened her legs and settled herself as comfortably as she could on the floor of the cockpit.

Footsteps on the tarmac: toecaps scrabbling up the fuselage: a man's shadow blocking out the light, and an amused voice which she recognized as Kenneth Oakman's.

"Ah, I'd know those legs anywhere!"

She shifted a couple of screws from between her teeth and lay looking up at him.

"Oh, sir," she said, "you have me at a disadvantage!"

He half squatted on the edge of the pilot's seat. "Don't let me interrupt you, Miss Barlow." His voice was deliberately flat. "Just carry on as if I weren't here."

She took the screws out of her mouth. "For a front-row seat," she said, "you have to pay. Hold these."

For a while they worked in silence, he holding the screws and inserting them one at a time into the holes already drilled in the instrument panel and she using her screwdriver to tighten them. Before long the aid was firmly in place.

She squirmed out then from under the dashboard, bringing with her a plethora of cables and leads which she began to connect up to her second box—a small battery-energized test set.

"Now let's see if my toy's going to work," she said.

"Actually there's no need for a ground check," he said. "The flight's off."

"What!"

"The starboard generator's u/s. Maintenance just told me."

Her lips thinned. "Now isn't that just fine!" She brushed the hair angrily out of her eyes. "I spend half the morning splayed out on my back like a beetle, breaking my finger-nails, getting my hair filthy with grease, then you come and say that for all the good I've done I might as well have stayed in bed."

"I'm sorry, Christabel." His voice was reasonable. "I didn't break the generator on purpose, you know."

The mildness of his reply took the wind out of her sails. Her anger, as suddenly as it had flared up, weakened and died. She picked up the festoons of cable.

"Damn it," she said. "But I'd better test."

"I'll give you a hand."

They crawled back to the navigator's seat and Oakman fed Christabel the leads one at a time, while she plugged them carefully into her test equipment.

Even inside the plane, noise from the airfield came through to them from time to time. Footsteps on the tarmac, the screech of welding from a nearby hangar, the occasional blare of the tannoy and once or twice the whine of jets as aircraft taxied past on their way to the end of the runway. After a while Christabel looked at her watch: half past eleven. We'll be finished, she thought, by midday.

The tannoy clicked. They could hear the whistling puff of the announcer's breath as he blew on the microphone to test it. They could hear the sudden increase in atmospherics as he thumbed the volume to maximum.

"Attention, please!" The raucous voice came through to them loud and clear even in the interior of the plane. "All heads of department are required at once in the director's office. All pilots to report immediately to Flying Control. I say again. All heads of department . . ."

Their eyes met—in hers, bewilderment; in his, fear, quickly veiled.

She smiled. "Somebody," she said, "must have been a *very* naughty boy."

22

Her smile wasn't answered. He slid quickly out of the aircraft. "Stay here, Christabel, till I get back."

She watched him run down the taxi track. She watched him jump into his staff car and hurtle off in the direction of Flying Control. In less than half a minute he was out of sight.

She shrugged, vaguely put out by such an unexpected turn of events. But whatever the flap is, she thought, *I* can't do anything about it. She crawled back to the navigator's seat, plugged in the last couple of leads and started her test.

The maps had barely begun to move across the screen when she heard footsteps on the tarmac, coming nearer—fast. But he can't be back already, she thought. She squirmed her way to the cockpit and, looking out, saw two mechanics running toward the plane. While still some distance away one of them shouted at her.

"Hop out, miss. Quick. We're starting up."

"But you can't. This one's u/s."

They came to a halt beneath her, panting, harassed and clearly somewhat perplexed.

"Know what the trouble is?"

"Starboard generator, I think."

"If that's all, we'll start her. Hop out pronto."

She slid obediently to the ground. Something was going on that she neither liked nor understood. Quite suddenly aircraft were starting up all around her; the whine of their jets rose like a discordant wail into the startled sky. Staff cars and maintenance crew were scurrying about like ants. A V-bomber and a pair of Scimitars came zigzagging down the taxi track; and a Bat—sister plane to Oakman's—took off in a deafening crescendo of sound. What on earth, she thought, can be up?

Suddenly, quite out of the blue, the words of the Defense Minister flashed through her mind: "In the event of nuclear

23

attack by rocket, the warning period will be roughly four and a half minutes." Now, Christabel Barlow, she rebuked herself, what a nervous little mouse you are to think of a thing like that. But her eyes, as she watched Oakman's aircraft start up, were troubled.

Her thoughts were broken by a shout from one of the mechanics. "Hey, miss! You know enough to keep this one running?"

"Sure."

For a moment the man peered at her doubtfully, then his face broke into a smile. "Miss Barlow, isn't it?"

She nodded.

"All right, ma'am"—he slid down to the tarmac—"hop in. But don't go trying to take off."

Before she could answer, the two mechanics had gone, running as though the devil himself were after them toward the nearest Canberra.

She clambered into the cockpit and sat on the very edge of the pilot's seat, listening to the whine of the jets.

Aircraft were passing her now in a steady stream, zigzagging fast down the taxi track and taking off in quick succession. She shivered. She felt like one who sees her fellow passengers abandon a sinking ship while she is forced to stand by and watch. She wished Oakman would hurry.

It seemed hours (but was in fact less than five minutes) before a car pulled up with a screech of brakes and out tumbled not only Oakman but also his navigator, Major Polhill of the United States Air Force. She peered out of the cockpit, uncertain what to do. Were they going to take off? Did they want her with them? And what should she do with her test gear, now linked up to the moving map?

"Stay in," Oakman shouted. "We want you with us."

What with the whine of their jets and the scream of a Scimitar taking off, she wasn't sure that she'd heard right.

24

"What?"

"Get into the back."

"But I've no kit!"

She could sense his impatience. She could see his mouth opening and shutting, but his words were whisked away in the slip stream. Then Polhill came climbing up the fuselage. He spoke quietly and reassuringly.

"Emergency test, Christabel. Get into the back fast. Fix the moving map, and don't ask questions."

There were any number of questions she *wanted* to ask. But she realized this wasn't the time. She nodded and disappeared into the maw of the plane like a rabbit into its burrow.

The Bat had been designed as a two-seater, with pilot and navigator-cum-engineer sitting side by side. But there was also a small and cramped third seat in the rear (sandwiched between the Doppler and the air-conditioning plant) which could be used to accommodate a second navigator. It was this seat which Christabel crawled to. And even before she was strapped in, the Bat began to move, taxiing fast along the perimeter. Before changing over the leads from test box to inertial navigator, she plugged in her intercom, anxious to hear what the others were saying.

Polhill was running through the take-off check list.

"Oil pressures normal.

"Oil and jet pipe temperatures normal.

"Generators— Say, Kenneth! Port generator's O.K., but the starboard's recordin' zero."

"It's u/s. But even if both pack up we can fly visually."

"Hmmm! The Lord help us if the weather closes in! . . . Brake pressures normal . . ."

By the time Polhill had worked through the check list, Oakman was ready for take-off. He lined up carefully—he was far too good and too experienced a pilot to be panicked into error. A quick look behind him: nothing coming in to land. A quick look at the airfield: the familiar outline of hangars, offices and laboratories dogtoothing the horizon. A quick look at the sun: a blood-red disc petrified like the flower of some exotic cactus into the frozen desert of the sky. Then he was concentrating on what lay ahead: the two-and-a-quarter-mile strip of concrete waiting to spring-board him into the sky. Brakes off. Throttles gently forward. The smell of kerosene, the vibration, the crescendo of sound, the surge of acceleration as the Bat gathered speed, wheels caressing the runway more and more lightly as their wingtips began to grip—then the softer, richer whine of the jets as the plane left the ground and rose sweetly into its natural element, the air. They raised wheels and flaps, trimmed for cruising and set course for the Dorset coast.

For some time they were too busy with routine matters of flying to think of Christabel. Then Polhill remembered her.

"You all right in the back?"

"I'm fine," she said. "And I just *love* being abducted. But where are we going?"

"As Jim told you," Oakman cut in, "we've got to test our emergency drill—fly west and orbit the Cornish coast. For about an hour, I expect. Afraid that's all we know at the moment."

"A *very* likely story!"

"I assure you"—in his most dignified voice—"it's true."

"Look," she said, "I'm not all that stupid. If this is only a *test* why take a plane that's unserviceable?"

A longish pause, then: "All right, Christabel. If you must know, there *is* some sort of flap on. We've been told to get west of Lands End by one o'clock and stay there till we're recalled. But what the flap's in aid of, nobody—not even the group captain—seems to know."

26

She considered this. It seemed to fit. "Well, let's hope," she said, "it *is* only a test."

"Yes. And listen, Christabel. There're masses of planes in the air, and Jim and I've a lot to cope with. So just sit still and keep quiet."

"Right," she said.

The Bat flew west: height 2,000 feet, speed 460 knots, course 250° magnetic.

There was, as Oakman had said, a great deal of activity in the air: planes of all sorts and sizes hurrying west. Most of them were flying higher than the Bat, but Oakman and Polhill had to keep very much on the alert—for visibility was none too good. And as they flew west, it tended to get worse, the mist closing in gradually and the sun losing its luster. By twelve o'clock, as they crossed the coast at Lyme Regis, they could see no more than a couple of miles in any direction—fifteen seconds' flying at the speed at which they were traveling. They reduced height and flew on, Oakman concentrating on the instruments, Polhill straining his eyes to probe the veil of mist, which gave the impression of parting in front of them as smoke in a tunnel disperses at the approach of a train.

It wasn't easy flying. Even from the back Christabel could tell that. But she drew comfort from the thought that she was in good hands. Oakman, she knew, had the reputation of being one of Farnborough's most accomplished fliers. While Polhill, now nearing the end of his three-year tour under the Exchange Officers Scheme, was a man of exceptional ability. He was leaning forward now, tapping the dial of their port generator.

"Low, and getting worse."

"Hmmm! What do you reckon's the trouble?"

"Could be overloading."

"Not so good . . . Christabel!"

27

"Hullo?"

"You got any electrical equipment switched on in the back?"

"I don't think so."

"What about that box of tricks you were playing with?"

"Wait a sec and I'll check." A pause, then: "My test gear works off its own battery, and it's disconnected anyway. The moving map's plugged into the inertial navigator, but it's not switched in. So the only things using current are the air conditioning and the radio. Why, what's up?"

"Port generator's dicky." He turned to Polhill. "If both generators pack up we'll have to land. Get a weather check from St. Mawgan."

We're in a bit of a mess, aren't we? Christabel thought. We can't see for mist, our generators are packing up and something nasty's likely to go off with a bang at one o'clock. She longed to talk to the others—to share her fears, to ask questions. What exactly had the pilots been told at Flying Control? Why weren't they using their radio to find out what was happening? How serious did they think the overloading was? But Oakman and Polhill had made it clear they had no time for talk. So she sat as much on the edge of her seat as her harness allowed, tense, keyed up, doing and saying nothing.

Polhill's conversation with St. Mawgan did nothing to reassure her. In fact the reverse. For the St. Mawgan controller came up with a negative landing report. Visibility over the airfield, he told them, was four hundred yards, decreasing. And it was the same throughout southwest England. The mist was closing in. The only airfield reporting anything like reasonable conditions was Culdrose, away in the south at the mouth of the Helford River.

Christabel realized there were little beads of moisture now on the palms of her hands. It won't be funny, she thought, if both the generators pack up and we're left with no instruments and nowhere to land.

After a while, to keep herself occupied, she began to check the navigational aids for a fault—hoping, very much against hope, to find the cause of the overloading. She could have done the check blindfolded—since for the last few months she'd practically lived with the Bat's Doppler and inertial navigator, D.R. computer and moving map (many of which incorporated innovations that had been brought about by her department's research work). She did the checks carefully and methodically, and with the expected result. She could find no fault. The fault, whatever it was, lay somewhere in the Bat's mile and a quarter of electrical cables, which ran with spider-web complexity beneath the cockpit flooring. So she was forced back to the edge of her seat, and to doing and saying nothing.

At twelve ten they passed the Wolf Rock. The sea was like oiled glass, with no hint of movement or color even where it lapped the hull of the lightship. And over the sea visibility was worse.

Her foot beat an anxious tattoo on the cockpit floor. If only, she thought, I had something to do; something to think of; something to take my mind off the generators and one o'clock.

From where she sat she could see the back of Oakman's head. Thank the Lord, she thought, he's a brilliant pilot; if things *had* to go wrong, I couldn't have picked a better man to be with. She studied the back of his head and smiled.

The idea came to her out of the blue. She could think about Kenneth Oakman. What nicer way of occupying her mind!

She had got to know quite a lot about him in the last few months. Some of it Farnborough gossip, some of it bits and pieces she had picked up during the half dozen times they'd been out together.

His names, she knew, were Kenneth Macaulay; and he'd been born in York, in 1933. From what Christabel could gather, he'd been one of those lucky children on whom the good things of life are showered in abundance: good health, good looks, brains, and parents who were happily married and more than comfortably off. His childhood sounded idyllic. A home overlooking some of the most beautiful moorland in the West Riding, a private school at which he had excelled without having to make any particular effort and summers spent with his parents in the valleys of the Loire and Indre. Then of course there'd come the war. But World War II had caused the Oakman family neither hardship nor inconvenience. Rather the reverse. As chairman of one of the largest steel works in Yorkshire, Oakman's father was far too important to be called up; his workshops simply switched from the making of car chassis to the making of tanks and Bren gun carriers, while his son was expeditiously evacuated to Canada. Kenneth spent five years in Canada. No bombing, no rationing, no blackout; but winter holidays skiing in the Laurentians, and summer holidays sailing among the Thousand Islands of the St. Lawrence. It was during these summer holidays that he became interested in flying.

Every July, he had told Christabel, the family he was living with took their motor launch to a boathouse on one of the Thousand Islands. And the Thousand Islands, in wartime, happened to be a low-flying area for pilots training at the nearby airfield of Kingston. Many holidaymakers regarded the pilots as a public nuisance. But young Kenneth was not among them. He loved the noisy, snub-nosed Harvards which came sweeping down so low that their propeller tips seemed to be almost feathering the water and which, on more than one occasion, very realistically "beat up" his dinghy. And he loved at night, from his bedroom window, to watch the red and green of their navigation lights winking away among the stars. But what gave him the biggest thrill of all was when one of them flew *underneath* the cantilever span of the International Bridge. He saw it done once out of a rising moon: the Harvard skimming no more than ten feet above the water, with the moon slung like a great ball of gold onto its tail plane and its shadow complete with navigation lights rushing ahead of it over the water. He decided that night to become a pilot. His father didn't like the idea much at first, having always assumed that Kenneth would follow him into the family business; but when it became clear that the boy's mind was made up, he wrote: "If you are determined to fly, you must do the job properly. That means Cranwell. I enclose a syllabus of the exams you will be expected to pass . . ." Kenneth Oakman studied hard. In 1951 he passed into Cranwell.

He was a shade over six feet by this time and exceedingly good-looking, with an athlete's wiry build, fair hair, and eyes of an enigmatic slate gray. He was clever, too, and a natural pilot. His instructors eyed him rather askance at first—everything seemed a bit too good to be true; but if there was indeed a flaw in Oakman's impeccable façade the instructors failed to find it. To say he did well at Cranwell would be an understatement. At the end of three years he walked off with an indecent number of prizes (including the Groves and the Sword of Honor). And what was more, walked off with them with the annoying ease of a man to whom honors are no more than his birthright.

Oakman's less gifted contemporaries would have taken more kindly to him if his laurels had been harder won. As it was, he soon found himself rather too much the blue-eyed boy to be popular. The result was that during his last year at Cranwell he began to withdraw into his shell, to shut himself up in a little self-contained world of his own. It wasn't that he failed to take part in the usual fun and games: the beagling and hunting, the beer drinking, the womanizing. But he took part in them with a detached, slightly superior air which others (especially women) found first intriguing, then infuriating. But whatever his personal idiosyncracies or shortcomings, his service career swept on at the flood.

In 1955 he was posted to Cyprus. He loved the island from the word go: the warmth and color of it, the tinder sky, the sapphire bays, the dusty green of the cedars, cypresses and olives. He loved the work, too. It was difficult work, with just sufficient danger in it to give each flight a tang of excitement: photographic reconnaissance mostly, with the odd low-level search or rocket attack. It was for a very special rocket attack that Oakman won his A.F.C. Eoka had captured a pair of important agents and taken them for questioning to an isolated farm high on Mount Olympus. The R.A.F. had been asked if they could wreck the half of the farm occupied by the guards and leave the other half intact. There had been all sorts of difficulties: time, weather and the locating of the farm by moonlight, to mention only a few. In the end two Vampires had taken off: the C.O.'s and Oakman's. The C.O. had got himself lost, but Oakman had found the farm *and* put three of his four rockets through the window of the room where the guards were sleeping. In the confusion the agents had managed to escape. It was a bit of luck for Oakman, the sort of luck that led to his being recommended for accelerated promotion. From then on, Christabel gathered, it had been roses, roses all the way. Eighteen months with the Black Arrow aerobatic team, a year as aide-de-camp to the A.O.C.-in-C. Fighter Command, a year with the Empire Test Pilots School, and then a post-

32

ing to the experimental flight at Farnborough. It was a story redolent with the sweet smell of success: a blueprint dangled in front of the eyes of all the keen young pilots joining the R.A.F.

And on the personal side? As the years passed, his *dégagé* air became more pronounced, so that on first acquaintance people often got the impression he was aloof and self-contained. A psychologist might have wondered what the aloofness was a cloak for; but the majority of people accepted it at face value and put whatever interpretation on it suited their books—his superiors that he was a bright boy playing it cool, his juniors that he was a stuck-up bastard.

As she studied the back of his head, Christabel wondered why he wasn't married. He was attractive to women. That was obvious. But perhaps, she told herself, the right girl just hasn't come his way. Instinctively, with a reflex action that made her smile at herself, she felt for her powder compact.

As her hand closed over it, she saw the tiny wisp of smoke spiraling up from the floor plates beneath the Doppler. Her smile vanished exceedingly quickly.

As she grabbed the microphone, Oakman's voice, curiously distant, came through on the intercom.

"Jim! The instruments!"

"The power's fadin'. Keep her steady."

A second of shocked disbelief, then: "Christabel! Switch off the electrics. Quick."

"Right!" she said.

But even as she leaned forward to knock up the switches everything became suddenly very quiet. All over the plane dials, instruments, computers, air conditioning and microphones went dead. And the smoke thickened.

As she switched on the emergency intercom her hands

were trembling, but her voice—she was glad to hear—didn't sound panicky.

"Smoke coming out of the deck plates. Under the Doppler."

She had never seen Polhill move so fast. He ripped off his safety harness, grabbed a Pyrene extinguisher and was kneeling beside the Doppler in a flash. But he didn't use the extinguisher. He hesitated. And Christabel knew why. A Pyrene spray ejects two and a quarter pounds of liquid CO_2 in the form of a concentrated cone; it isn't a thing one uses lightly.

"Is the smoke gettin' more or less?"

She stared at the wisps of white. "It got worse a moment ago. But I think it's less now."

He passed her the spray. "If it gets worse, give it a squirt."

She moistened her lips. "Jim! The generators have blown, haven't they?"

"Yes. No risk of fire now."

"But Ken can't fly without instruments?"

"If I help him he can." He smiled at her. "Don't worry. Ken and I've been in worse trouble than this. We'll be O.K."

As he crawled back to his seat, the Bat lurched uneasily.

She leaned over the Doppler, watching the innocent-looking coils of white, like smoke from a circle of cigarettes, seeping out of the floor plates. After a while the smoke got less, but not her anxiety. Can a pilot control a high-speed jet in mist, she wondered, without instruments? She doubted it. And the Bat, as if to confirm her fears, toppled suddenly seaward. Polhill's voice, sharp and anxious, came through the intercom.

"Level off! We're down to three hundred."

The plane pulled out of its dive, altered course, and went

34

teetering off on a new heading. As she listened to the exchanges between pilot and navigator, Christabel got the hang of what was happening.

They had lost height, so that Oakman could see the sea—which gave him some sort of datum to fly by. And they had turned back for Cornwall. Their electrical instruments, of course, had packed up; but they could steer a course by their stand-by compass (a direct-reading variety which depended on magnetism rather than electrically operated gyros). And so, like an owl caught out in the glare of noon, they began to limp erratically toward the safety of land. Oakman flew visually, and every time he wandered too far off course or lost or gained too much height Polhill called through a correction.

It was hot in the Bat, hot and suffocating. For their air conditioning had gone the way of their instruments. Christabel moistened her lips, dabbed the sweat out of her eyes and held on tight to her Pyrene spray. Whatever I do, she thought, I mustn't faint—at least not till the smoke stops. It was getting less all the time, and soon only a single dying coil was struggling out through the cockpit floor. I only hope, she thought, Polhill's navigation is spot on. Some Cornish cliffs rise sheer from the sea. If we hit the wrong part of Cornwall there'll be one God Almighty bang. She tried to blow the hair out of her eyes, but it was plastered onto her forehead with sweat.

They were almost on top of the coast before they saw it. Then the gray of the sea turned suddenly to green, and they were flashing low over a blurred mosaic of copses and fields. The Bat wheeled away, circled once, then began to follow the coast from about two hundred yards offshore.

After a bit they were able to pinpoint their postion: midway between The Lizard and Lands End.

The coastline gave Oakman some sort of horizon to fly by.

And that helped. But following the ins and outs of the frequent promontories and bays was far from easy. For the mist was patchy, and at speeds close to stalling the Bat was sluggish on her controls. One moment they'd be heading blind into apparently open sea, the next they'd be unpleasantly close to the wooded slopes of the hinterland. Christabel could see the drops of sweat rolling down Oakman's neck. And it came to her again how lucky she was that her life was in *his* hands, and not in the hands of some no-better-than-run-of-the-mill pilot, who would surely have piled up and killed them long ago.

She was pressed hard into her seat as the Bat banked violently away from a cliff that came rushing at them out of the mist.

"Jim!" Oakman's voice was tense. "We've got to get down."

"It's only half past twelve. What about the emergency?"

"This *is* an emergency. Look up Culdrose."

Polhill thumbed through his list of airfield layouts. "A naval drome, skipper; on the Helford River."

"Ugh! Short runways!"

"Yes. Six thousand feet."

"Six thousand feet!" There was a hint of panic now in Oakman's voice. "With no tail chute we'll never pull up in six thousand feet."

Silence, and the mist flashing past like streamers of gun-smoke. They were in trouble.

They went over the alternatives. With instruments and radio aids they could have landed blind at pretty well any airfield in southern England, but their instruments and radio were useless. If they'd been in a V-bomber they could have stayed airborne long enough to fly into a mist-free zone; but the Bat, being a low-level bomber, would soon be getting low on fuel. The rear navigator's seat wasn't

36

equipped for ejection; so they couldn't use their parachutes.

Alighting on the sea was out; tests with a model Bat in the water tank at Farnborough had shown that the moment the Bat touched the water it would nose over violently and kill its occupants. There was only one thing they could do.

"Let's have a look," Oakman said, "at Culdrose."

They hoped visibility at Culdrose might be better. But it wasn't. In the half hour since they'd been in touch with St. Mawgan, the mist had drifted down into even the southernmost tip of Cornwall. They turned in at the mouth of the Helford River and were almost on top of the drome before they saw it. Then the dull red glow of the identification beacon flashed briefly up through the mist and was gone. They had a blurred glimpse of lights from huddled buildings, fragments of runways and a line of sodium flares disappearing into the mist; then everything was white and featureless, and they were forced to circle away to the comparative safety of the sea.

"We'd never make it." Oakman's anxiety was naked now. The sweat was running down his neck; his hands were clenched tight around the control column, and his eyes were frightened.

In the silence the mist seemed to close in and the atmosphere in the plane to grow even more claustrophobic.

"You'd better start praying, Jim." It was hard to tell whether Oakman was mocking or serious. "I don't know what else'll save us."

Another and longer silence. Then Polhill began to run his pencil over a map. "Say, Captain, there's a road here, straight for three or four miles, and about in line with the Culdrose runway."

"So?"

"How about a timed letdown over the road?"

"With no instruments!"

"We've a watch, a magnetic compass, a pressure altimeter."

"What about radio masts, and the Telstar receiver pylons? I don't like it."

They none of them liked it. But what was the alternative? Twice while they were arguing the pros and cons the Bat had to cartwheel away from slopes of green which came rushing at them through the mist like great combers rising out of a night sea. Once, too, Oakman completely misjudged their height, and they almost flew into the water.

"Don't you think," Polhill said quietly, "we'd better give it a try?"

Oakman moistened his lips. "With no instruments and no moving map, it just isn't on."

They both got there together: Christabel and Polhill. Their voices blared through the intercom in an excited duet.

"The test equipment!" It worked off its own battery; if they changed over the leads it would give them sufficient current—for a short while—to work the moving map.

It wouldn't be easy. They saw that at once. There were all sorts of technical difficulties—they'd have to feed in course and air speed rather than track the ground speed, and they'd have to fly slap over a preselected spot in order to reset the equipment. But if they *could* get the map unwinding, so they could tell exactly where they were and could see exactly what hazards were coming up ahead, it would very likely save their lives.

Quickly Christabel switched over the leads from inertial navigator to test box. Then, as Polhill called through their courses and air speeds, she fed the information by hand into the box. And across the miniature screen on their instrument panel the maps began to move.

So far, so good.

38

Their next step was to locate and fly over a check point, so that the center of the map could be set under the cross wires on the screen which marked their position. And this, at low level and in poor visibility, was easier said than done.

They reduced speed and gained as much height as they dared, so that the landscape beneath them gave the impression of passing more slowly. Then they headed along the coast for the check point they'd chosen: the Manacles, a reef of rocks jutting due east into the Channel. They missed the Manacles the first time; but Oakman circled back, and at the second run-in they spotted them: twin lines of reef, knifing the water. The Bat swung close inshore. As they passed low over the largest rock—the Shark's Fin—Polhill re-set the map under the cross wires, while at the same time Oakman adjusted his altimeter so that when they touched down at Culdrose it would read zero.

They weren't out of the woods. But they'd taken a first step on the road to safety.

They wasted no time—for they knew the test box had only a limited supply of power, and wouldn't go on motivating the map for long. So they swung straight in to The Lizard peninsula and made for the road—the four straight miles of B.3293 which led across the Downland to Culdrose. If it hadn't been for the moving map, unrolling like a film strip on the instrument panel, they'd have had no idea where they were. As it was, they could tell there were no high obstructions ahead. They let down to four hundred feet and carefully rehearsed their letdown procedure—Polhill to watch the map and call out landmarks as they were due to come looming out of the mist; Christabel to keep check on their course, speed and height; and Oakman to concentrate on visual flying. And at the end of their letdown—*if* everything went right—they ought to be over the Culdrose identification beacon, fifty feet up, in line with the runway and ready for touchdown. But the slightest miscalculation or the slightest inaccuracy in flying and, Christabel knew, they'd very likely end upside down in the hangars or burned out at the foot of the radio masts. But with Kenneth as pilot, she thought, that's just not going to happen.

They flew blindly over an unidentifiable mosaic of grassland and field. Thank the Lord, she thought, they're used to this sort of thing. Most pilots, as she knew, had to do all their flying at high altitude nowadays, and low-level work had become something of a lost art, a relic of the past. But the Bat had been expressly designed as a low-level strike aircraft, capable of sneaking in undetected beneath the enemy's radar; and ever since the first production models had been delivered to the experimental flight at Farnborough, their crews had specialized in low-level flying, both by day and by night.

Her thoughts were interrupted by Polhill. "Should see the road any second now. Coming in from the right."

It came slanting out of the mist at the tip of their starboard wing—straight and welcoming, a pointer to safety. As they swung parallel to it, Christabel reached for the intercom.

"Four hundred feet," she said. "Course 280. One minute thirty seconds to go."

The moment they hit the road Polhill started his running commentary. "A few seconds, Captain, and a little stream comes in from the right. . . . There it is. . . . In a moment there'll be woods either side of the road. . . . Get over to starboard a bit. . . . There're the woods. Hold her level now. We're spot on."

As the Bat sank lower they could see the fields more clearly. In one there was a pair of hunters: a bay and a sorrel. At the scream of jets they kicked up their heels and disappeared under the Bat's wing as though at the start of a point-to-point.

"Two hundred feet," Christabel called. "Course 275. One minute to go."

"We're still spot on. In a second there'll be a crossroads and we turn a fraction to starboard—about fifteen degrees. There's the crossroads now. Turn starboard, and down to one fifty."

Flying the aircraft by feel into its turn, Oakman saw the road come sliding under his wing. He steepened his turn, overshot the road by a good fifty yards, regained it and straightened up. He wiped the sweat out of his eyes.

"Down to one fifty." Polhill's voice was sharp.

He throttled back. The deceleration swung them aside. As he corrected he heard Christabel's final check: "One hundred feet. Course 310. Thirty seconds to go."

He peered into the mist. He could see no beacon, no runway. If we're not lined up dead-right, he thought, we've had it. Plenty of trees are a hundred feet high, and plenty of buildings and radio masts. But it's now or never. He called for full flap. Now, he thought, as Polhill jerked back the lever, we're committed. Now we've *got* to make it.

The Bat slowed; her nose tilted up and her controls took on the familiar sogginess which warned him they were close to stalling. But if I don't lose speed to the very edge of stalling, he thought, we'll never pull up in six thousand feet, even if we do hit the runway. He cut his air speed till the stick began to tremble.

"The beacon!"

He saw it at the same second as Polhill: the long and the short red flashes blurred and diffused by mist. And beyond the beacon, the sodiums: the spluttering, welcoming daubs of refracted light leading in to the runway. He banked in between the lights. He cut the throttles. He kicked the rudder to correct for residual drift. He eased forward on the stick. And waited.

And the runway came rushing toward them out of the mist.

They cleared the boundary by less than a couple of feet. Then their tires brushed the welcoming tarmac. And they were down.

He eased the stick forward and squeezed on the brakes. He squeezed till the veins stood out on the backs of his hands like rivers of ink, and sweat, cold and salt, poured into his eyes and into his mouth. And the Bat began to lose speed.

But slowly.

Too slowly, it seemed to Oakman. The runway lights were still flashing by, fast as headlights on an autobahn. How many lights were there, he wondered, to the end of the runway? And how did the runway end? In a stone wall? A railway cutting? A sheer drop to the river?

"Second intersection," Polhill said quietly. "Five hundred yards to go."

The lights were passing more slowly now; they were no longer a continuous ribbon of white but had a separate existence. The tail of the Bat rose higher. The brakes gave a last protesting squeal. A smell of burnt rubber seeped into the cockpit. And then, quite suddenly, everything was very still and very quiet.

"Well done, Kenneth," Christabel whispered.

They didn't realize at first just how near a thing it had been. Then they saw the lights, the red lights that marked the end of the runway, staring at them from out of the mist less than a dozen yards ahead.

They were still sitting there, cold and shivering with shock, when a naval utilicon came nosing out of the mist and signaled them to follow her to Flying Control.

They trailed the utilicon thankfully, around a twisting

42

perimeter track, until the lights of the control tower flowed warm and welcome through the mist. Oakman swung into the parking circle for visiting aircraft. As he cut the Bat's engines, he glanced at his watch; it needed a few minutes to one o'clock.

4

It needed a few minutes to one o'clock as the lady of indeterminate age and her poodle were brought to a halt at the entrance to Hyde Park.

"I'm sorry, ma'am." The policeman was courteous but firm. "The park is closed this afternoon."

The lady's umbrella beat an impatient tattoo. "But this is ridiculous. Suki and I have been coming here for years." Her glance went past the policeman and came to rest on the army truck, the little emplacement of sandbags and the man with a tin helmet on which the letters C.D. were painted in bright red. Then she noticed the mobile radar scanners. Her eyes widened and her voice took on a touch of eagerness. "But what's going on? Are we starting another war?"

"I'm sorry, ma'am. I only know I've orders not to let anyone in the park. Now will you please move on."

She drifted away, reluctantly, grumbling, but warmed nevertheless by a touch of something very akin to nostalgia—a memory of W.V.S. canteens and cups of tea and sirens and the companionship of nights in communal shelters.

The same sort of nostalgia, one might have thought, was warming the heart of the little man in the tin helmet. He was a Civil Defense warden, and very busy. He was in

44

charge of a defense post at the Albert Gate approach to the park; and he had in his little kingdom—as well as his tin hat—a radio, a whistle, a geiger counter, and a couple of privates whom he was exhorting to sandbag up his post.

"Come on! Come on, you two." His voice was chiding. "Step lively now."

The privates, one gangling and taciturn and the other thickset and loquacious, eyed him without enthusiasm.

"All right for you, cock," the thickset one grunted. "What abaht givin' us a hand?"

The warden was indignant. "Me, give a hand! Goodness gracious, I've more important things to do." He looked at his watch, disappeared like a startled rabbit into his post and began to tinker with his radio.

The thickset private spat. "Little runt's enjoying his-self!"

"Ahh!"

"Mucking use 'is sandbags'll be if an atom bomb lands on 'is 'ead!"

"Ahhh! Nor 'is tin hat, either."

A police car came into sight. It moved slowly down the road running parallel to Hyde Park. "Attention, attention!" its loudspeaker blared. "The public are advised to take shelter for a few minutes. Keep indoors and away from windows. An experiment is taking place in Hyde Park. Attention, attention! The public are advised to take shelter . . ."

There was little confusion, and no panic. A fair number of people indeed chose to ignore the warning and remained clustered in doorways, peering toward the park with a sort of puzzled and slightly apprehensive interest.

In the defense post the radio gave a sudden crackle. The warden thumbed up the volume and a disembodied voice announced briefly: "Missile located. Target area London. Warning period two and three quarter minutes."

The warden ran out of his post. He adjusted his tin hat. He took out his whistle and began to blow a series of long piercing blasts. Then he noticed the privates staring at him. "Get on with them sandbags," he said.

"Come off it, cock!" The loquacious one put his hands on his hips. "If this is a test, we don't want to rupture ourselves, see. If it's the real thing, a few mucking sandbags won't do us no good."

The warden's reaction was surprising. He almost ran up to the private. He thrust his face forward, his chin jutting out, his cheeks flushed. "Listen, you stupid bugger," he hissed. "I'm not enjoying this any more than you are. But if I'm due to buy it I'll go out doing a useful job, not loafing about and moaning. And you two'll ruddy well do the same. Now get on with them sandbags."

The privates were so surprised they picked up a sandbag and almost ran with it toward the defense post.

The warden went on blowing his whistle. He blew it until he was flushed with shortage of breath as well as with anger—an anger which was kept banked up by the fact that people seemed to be taking so little notice of him. The windows and doorways overlooking the park were full of interested spectators; there was even a small number of people still on the streets. His radio crackled again. "Target area London. Warning period thirty seconds."

"Come on, you two." The warden gestured toward his defense post. "Inside."

Caught up in the tide of his urgency, they obeyed without question.

"Lie on the floor. Cover your eyes."

Even the loquacious one was too overawed to object.

They lay stretched out on the beaten-down earth, which

was still slightly damp from the rain of the night before, waiting.

Everything was very quiet.

They felt slightly ridiculous.

The seconds passed.

Then a clock in the nearby barracks started to chime the hour. It's a false alarm, the warden thought, much ado about nothing.

But even as his thought took shape, the defense post was filled with a sudden whistling, shrill and high-pitched. A great crash, like the collapse of an ice wall, reverberated from the direction of the park. Then the sonic boom: a double wave of tortured sound, surging up to an unendurable crescendo. Dust rained down from the roof of the post. From the houses facing the park came the clatter and ring of breaking glass. Then silence.

They lay pressed tightly against the earth, helpless, appalled, waiting for the blast of heat and flame that would shrivel them into so many thimblefuls of radioactive dust. But there was no heat, no flame—only silence. After about a minute the warden got slowly to his feet. He uncovered his geiger counter. He turned to the others.

"Stay inside," he said.

He walked out of the defense post. He looked at the sky. It was serene. There was no nuclear thunderhead. His geiger counter was silent. He felt like falling down on his knees and thanking God. Then he saw the parachute.

The sun was shining on it, turning the silken canopy into an inverted bowl of light. It had been ejected by retro-rocket, he guessed, from the missile head. Now it was floating gently to earth. He watched, fascinated; too intrigued to remember the "no fall-out" report which he ought to have been transmitting.

The parachute drifted against a tree. It collapsed, bringing a small metal container to rest on the grass.

For perhaps half a minute there was neither sound nor movement; then from the far side of the Albert Gate came the sound of engines starting up, and a second later a pair of army trucks moved slowly into the park. One headed toward the crater left by the rocket head, the other toward the parachute. The warden couldn't watch both at the same time, so he concentrated his attention on the truck approaching the chute.

It pulled up about twenty yards short. Three men clambered out; the warden could recognize them by their uniforms—a police officer, a Civil Defense worker and a technician from the Bomb Disposal Unit. They approached the parachute with all the mistrust and circumspection of a patrol reconnoitering an enemy strong point. Very carefully they cut the shrouds and released the metal container. Then even more carefully they opened the container.

The warden couldn't, of course, see the single envelope (addressed to the Prime Minister) which was inside. But he did see the police officer transfer something from the container to his brief case. For perhaps a couple of minutes the three men stood in a little cluster on the grass, talking. Then a police patrol car drew up beside them and the police officer, clutching his brief case, climbed in and was driven away through the Albert Gate and out of sight.

The "experiment" was over. And the warden, wondering, went back to his post.

The Prime Minister was not easily ruffled. He had a reputation for *sang-froid* which had long been the joy of political cartoonists (who delighted in depicting him in the most outrageous situations raising no more than a well-bred eyebrow). But his *sang-froid* had deserted him now; his

48

anxiety was naked. His hands as he slit open the envelope were trembling.

The Soviet Chairman's note was longer this time. And its tone, from the first sentence to the last, was abrasive.

My dear Prime Minister:

Bear in mind how this message, in spite of your efforts to stop it, was delivered to you and your colleagues in Washington, Paris and Bonn; and do not doubt that the U.S.S.R. has the ability to deliver the most devastating weapons, with complete accuracy, anywhere on the surface of the earth. (This fact we will further demonstrate by landing harmless missiles at specified points in your territories in the course of the next few days.) Your outmoded fighters and anti-aircraft defenses are quite powerless against our missiles; we can land them where we wish.

You do not have this capability against us. Your V bombers are outdated, while your few offensive weapons (on loan from the United States) lack accuracy and range and cannot penetrate our latest anti-missile defenses.

Thus while you are wholly vulnerable to an attack from us, you have no means of attacking or of deterring the U.S.S.R.

In view of these facts, the peace-loving Russian people are at last in a position to remove the threat of war which has been hanging these last years over the human race. We are strong enough to ENFORCE peace.

I therefore require you and your Cabinet and Chiefs of Staff to present yourselves here at the Kremlin within seven days of receiving this message—i.e., by midday on October 30—when I shall outline my proposals for establishing a modus vivendi in keeping with the times. Unless you accede to this request I shall reluctantly be compelled, my dear Prime Minister, to give instructions (which would be carried out at that precise time— namely midday on October 30) for the complete obliteration of your country from the surface of the earth.

If you doubt the validity of the above contentions I suggest

49

you attempt to answer this note by the same method that I have used to communicate with you: i.e., by landing your reply, in a single missile, in Red Square, Moscow, within the course of the next seven days. Only if you are able to do this, thereby demonstrating that the West has indeed a genuine deterrent, will I be willing to consider alternative proposals.

I look forward to seeing yourself and your colleagues on October 30. For the sake of your country and peace-loving people everywhere in the world, do not be late.

He read the note twice. Then for a long time, feeling physically sick, he sat staring out at the park. The sun was gold, the grass was green and the trees were copper and russet; but the beauty of the afternoon served only as a whetstone to his apprehension.

He saw the situation quite clearly. Russia and the West had long been like two duelists, each with his cache of weapons. For years these weapons had been of roughly equivalent frightfulness (each had had nuclear bombers, nuclear missiles and multimegaton bombs) and so peace had been preserved by a balance of terror. But now—or so the Russians claimed—their scientists had got so far ahead in the missile race that the balance of terror was no longer held even; for the Soviet could hit the West and the West couldn't hit back . . . or so the Russians claimed . . . and the West had seven days to prove them wrong.

Seven days, he thought. Maybe only seven more times to see the sun rise and set, to feel the wind on my face, to wake up in the morning with my wife lying beside me in bed. It isn't long. And yet, a voice whispered, it *could* be long enough. Seven days: the amount of time the world was created in. And should it be more difficult to conserve than to create?

Oh, God, he thought, give us wisdom these next seven days; give us wisdom, patience, understanding and strength.

He gave orders for the alert to be ended, and for the calling of an immediate meeting of Cabinet and Chiefs of Staff. Then he pulled out a sheaf of foolscap and began to make notes.

(1) [he wrote] Under no circumstances will Her Majesty's government be the first to make use of offensive nuclear weapons.

(2) The one wholly satisfactory answer would be to land our reply, as challenged, in Red Square.

He had covered three pages with his neat sloping script, and had conferred with his opposite numbers in Washington, Paris and Bonn, when his secretary told him that the Cabinet and Chiefs of Staff were assembled and waiting.

5

At about the time the Cabinet and Chiefs of Staff met at No. 10 Downing Street, Oakman was getting a maintenance report on the Bat.

The trouble had been located: generator leads which had been frayed almost to the breaking point by the vibration of a loose cross member under the cockpit floor. Repairs wouldn't be difficult; but they'd take time, especially as naval maintenance crews were unused to working on Bats and lacked both wiring diagrams and spares.

"Be all of twenty-four hours, I'm afraid, sir," a chief petty officer told Oakman.

He pulled a long face. But he knew better than to try to hurry the senior service.

The prospect of being stranded at Culdrose for twenty-four hours didn't please them. They were outsiders, caught up in a situation over which they had no control. And the situation struck them as being none too pleasant. For they didn't need to be hypersensitive to realize that although one o'clock was safely past, some sort of crisis was still in the offing. What the crisis was they didn't know, and nobody seemed able to tell them. But there was tension in the air: an atmosphere of anxiety, of not knowing what was happening. Things would have been a lot easier, of course, if they'd been at Farnborough. They would have known where they stood there, and they'd have had jobs to get on with. At Culdrose they could only mooch about, feeling uncertain and in the way. It wasn't that the Navy were unhelpful (everyone, on the contrary, went out of his way to be nice to them); but the people they spoke to all seemed preoccupied with their particular jobs, and appeared to know nothing of the situation as a whole. Eventually, however, Oakman managed to have a word with Culdrose's commander flying—who was one of the few people on the airfield able to put him in the picture.

A Soviet missile, the commander said, had landed in the middle of London. The missile itself had been harmless. But it had contained some sort of ultimatum. Nobody knew details. But the Prime Minister was broadcasting to the nation at six, and his broadcast was being relayed throughout the station. They'd know details then. In the meanwhile officers were expected to discourage the spread of rumors, to keep off the telephone and to get on with their jobs.

"I know it's difficult for you chaps," the commander added. "But why not lend a hand with your plane?"

They spent the rest of the afternoon crawling up and down the fuselage of the Bat, sometimes being useful, sometimes getting in the way. It amused the maintenance crew. And it killed time.

They knocked off at five and congregated, together with nearly a couple of hundred others, in the wardroom—waiting.

Shore leave had been canceled; and pretty well the whole strength of the air station was there, from the commander down to the most junior snotty. There was a good deal of speculation as to what the Prime Minister was going to say. For already, and in spite of precautions, rumors had started to circulate. The stock exchange, a paymaster was saying, had crashed. So, a pilot capped his story, had a Soviet sputnik.

As the first of the time pips came through, the chatter and clatter subsided, and the wardroom grew suddenly quiet.

How does one tell a hundred million people that they may have less than a week to live, that in six and a half days' time they and those they love may be completely obliterated from the surface of the earth? Even the packaging consultants couldn't wrap that one up to look very pretty.

All sorts of evasions and subterfuges had occurred to the Prime Minister. But in the end he'd decided simply to tell the truth—with the Soviet-controlled radio and press trumpeting the facts world-wide in thirty languages, he didn't in fact have any alternative. So he broadcast the text of the Soviet note, and the text of his dignified and very diplomatic reply. And he didn't try to disguise the fact that the world was now poised on the brink of Armageddon. He did, however, give two assurances: that the United Kingdom would never be the first to use offensive nuclear weapons; and that a reply *would* be landed, as challenged, in Red Square. And the landing of this reply, he ended blandly, would of course solve everything in the happiest possible way.

But *how* it would be landed he didn't say.

In the wardroom at Culdrose his talk was listened to in a numbed silence. Then, as the radio was switched off, came the deluge: the spate of anxiety, recrimination, threats and fear. The firebrands advocated action: "Get in with our bomb first." The fainthearted advocated surrender: "Let the government go to Moscow; *anything's* better than a nuclear war." But once the initial shock had receded, the firebrands and the fainthearted were seen to be a minority.

54

Most people that first evening took the common-sense attitude: "It's damn worrying, of course. But the government have said they can land a reply. So let them land it. Then everything'll be fine."

A good few naval pilots tried to pump Oakman, anxious to get another service's point of view. But he was cagy, preoccupied, and after a while he suggested to Christabel and Polhill that the three of them take a stroll over the airfield. Something, they realized, was on his mind—something he didn't want to discuss in public.

The airfield was wreathed in mist: cool, damp and autumnal. The taxi-track lights glowed blue and gold, refracted and diffused in the heavy air.

"The Russians have picked weapons cleverly," Polhill said. "Their missiles are far ahead of ours."

They went over the possibilities. British V-bombers: too slow and outdated for anything but a massed attack. American bombers: not likely to be able singly to penetrate an alerted Russian defense. Atlases, Thors, Titans and Minutemen: lacking in accuracy. Skybolts: too unreliable and being scrapped anyway. Carrier-borne strike aircraft of the U. S. Navy: a possibility, but every carrier would almost certainly be shadowed by a Soviet submarine which would give warning if the planes took off. Polaris: another possibility, but could they fit non-nuclear warheads and get a submarine into firing position in time? And anyhow, the Russians claimed they could shoot down single missiles. And so it went on. Every method they thought of came up against some technical snag.

They had just about run out of ideas when Oakman said casually:

"There's one other possibility, of course. The Bat."

6

The Bat.

The idea was conceived. It took shape in their minds. It put out roots. It grew.

"Of course," Christabel whispered. "It's what she was built for. *Under* the Soviet radar. With a standoff bomb. But carrying a message instead of a warhead."

"Hmmm!" Polhill rubbed his chin. "What about navigation?"

"Same as we used this morning. The moving map."

They stood in a little circle, with the lights of the taxi track winking away and the mist swirling in from the sea. Christabel reached for Oakman's hand.

"It's the answer, isn't it, Ken?"

"Could be."

"Will you put it to the group captain?"

He shivered. "You go too fast, Christabel."

"But we've got to move fast. We've only six days."

"If we stay here much longer," Polhill cut in, "we won't move at all. We'll freeze solid."

They agreed to go back to Oakman's cabin.

The cabin was warm and comfortable, and they weren't likely to be disturbed. Oakman drew the curtains and pulled up a couple of chairs to the small electric wall fire. Then he puttered about, offering cigarettes and wasting time with small talk. His attitude puzzled Christabel. The idea of using the Bat had been his in the first place. Yet he seemed now almost to have lost interest in it, to be thinking of other things. Certainly he wasn't following it up with what she considered the proper urgency.

"Well now," she said brightly, "I'd say the main snags'll be refueling and navigation."

"And I'd say you're rushing your fences."

"Oh?"

"My dear girl! Flying the Bat to Moscow isn't a simple little thing to be agreed on just like that. There're a thousand and one things to be taken into account."

She flushed. "Sorry. I was only trying to help."

"I think what Ken means," Polhill said, "is that we shouldn't *start off* by assuming the flight's on. That's the last step, not the first."

Oakman nodded. "The first step, surely," he said, "is to decide if a reply has to be sent to Moscow at all."

"But that's obvious! Unless you want to be completely obliterated."

Oakman pushed back his chair. He began to pace the cabin, up and down, down and up—eight feet one way, eight feet the other. He wasn't so much arguing a brief as thinking aloud, throwing ideas into the melting pot.

"Isn't it possible the Russians are bluffing? Take the way their notes were delivered. Four rockets landing simultaneously in the middle of four capitals. Spectacular, but pointless. Because we've known for years, haven't we, that the Russians can lob missiles pretty well into a bucket from halfway across the world. Remember the Berlin crisis, when they lobbed a rocket a week into a square mile in the Pacific, just to impress your people in Washington, Jim? So the way the notes were sent doesn't add up to anything new.

"Now take what the notes say. 'We can lob missiles into your cities; you can't lob missiles into ours. Therefore you've no deterrent.' But if you work it out, that's nonsense! It's a *non sequitur*. Our missiles aren't dead-accurate, agreed. The Russians say they can shoot some of them down: we'll agree to that, too—the Russians don't usually make claims they can't substantiate. But if we chose to launch a massed attack, *some* of our missiles would get through *somewhere* near target. And you don't need to be all that accurate, do you, with a thousand square miles of fall-out! So surely the fact's this: in spite of the note, we *have* still got a deterrent, and Russia and the West are in the same old impasse they've been in for years—neither dares start anything for fear of the counterattack. So if we've the nerve to sit tight and do nothing, we'll be O.K. The Russians won't *really* start a war. They're only bluffing."

There was a longish silence. Then Polhill said quietly, "Personally, I agree, Ken. I reckon they're bluffing too. But we can't be certain, can we?"

"Not a hundred per cent certain."

"Exactly. And that's what the Russians'll bank on. The fact that we can't be sure, and that we'll give in rather than risk a holocaust."

"Hmmm!" The argument worried him, but it didn't entirely convince him.

"And another thing," Polhill went on. "You can bet your life the Russians have been preparing for this for years. In the next six days we'll have the whole weight of their propaganda thrown at us. There'll be sputniks, more rockets, strikes, demonstrations and your Committee of a Hundred lying down left, right and center. Until there'll be such a panic and such pressure from the public, the governments will be forced to go and negotiate—unless we can land a reply."

58

"As I see it," Christabel cut in, "if we *don't* land a reply, the man in the street'll strip the issue down to this. 'The Russians can lob rockets into our cities; we can't lob rockets into theirs. Therefore we're defenseless. Therefore—unless we land a reply—we'll *have* to give in.' "

"Do you agree with that, Jim?"

Polhill drew on his pipe. It was quite a while before he answered; but when it did come, his reply was unequivocal. "Yes," he said. "When it comes to the point, I think most people would prefer *anything* to the risk of a nuclear war."

Silence. The mist had turned to a fine drizzle now, pattering gently onto the cabin roof and trickling along the gutters with a muted gurgling.

"Right." Oakman seemed suddenly to make up his mind. "So we have to land a reply, or go to Moscow. But there's another point: would going to Moscow be all that terrible?"

Christabel looked at him curiously. "It would be the end of a lot of things we value."

"Such as?"

"Freedom, democracy, the importance of the family—all the things that matter most."

He sighed. "You're very sure of what's right and wrong, aren't you, Christabel?"

"I can tell black from white."

"Lucky girl, to have never heard of gray!"

"Oh, Ken! Of course I don't think everything's black or white. But some things are good, aren't they; like freedom? And some things are bad, like oppression. Remember Hungary. And unless you're a fellow traveler you can't *really* want to kowtow to Moscow."

He turned to Polhill. "You're a levelheaded chap, Jim. What do you say to toeing the Moscow line? Mightn't it give your kids a better expectation of life?"

Again Polhill took his time over answering; and again his answer, when it did come, was unambiguous.

"I don't think it would work, Ken. I get your point about its being the end of the cold war and nuclear stockpiling. But I think we'd still be left with a lot of tension, jealousy and fear. And the bomb in the background. And China. I think, too, we'd lose a lot of worthwhile things apart from the ones Christabel mentioned."

"Would we? I wonder just what *would* happen if the government went to Moscow."

"To start with, I suppose, we'd just have our stings drawn: the services disbanded, no nuclear stockpiles, no missiles, not even the old Bat! Then I expect we'd be weakened economically, and our standard of living would drop. I don't imagine the other changes would be all that drastic at first. They'd be gradual. And I guess maybe I could stomach them all—except for one. We'd be driven farther from God."

"Hmmm! Aren't the churches in Moscow often full?"

"Maybe. But in Russia they put Communism first and God second. If there's a conflict of interest, it's God who gives way."

"I suppose that's true." A longish pause, then: "Of course, in some ways Communism and Christianity have a lot in common."

Christabel blew the hair out of her eyes. "Oh, Ken! How naïve can you get! What sort of Christianity is it that puts God second?"

" 'In my Father's house,' " he said, " 'are many mansions.' "

She was angry. She wanted suddenly to hurt him, to get through his armor of detachment and self-sufficiency. "Aren't you in the wrong uniform?" she said nastily. "Shouldn't you have little red stars on your shoulder?"

"If I'd been born in Kiev instead of York," he said, "I very likely would have."

60

She stared at him. I know what's the matter with him, she thought. I know why a lot of people don't like him, why he's not got all that number of friends, why he's never married. He's uncommitted. He doesn't believe in things. He doesn't *give* anything. He doesn't *need* anybody. He just drifts along in a self-contained world of his own, looking after number one. She listened to him discussing details of Communist life with Polhill. As if it mattered! she thought.

"I know why you've gone off the Bat," she said suddenly. "You're scared."

He wasn't angry. He considered the matter with care. "You may be right," he said mildly. "Though I prefer to think I'm cautious. I've only one life, you know. I don't want to throw it away on something not worthwhile."

Damn you, she thought, for always being so clinically right.

She simmered gently, listening with only half an ear to their conversation. She was too angry to take much in; only occasional fragments got through to her . . . "It's a risk we daren't take." This was Polhill. "If I'd been born in Russia I know what I'd be thinking: what a wonderful thing it was we had a chance to end the cold war and *force* the world to see sense." This, of course, was Oakman. She was fast losing both interest and patience, when Oakman said unexpectedly, "All right then, I'm convinced. We must try to land a reply. The next point is how."

She blinked. At last, she thought, he's seen sense, at last we're getting down to brass tacks.

The conversation that followed was technical. They all knew what they were talking about; they were all *au fait* with the latest weapons—both offensive and defensive; and they all seemed convinced now of the urgency and importance of what they were trying to do. They racked their

61

brains to think up a way of getting a message into Red Square. But there were always snags.

"You reckon they *can* shoot our missiles down, Jim?" Oakman asked.

"I'm sure of it. Single missiles, that is. Of course, if we launched a massed attack—Thors, Titans, Jupiters, V-bombers, the lot—*some* would get through. But that doesn't help us now. We've been challenged to land our reply 'in a single missile.' As I see it, if we start launching rockets and planes by the dozen, we'll very likely trigger off a hot war."

A long silence. And the cold and damp of the mist seeming to seep into the cabin.

Christabel shivered. "Maybe the Americans'll have something up their sleeve."

Polhill relit his pipe. "I don't think we should count on it. Our strategy's based on the massed deterrent. If it came to a shootin' war, we could knock Russia cold—several times over. But this affair of lobbin' a single missile into Red Square with the Soviet defenses all lined up to stop it . . ." He shook his head.

"So it looks," Oakman said thoughtfully, "as if we're left with the Bat."

Another silence. Broken this time by Christabel. Her voice was bitter.

"God, what a mess we've got ourselves into! Twenty years after the German V-2's and the R.A.F. *still* hasn't a single decent rocket. All we've got is a lot of damned silly piloted planes. All right for the sons of air marshals to fly upside down in. But about as much use for war as bows and arrows! Daddy saw it coming ten years ago. And all they did was try to court-martial him!"

"Don't get so het up," Oakman said quietly. "And remember it may be one of your 'damned silly piloted planes' that gets us to Moscow."

He thought she'd be furious. But her anger, unexpectedly, gave way to contrition.

"Sorry, Ken. Of course the Bat isn't silly. I didn't mean that."

For a moment her change of face had him puzzled. Then he got it.

Deep down at heart she hadn't much faith in planes. She was a child of the missile age, steeped in the mechanics of push-button technology; yet she felt that this time perhaps the Bat was their only hope. And she wanted him to fly it to Moscow. Just why she wanted him to fly it to Moscow he wasn't sure. But that was the fact of it. From the moment he'd first mentioned the idea on the taxi track, she'd been trying to push him into the air. He wondered why. Partly, of course, because she felt the flight was vital, and had to be made by someone. But that, he could tell, was only the half of it. There was a personal tie-up as well. She wanted *him* to do the flying. Perhaps, he thought, she wants me to prove myself—like the knights of old, whom no self-respecting maiden would walk out with till they'd slain a couple of dragons. He looked at her curiously.

"Let's work out a flight plan," she said. "The main snags are refueling and navigation. But we can get around them."

He envied her her confidence and her singleness of mind. At first he took only a halfhearted interest in the plan which began to take shape; but after a while he found himself swept along—at first reluctantly, then with increasing interest—in the tide of her enthusiasm.

They went on talking late into the evening, till the rain stopped and the mist began to lift and a haloed moon was shining frostily out of the sky.

It was eleven o'clock before they turned in.

And the flight of the Bat by then was something more than a pipe dream.

63

7

She washed, brushed her teeth and climbed into her newly bought pajamas. She was exhausted, paid out both physically and mentally. Yet for a long time sleep wouldn't come. Resolutely she shut her eyes, counted up to five hundred, and lay first on her stomach, then on her back. But Helston clock kept tolling the sleepless hours: twelve o'clock, one o'clock, two. It was close on 3 A.M. before she fell into an uneasy sleep.

And in her sleep she dreamed.

She was holding a box: a black metal box about nine inches square—rather like the navigational aid she'd fitted that morning into the Bat. She wondered what was inside it. She picked it up, and it was very light. She shook it, and it made no noise. I don't believe, she thought, there's anything in it at all. "Don't open the box, Pandora," a voice said, "or you'll regret it." But my name isn't Pandora, she thought; and why shouldn't I open the box? It's mine. She raised the lid. There was a muffled explosion, and a circle of flame. "Those who play with fire," the voice said judicially, "must expect to be burned." In her sleep she moaned, and her hands opened and closed. The flames spread. They got larger and fiercer. Feeling their heat on her face, she shrank

64

back. And then, in the middle of the flames, she saw the man. He was in flying overalls. And his body was white-hot and disintegrating. She screamed. She tried to rush into the flames. But hands gripped her shoulders and held her back. "This is your fault, Pandora," the voice said, "for opening the box." She twisted, screamed and sobbed. Then a light was flashing in her eyes, a woman's hands were on her shoulders and she was sitting up in bed, trembling and damp with sweat.

"It's all right," a voice was saying over and over again. "It's all right. You're awake now."

Relief that she'd only been dreaming flooded over her. Then, unaccountably and much to her embarrassment, she burst into tears.

"I'm sorry"—she scrabbled for her handkerchief—"I'm terribly sorry."

The Wren officer, who had come from the next cabin, looked at her without overmuch sympathy. "You quite awake now?"

She nodded.

"I'll get you an aspirin."

"It's good of you."

From the adjoining cabin she heard a drawer being opened and shut, then the sound of running water. A moment later the Wren returned with a glass and two aspirins.

She took them like a child, thankfully and without question.

"You all right now?"

She nodded. "Sorry to be such a fool."

The Wren officer smiled. "I expect a lot of people are having nightmares tonight. . . . The aspirin'll soon send you off."

She nodded. She pulled the bedclothes up to her chin and curled herself into a ball. She didn't care what the Wren thought of her. She wanted only to shut the dream out of her mind; not to think of its implications, not to think of anything. Just to sleep, to sleep and forget.

This time, almost as soon as her head touched the pillow, she fell into the sleep of the utterly exhausted.

8

She pulled the curtains, and the morning sun came slanting into her room.

It was a peaceful scene she looked out on. The mists of yesterday had vanished, and the airfield lay bathed in light. Vanished, too, had her midnight fears and the memory of what she had dreamed.

She dressed leisurely, breakfasted late, then strolled down to the hangars to get the latest news on the Bat. As she had half expected, Oakman and Polhill were already there; and the news was good.

"She'll be ready in a couple of hours," Oakman told her. "I've fixed take-off for half past one."

The rest of the morning passed slowly. They were all of them eager to get back to Farnborough and put their plan for using the Bat to the authorities. If left to himself, Oakman would have done nothing until their return; but Christabel gave him no peace until he had rung Group Captain Pellew (Farnborough's C.O.) and arranged to see him the moment they landed.

Polhill also did some telephoning: to his wife.

In ten years of service life, Jennifer Polhill had got used to her husband's being whisked away at a moment's notice.

But the circumstances yesterday had been unusual, and she'd been scared out of her wits.

"Jim! Where are you ringing from?"

"Culdrose. An airfield in Cornwall."

"Thank God you're all right. I'd visions of you going east, not west."

He told her not to worry; that he'd be home in the evening; that he'd give her the news then. And she knew better than to ask too many questions over a public line. After a while they began to gossip of trivialities.

"I had a visitor," she said, "last night."

"Not Mrs. Harley?"

"Who else!"

Mrs. Harley was one of Jennifer Polhill's lame ducks—an angular, friendless woman who had come to call on the Polhills soon after they had settled into their home near Farnborough. She was a widow, accustomed, she was quick to let the Polhills know, to better things than the drably genteel hotel she was now incarcerated in; and Jennifer, feeling sorry for her, had gone out of her way to be friendly. The result was that Mrs. Harley had attached herself with the limpet-like tenacity of the Old Man of the Sea.

"I hope," Jim said, "she didn't keep you up half the night."

"No, she pushed off when I fed Anne."

"What did she want?"

"The usual: someone to talk to. The Russian note has scared her stiff, of course."

"Hmmm."

"And you'd better look out! She's going to pump you about how the R.A.F. intend to land the reply."

"I'll refer her," he said, "to my commanding officer!"

They talked for a while of the children, of whether last night's frost had hurt the apples which they hadn't had time to pick, of what time he'd be home. Then they said their good-byes.

"See you tonight, darling."

"I'll look forward," she said, "to that."

"Bye."

"Bye for now."

An hour later the Bat rose sweetly clear of her shadow, circled the airfield and set course for Farnborough.

Group Captain Pellew heard the whine of the low-level bomber's jets as she came into the landing circuit. He walked across to the control room and watched the television-like screens as the plane touched down. Ten minutes later came the expected knock on his door.

"Ah, Oakman. Come in and sit down."

"Thank you, sir."

"Cigarette?"

"No, thanks, sir."

Pellew began to pack his pipe. Over the rim of the bowl he studied Oakman carefully. He didn't care for the fellow—too much the blue-eyed boy for his liking—but his likes and dislikes, he reminded himself, were neither here nor there.

"Now what was it you wanted?" he asked.

"I've been thinking about getting this message to Red Square, sir. Couldn't we use a Bat?"

"The thought *had* occurred to some of us here. But I doubt if it's practical."

"Well, sir"—Oakman turned on his most charming and deferential smile—"while we were stuck in Cornwall my navigator and I worked out a plan in detail. It wouldn't be easy, of course. But I'd have thought it was on."

"What about refueling? And navigation?"

"Those are the snags, of course. But couldn't we rendezvous with a tanker in mid-Baltic—say over Gotska Sandön?

And for navigation, couldn't we use the moving map? It makes the hell of a difference to low-level work. We'd need a couple of check points en route, of course, to reset the map. But I dare say Instruments could fix that. And with luck and good weather I reckon we'd stand a chance."

"But Bats aren't operational yet. They're barely out of the egg."

"There are three here, sir—in the experimental flight. Why not one of them?"

"Hmmm!" Pellew tipped back his chair. Now, he thought, for the sixty-four-thousand-dollar question. "And who's going to fly this Bat?"

"That's not for me to say, is it, sir?"

"No, but whom do you suggest?"

"I suppose the most experienced crew."

"Which is?"

"Ellis and Maynard."

An artery in the group captain's forehead started to throb. Now steady, he told himself. Ellis and Maynard *are* the most experienced crew, and the most senior; they couldn't possibly be passed over. *You* may think this fellow's a bit of a bastard, coming up with a suicide scheme which he won't be involved in. But the scheme's a good one. And it's that that counts.

"Of course, sir," Oakman added, "I hope Polhill and I could be a stand-by crew. Or something like that."

It'll be a one-plane operation, Pellew thought. The standby crews'll never get off the ground. He pushed back his chair and walked to the window. He wanted time to think.

"This plan of yours," he asked after a while, "is the whole thing cut and dried—times, tracks, firing point, the lot?"

"Pretty well."

"And you want it put to the Air Ministry?"

"Yes."

70

Pellew swung around, his mind suddenly made up. "Then get cracking. Now. Pull in all the help you need. Shut yourselves in the ops room and don't come out till the whole thing's on paper. I don't want a Staff College layout. I want something simple"—he grinned—"something that even an air marshal can understand! If I like it, I'll take it to London myself. Tonight."

He cut short Oakman's thanks.

Long after the squadron leader had left, he stood by the window, looking down at the golden glow of the runway. The mist had started to thicken again, and although it was not yet dark the sodiums had been lit. Pellew sighed; he wished to God he were ten years younger and had more experience on Bats.

Oakman, Polhill and Christabel, meanwhile, had shut themselves in the ops room. They drank cup after cup of coffee and drew up and tore up draft after draft, and the hours passed. What they had to do wasn't easy. For as Polhill pointed out, the thought of the Chiefs of Staff would be centered on rockets and missiles, and the idea of using an experimental low-level bomber would strike them, at first, as being something out of the ark: a throwback to World War II. They therefore decided to put forward their scheme in two sections: *section a* to "sell" the *idea* of using a Bat, and *section b* to prove it practicable. They sucked the ends of their pencils, and rephrased this passage and that; and it was three hours before Oakman, clutching his notes, knocked for the second time on Group Captain Pellew's door.

Pellew waved at a chair, picked up the notes and started to read:

AIM: *To land a message, as challenged, in Red Square.*
METHOD: *It is suggested that the message could be safely and accurately delivered by a low-level bomber, the Bat, carrying*

71

a standoff bomb, the warhead of which was replaced by a canister containing the message.

OUTLINE FLIGHT PLAN: *The Bat should take off from an airfield in northeast Scotland at dusk, cross the North Sea and southern Sweden at a height of 200 feet and rendezvous with a tanker aircraft in mid-Baltic; refueling would then take place below the height at which either plane could be detected by Russian radar. The Bat should then fly low up the Gulf of Finland, pass over a navigational check point in order to reset its moving map, and cross the Russian coast at a preselected spot a little north of Narva. (The success of the operation will be contingent upon accurate navigation on this leg: i.e., on the ability of the Bat to get an accurate navigational check so as to ensure an absolutely correct landfall and subsequent accurate navigation over Russia.) After crossing the coast the Bat should increase speed to maximum, Mach 1.3, and reduce height to minimum, 100 feet. On reaching a firing point ten miles south of Moscow the aircraft should release its bomb and return. Refueling on the flight back again to take place in mid-Baltic.*

ADVANTAGES OF PROPOSED OPERATION:

(a) *Rockets and guided missiles are the conventional weapons of today, and against these the Russians will have prepared massive countermeasures. The development of a low-level bomber, on the other hand, has been a secret British venture which runs contrary to the main stream of aeronautical progress. The Russians may know little about it, and they are not likely to consider the Bat operational; a British low-level bomber operating from an airfield in the U.K. might therefore easily take them by surprise.*

(b) *If too many missiles, etc., are fired at Moscow, the Russians may fear they are being attacked and may retaliate, thus starting a nuclear war. The use of one single bomber, on the other hand, entails no risk of triggering off a hot war.*

(c) *Tactically a Bat has these great assets:*

1. *It flies so low it cannot be picked up by radar.*

72

2. *It flies so low it cannot easily be picked up visually on account of the curve of the earth and natural objects such as houses, trees and hills.*
3. *It flies so low it leaves no vapor or contrails.*
4. *Since it flies faster than sound there is no noise ahead of it and therefore no warning of its approach.*
5. *Unlike a preset missile, it is a flexible weapon. Its pilot can change plan, weave and alter course. This unpredictability is bound to confuse the defenses.*
6. *It is very difficult to hit with defensive weapons because it flies so low that guns cannot be aligned on it accurately in the few seconds it is in sight, and proximity and nuclear warheads cannot be used against it for fear of destroying those on the ground."*

This, Pellew thought, is good stuff. He turned to the fourth section.

DIFFICULTIES TO BE OVERCOME: *Apart from the question of time* [he read] *success will depend on three factors: the ability of a Bat to refuel en route; the ability of a Bat to locate a preselected spot on the Russian coast and pass over it accurately; and the ability of a Bat to release its standoff bomb with precision.*

(a) REFUELING: *The range of a Bat is 1,100 miles (it is hard to improve this, since the weight of extra fuel tanks involves a sharp increase in consumption). Refueling en route is therefore essential. It is roughly 850 miles from northeast Scotland to mid-Baltic, and 1,000 miles from mid-Baltic to Moscow and back again. Mid-Baltic is therefore the best place to refuel. Given good weather and experienced crews, it should be possible for Bat and tanker to rendezvous at a height of 100 feet off the island of Gotska Sandön. Refueling (both going in and coming out) could then take place safely, beyond the range of Russian fighters and below the level at which Russian radar is effective.*

(b) NAVIGATION: *This is the big problem. A high-flying*

73

V-bomber armed with a multimegaton bomb doesn't need to be all that accurate in its navigation (an error of a few miles in its point of release won't matter). But a low-level bomber armed with a standoff bomb does need to be accurate, especially on this operation, when the target area is limited to a few hundred square yards. Now if a low-level bomber is equipped with the latest moving-map presentation, navigation is simple PROVIDED THE PLANE KNOWS EXACTLY WHERE IT IS ALL THE TIME. *But once the plane becomes lost difficulties snowball—for the aircraft either has to climb to get a look at the surrounding country, and this leads to its being detected and shot down, or if it stays low it has to fly blindly about in search of a pinpoint, and this leads to its wasting fuel and running the risk of flying into an unknown hazard. A prerequisite of success, then, is that the Bat should be able to navigate accurately all the time.*

For the first part of the flight this would be easy. Doppler, etc., could be used, and visual checks made on the Scandinavian coast. After leaving Gotska Sandön, however, the Bat would be faced with over two hundred miles of blind flying over the sea, then nearly three hundred miles over the Russian plains. And after Gotska Sandön, Doppler, radar and radio, etc., couldn't be used for fear of the Russians picking them up. Navigation on this second part of the flight would therefore depend on dead reckoning and the moving map. This latter is ideal for the flight over Russia. But it has one weakness. Its accuracy decreases with the distance flown from the last point at which it was set. It is therefore essential on this second part of the flight for the Bat to obtain a number of accurate fixes, so that the moving map can be readjusted. One such fix MUST *be obtained as the plane crosses the Russian coast; otherwise it will quickly become lost and the operation will stand no chance of success. The Instrument Department at Farnborough are confident they will be able to devise a type of screened beacon which could be dropped off the Russian shore and which the Bat could home on, thus enabling the plane to make*

74

an exact landfall. [This last had seemed a bit overoptimistic to Oakman; but as the others pointed out, too many doubts and qualifications would only put the Chiefs of Staff off.]

(c) RELEASE OF STANDOFF BOMB: *This should present no problem. Trials have demonstrated that a bomb released ten miles from target is accurate to within fifty yards. There should be no difficulty, therefore, once the release point has been reached, in landing a bomb in Red Square. All that's needed is for the nuclear warhead to be replaced by a canister of similar weight and aerodynamic behavior.*

The notes ended with a detailed flight plan: a schedule of times and tracks and refueling points.

Pellew read every word of it—twice; from the formal opening right through to Oakman's neat and careful signature at the foot of the final page. And the conviction suddenly came to him that this was it; that this was the answer; that this was a straw at which the Cabinet and Chiefs of Staff would clutch, blindly and thankfully and with a grip which would never weaken.

He looked up at Oakman and smiled. "I'll take this to the Air Ministry right away," he said. "I'll have it through to the old man tonight. And I've an idea he'll like it."

9

"The old man"—Air Marshal Sir Basil Timperley—sat in the oak-paneled committee room of No. 10, clutching his brief case. His foot tapped impatiently on the parquet floor.

It had been after ten the previous evening before Oakman's scheme had reached him—for he had been presiding over a staff conference at Bomber Command. He had liked the idea of using the Bat from the word go; but it had been close to midnight before he'd satisfied himself that every detail was watertight, and too late that day for action. He had, however, telephoned the Prime Minister, and they had agreed to discuss the scheme at the cabinet meeting first thing the next morning.

The Cabinet and Chiefs of Staff met at nine thirty. By this their third meeting they had fallen into a routine. The Prime Minister was setting the ball rolling with a résumé of what had happened in the previous twenty-four hours; ministers and Chiefs of Staff would then answer semi-technical questions which concerned their departments, and finally they'd talk of the future—of what immediate and long-term measures they could take to deal with the crisis that had so suddenly engulfed them. Not till they had reached this final stage, Timperley decided, would he put forward the idea of using the Bat.

The Prime Minister's résumé could hardly be called cheerful. His opening gambit—"I'm afraid I have no good news for you"—set the tone for what was to come. So far, he told his audience, every attempt to land a reply in Red Square had failed. The Americans had launched four rockets; NATO, three. All had been intercepted. The Russian claim that they could shoot down single missiles had been substantiated. That numbers could swamp the Soviet defenses if it came to a hot war, nobody doubted; but it began to look as though single missiles just wouldn't get through.

The tap of Sir Basil's foot increased in tempo. All this made the scheme he had in his brief case the more attractive.

The Prime Minister's voice, unemotional and matter-of-fact, continued the catalogue of gloom. It seemed that Russian missiles, on the other hand, could land where they pleased. One had landed last night, exactly as predicted by Moscow Radio, beside the launching ramps of Cape Canaveral, another off Woomera, another off South Uist. The West's anti-missile defenses (still in embryo) were proving ineffective. It wasn't unexpected. But it *was* disheartening. And frightening. And the Communists were making capital out of the West's discomfort.

This, the Prime Minister said, was the most serious development of all: the way the Communists were exploiting their supremacy in missiles to whip up apprehension and defeatism all over the world. Already, in the first forty-eight hours, there had been rallies, strikes and protest marches, meetings, demonstrations and petitions: all with a single theme: Don't be obstinate; don't risk the holocaust of a nuclear war; go to Moscow. It was a theme which found an echo (albeit in some cases a grudging one) in the heart of every man, woman and child in the world. It was a theme which would, he knew, be repeated, *accelerando* and at mounting pitch, in the days to come.

"And yet"—the Prime Minister's voice took on a sudden urgency—"I'm still convinced the Russians are bluffing and that if we stand firm they'll climb down. We've been over the arguments before. What held good on the first day will still hold good on the last. We mustn't be swayed by public opinion. We must refuse to be intimidated by threats. On that, I'm sure I have your support."

His eyes flickered from face to face, staying longest on the face of the Leader of the House. He sighed, and went on to speak of diplomacy.

Every effort to negotiate with Russia had drawn a blank. On the credit side, however, a definite policy had been worked out among the leaders of the West. He explained this policy now, carefully, anxious that no one should get hold of the wrong end of the stick. The Americans, he said, had decided to make a limited effort only to land a reply; they were keeping their big guns in reserve, in case of a hot war. It wasn't a case of contracting out. He emphasized that. It was a case of common sense. For the surest safeguard against war was still the deterrent—the overkill capacity of a massed attack by American bombers and rockets—and for these same bombers and rockets to be rearmed with harmless instead of nuclear warheads would be like leaving the hive to be guarded by bees without a sting.

"This doesn't mean," the Prime Minister added, "that the Americans are doing nothing. Far from it. They're working on several projects, including one we've great confidence in—they've sent a Polaris submarine under the icecap, and she should be in firing position tomorrow night—but it *does* mean that they're leaving us in Europe to make the main effort. And that's only common sense. For the experts think that short-range missiles have a better chance of getting through than long-range."

The discussion got technical. Why were short-range mis-

78

siles a better bet than long-range? Why had the Russian missiles got through whereas ours had failed? Sir Basil bided his time. He was out of his depth and out of sympathy. Missiles, missiles, missiles, he thought: soulless creations; symbols of a sick world; terrifying, unreliable, not to be trusted in an emergency.

Soon they were talking of plans for the future. And every plan was for the firing of this, that or the other missile. They're losing touch with reality, he thought; they're being blinded by science. He said nothing; he waited for his cue. And at last the Prime Minister turned to him.

"You're very silent, Basil. What about this scheme of yours?"

He laid his brief case carefully on the table.

" 'Men make the city,' " he said slowly, " 'and not walls or ships without men in them.' "

He savored the moment of silence: the two dozen faces staring at him in blank astonishment. He unfastened the clasp of his case. "I have in here a scheme which relies not on missiles but on men. And I've faith in it."

He pulled out the neatly typed pages of Oakman's scheme. " 'Aim,' " he read, " 'to land a message, as challenged, in Red Square.' "

Their interest at first was polite and skeptical. A single low-level bomber, they thought; sounds like a throwback to World War II; and what sort of chance would it stand against the whole weight of the Soviet defenses? But gradually, as the technicalities of the scheme unfolded and they were able to grasp the peculiar advantages of a low-flying aircraft for this operation, their interest quickened. Here was something within the range of their comprehension. Missiles they could take only on trust, relying on the obscure calculations of scientists which they could make neither head nor tail of; but a low-level piloted plane was a thing they could understand. And what they could understand they grasped at, thankfully. By the time Sir Basil came to the end of the flight plan, he was preaching to the already converted.

When he had finished there was a short silence; then the Prime Minister said simply, "What chance would *you* give them, Basil, of getting through?"

"If all goes well and we achieve surprise, better than fifty–fifty."

"And of coming out of it alive?"

"Much the same. *If* all goes well. That's the crux of it. With an operation like this, all's well if all's well. But once things start to go wrong, snags snowball. And if that happens they've had it."

Another silence. Then the Leader of the House said judicially, "It's a justifiable expenditure: one air crew against the survival of the West."

Nods. Grunts of assent. And it all happened as Pellew had predicted: the Cabinet and Chiefs of Staff gave the scheme their blessing, wholeheartedly, thankfully, and with an optimism which the facts by no means entirely justified.

As the meeting was about to break up, the Prime Minister said, "I suppose you'll ask for volunteers?"

Sir Basil shook his head. "For a mission like this," he said, "we'll pick the most experienced crew."

10

In the control tower at Farnborough everyone kept out of Pellew's way—for word had got around that the old man was in one of his moods. It wasn't altogether true. He was more keyed up than irritable: on edge, preoccupied, grabbing the phone off its cradle the second it rang. It was midday before the call he was waiting for came through, and S.A.S.O.* Bomber Command was telling him on the scrambler that the flight of the Bat was on.

From that moment things moved fast.

Within an hour two teams, which had been provisionally alerted the night before, were set up: an operational team whose job was to work out a detailed flight plan, and a technical team who were to see that the aircraft itself was at peak efficiency and its standoff bomb suitably modified. Then came the question of air crew. S.A.S.O. had been emphatic on this point: "You're to pick your most experienced crew." "And what," Pellew had asked, "about the chap who thought the scheme up?" "He can be a stand-by." In the end Pellew decided to call in three crews: Ellis and Maynard, Robinshaw and Taylor (the second most exper-

* Senior air staff officer.

ienced pilot and navigator), and Oakman and Polhill. And it was these six who were called to the operations room.

S.A.S.O. himself came down from High Wycombe to brief them. He didn't waste time and breath telling them how much depended on what they were going to try to do. That they knew. He was strictly practical. They need only worry, he told them, over the physical act of flying the plane. Everything else would be worked out for them. Details of refueling, navigation, bomb release, radio and emergency drills—all these would be handed them on a plate, leaving them free to concentrate entirely on the flight itself.

"Now the requisites of success," S.A.S.O. went on, "are three. Rehearsal. Speed. And secrecy."

He dealt with them one by one, like a schoolmaster developing a thesis. Operations in the last war, he said, had proved the value of rehearsal. If the impossible was rehearsed often enough and meticulously enough it became the commonplace. In this case they obviously couldn't make trial runs to Moscow, but they could do the next best thing: rehearse the vital parts of the flight stage by stage—the low-level refueling, the finding and passing over a preselected check point and the actual release of the bomb. They could also fly a trial run over a similar distance—say, to Iceland. And the photographic staff were preparing a scale model of the Gulf of Finland and the run-in to Moscow, which they could memorize.

"Now for the second requisite: speed. We've only four days—four days to Armageddon. So we must get cracking. We've worked out a schedule of tests, starting the moment this briefing is over. If there're snags we'll iron them out at once. If there's special equipment needed we'll have it made. And we'll make the attempt the moment we're in the clear. While the good weather holds. The sooner, the better.

"As for security—your lives depend on it. For if the Russians get to know what we're planning, we can write R.I.P. to the whole affair." He went on to detail a comprehensive range of security measures.

And to end up, he assessed their chances of success. "Don't imagine," he told them, "this is a forlorn hope you're being sent on. Or a suicide trip. If all goes smoothly you've every chance of getting away with it. If all goes smoothly . . . That's the key. And that's the reason for all this rehearsal. Before you take off we want to be sure that every detail of the flight goes like clockwork. Unless it does, you won't, I promise you, take off.

"And now I'll ask Group Captain Pellew to tell you about the tests laid on for this afternoon and tonight."

In the afternoon, Pellew told them, they were to test the accuracy with which they could release a modified stand-off bomb (with its nuclear warhead, of course, replaced by a canister and parachute release gear). In the late evening, after a couple of hours' rest, they'd take off for a practice low-level refueling over the sea. He went into details.

While the group captain was talking, Oakman studied his fellow air crew. Robinshaw and Taylor were quietly making notes—it would take an atom bomb, he reflected, to shake *them* out of their well-bred *sang-froid*. Maynard and Polhill, too, were scribbling away, as happy apparently as schoolboys at a technical class. Ellis, on the other hand, was fidgeting, and his face was pale and strained. He looks ill, Oakman thought. Anxiety welled up in him. Perhaps he *was* ill? He studied Ellis clinically, and after a while his anxiety receded a little. Much more likely, he told himself, the Winco was simply overworked and tired. And in any case, why worry? Even if he *was* ill, Robinshaw and Taylor would surely be next on the list.

Pellew was talking now of the low-level refueling to be

practiced later that evening. He was giving them take-off times and points at which to rendezvous. The navigators' pencils moved busily over their kneepads. A few questions, a few technical explanations, and the briefing was over; and the air crew were walking out of the control tower and over the sunlit tarmac to their planes. Ellis, Oakman noticed, seemed to be having trouble carrying his bone dome; after a while he handed it to his navigator.

"Kenneth!"

"Hmmm?" He was preoccupied, staring at Ellis.

"Wake up, man." Polhill tapped him on the shoulder.

"What is it?"

"I thought *we* were making this trip. It was our idea."

"Hmmm! I suppose the high-ups stuck to the book: picked the crew with most experience."

"I don't like it." Polhill's usually cheerful face was anxious.

"We thought the scheme up. I took it for granted we'd do the flying."

Oakman shrugged. "Why worry?" he said briefly. "The decision's out of our hands."

He clambered into the cockpit, jerked the pin from the back of his ejector seat and started his preflight checks. It was obvious that the matter, to his way of thinking, was closed.

Half an hour later they were circling Boscombe Down at ten thousand feet, waiting their turn to launch.

It was a lovely afternoon: blue sky, patches of cotton wool cloud, and far below them the green-gold mosaic of the Wiltshire plains, shimmering in the heat haze of an Indian summer. After a while they picked out Ellis, a pinhead of silver aglint in the sun, starting his run-in. They followed him for perhaps a dozen miles; then a layer of cloud drifted between them, and he was gone. A few minutes later the range came through on the R.T. telling them to reduce height and orbit the waiting area.

The Bat spiraled down through four fifths cloud, like a great bird searching for somewhere to nest. Soon they could pick out the familiar landmarks—the tall thin spire of Salisbury Cathedral and the monoliths of Stonehenge. They checked altimeter and compass, and reset their moving map.

The procedure for launching their bomb was simple. All they had to do was fly the Bat over a preselected spot on the ground, at a known course and speed, and the moment they were over the spot press their release button. The standoff bomb would then shoot off, propelled by its own rockets, stabilized by its own gyros and guided by its own computers onto a target ten miles distant. It was simple in theory. Simple, too, in practice—so long as navigation during the run-in, right up to the moment of release, was one hundred per cent accurate. Everything depended on that. (It was this procedure of release, of course, which occasioned the need for such accurate navigation during the flight to Moscow. It was no good the Bat's getting somewhere near the outskirts of the Russian capital and firing its message blind; it had to fire it accurately, flying a known course over a known spot; and this was possible only if navigation had been exact during the run-in.)

"O for orange." The voice of the controller filled the cockpit. "Come in now."

Throttles three quarters open, the stick eased forward, their speed building up, the plains blurring, the vibration, and the shriller whine of their jets as they swept low and fast into the launching approaches. Polhill's eyes flickered from compass to stop watch to unrolling map; Oakman's followed the landmarks as they flashed by under their wing tips, blurred by proximity and their speed of approach.

85

The aircraft hammered uneasily in air movements close to the warm ground. The instruments vibrated. As he held the Bat hard on course, Oakman felt the familiar stir of exhilaration. He had done it all before. Often. Yet each time something of the original thrill and wonder and sense of power remained.

"Height O.K. Course O.K. Speed 590 knots."

He eased back a shade on the throttles. Mach .9 (570 knots) was the speed they wanted. If they came in too fast they'd very likely cause damage on the ground, possibly even breaking glass and eardrums with the force of their sonic boom.

"Five seconds, four seconds, three seconds," Polhill chanted. "Two, one, fire."

His finger tightened on the release button. Flame and smoke lapped briefly around the bomb and it was gone, and the Bat, freed of its load, rose sweetly into an effortless climbing turn.

A few seconds later, over the range, the standoff bomb broke in two. A parachute opened. And a small container drifted slowly to earth.

"Looked pretty good from here."

Oakman nodded, easing back on the throttles as they soared up through ten thousand feet and set course for Farnborough.

An hour later results were being analyzed in the operations room.

Things had gone well. Although the Armament Department had been given less than twenty-four hours in which to modify the standoff warheads (Pellew in fact had jumped the gun by telling them to start work the previous evening), the release apparatus which they'd installed had worked perfectly. In each case a canister had been parachuted squarely into the target area. Ellis's had landed seventy yards off center, Robinshaw's thirty yards and Oakman's forty yards. Which, as Pellew pointed out, was accurate enough for the real thing. He went on to say that there'd be further trials tomorrow, more realistic ones, with the Bat flying flat out and at the same course and height as she'd use over Moscow. These trials, he added, wouldn't be done at Boscombe Down, or the Air Ministry would have a nice little bill for broken glass; they'd be carried out secretly over the sea, and the Navy was already buoying them up a target area at the approaches to the Channel.

He went on to brief them for the refueling tests which were scheduled for later that evening.

When the briefing was over they were left with four clear hours before taking off for the refueling rendezvous with their tankers. "Get as much rest as you can," Pellew had advised them. But four hours is an awkward time to rest in, and Polhill suggested that they find Christabel and the two of them come home with him for supper.

After a couple of phone calls they located her in a laboratory of the Instrument Department. She was none too keen on the idea at first.

"I'm busy playing with my little black boxes," she told Oakman.

"You've got to eat sometime."

"But not now."

Oakman, however, was persuasive, and a quarter of an hour later the three of them were driving out of the gate by the R.A.F. mess.

As they pulled into the stream of rush-hour traffic, Christabel looked back at the hospital block. About a dozen cars were parked in front of it, including an ancient Lagonda.

"Isn't that Ellis's?" she asked.

Oakman peered out of the rear window. "Yes," he said

slowly, "I think it is." And for the rest of the drive to the Polhills' he was unusually quiet.

Jim and Jennifer Polhill lived in a large, Tudor and slightly dilapidated farmhouse, together with their three children, two dogs, two tortoises, a pony and a colony of fantail pigeons. They had ten acres of grassland and beech woods: too much for them to cope with, really, but wonderful for the children. A good few people had smiled when the Polhills first bought Dragonfly Farm shortly after Jim's arrival from Wright Field: another American, they'd told one another, going to ape the country squire. And when Jim had appeared on his land complete with tweeds, pipe, shooting stick and springer spaniel, their impressions had been confirmed: it was quite usual, local people reminded themselves, for the exchange officers to discard their Chevrolets, baseball caps and cigars and try to become more English even than the English. What these people didn't realize at first (though the truth got home to most of them before long) was that the Polhills weren't putting on an act at all: they were simply living the sort of life they'd been used to living in New England, where they'd both been brought up and had spent the greater part of their lives, and that Polhill's tweeds and "Oxford" accent weren't in fact affectation at all—he'd always dressed and spoken that way.

It had just struck seven as he pulled up beside the lich gate, and the children were upstairs—the youngest asleep in her cot, the others (Robert, aged seven; and Nicola, five) peering out of their bedroom windows. Jim went upstairs to say good night to them, while his wife offered Kenneth and Christabel drinks.

Jennifer Polhill was an attractive girl, with chestnut hair, a heart-shaped face and large deep-set eyes, the whites of which were slightly blue, like a newborn baby's. She looked far too young to have three children. While Jim was up-stairs she kept the conversation going easily enough, but without a great deal of animation. The moment her husband returned, however, his presence seemed to spark off in her a sort of spontaneous gaiety. It was noticeable only in little things: in the added bite to her conversation, in the way she smiled at him as their eyes met over their cocktail glasses, in the way she moved as she offered cigarettes. She must, Christabel thought, be very much in love with him—and this surprised her a little, to think that a woman rising thirty should still take on a sort of radiance, like a bride, merely because her husband was close to her.

During supper their conversation got around to the tests. Christabel and Kenneth were a bit security-conscious at first; but it soon became clear that Polhill had no secrets from his wife, and before long the four of them were deep in technicalities. Once or twice, as they spoke of this problem or that, Jennifer Polhill eyed her husband curiously, as if something was puzzling her.

"I take it," she said at last, "the tests were a success?"

"Yes."

"Then what are you worried about?"

"Nothing," he said quickly, "that's at all important."

Jennifer would have been happy to take the hint, but Christabel jumped in with both feet.

"Come on, Jim," she said, "I've noticed your long face too. What don't you approve of?"

There was an awkward silence.

"I think he's put out," Oakman said at last, "because Ellis and Maynard are making the trip, and not us."

Jennifer didn't move. Her eyes were fixed on her hus-band. Her voice was curiously breathless. "Is that a fact? You're not going?"

"No."

"The high-ups evidently wanted the senior crew," Oakman said easily. "You know what sticklers they are for protocol."

Jennifer pushed back her chair. She gave Christabel a vague, half-apologetic smile.

"Excuse me," she said. "I think the baby's crying."

She went upstairs to the nursery.

The baby wasn't crying at all; she was asleep in her cot. Jennifer let down the side bars and dropped to her knees and pressed her face into the jumbled-up blankets. Thank God, she thought. Thank God the whole thing's off—at least for Jim—and he's not going to be killed. Tears of relief ran salt and wet over her lips. She knelt by the cot for several minutes, her face pressed close to the baby's; then slowly she got to her feet. Now pull yourself together, she thought, and go back to the others, or Jim'll be worried. She splashed water over her eyes, touched up her make-up and gave the baby a teaspoonful of gripe water; then she came slowly downstairs.

"What was it?" Jim asked her. "Wind?"

"I gave her some gripe water," she said. "And now she's fine."

After coffee she suggested that they walk around the garden. It was dark, but the western sky was aglow with the lights of Aldershot, and a great three-quarter moon was rising out of the beech woods. There was an autumn coolness in the air, and already little patches of mist, harbingers of the frost to come, were forming in the hollows. After a while Jim and Jennifer left the others beside the house and went off to the bottom of the garden to pick some apples for the children to take to school the next morning.

"I wish," Jennifer said, "you didn't have to go up again tonight."

He took her hand. "So," he said, "do I."

90

They smiled at each other, sharing the same thought.

The shrill of the telephone brought them down to earth with a bump.

"Shall I answer it?" Kenneth shouted from the terrace.

"Sure. Go ahead."

Kenneth Oakman walked through the french windows and into the hall. He picked up the phone. "Farnham 0317," he said.

"Is that Squadron Leader Oakman?"

"Yes."

"Pellew here. I've important news for you. Be careful what you say on a public line . . ."

Left to herself, Christabel was uncertain what to do. She thought of joining the others as they came up from the orchard, but her instinct warned her she'd be *de trop*. Yet it was cold on the terrace, so after a moment's hesitation she followed Oakman through the french windows. The door which led into the hall was open, and she could hear his voice quite clearly. Not wanting to listen in to what she thought might be a private conversation, she walked across to the door, intending to shut it. But as her fingers closed around the handle she pulled up short. For something had happened to Kenneth Oakman's voice. It had gone choked and muffled, as though he were having to fight for breath. She peered anxiously around the door.

The Polhills' hall was L-shaped, and from the door of the sitting room she couldn't see the telephone directly. But she could see it—and Kenneth Oakman—by reflection, in a gilt-framed mirror hung on the opposite wall.

She caught her breath. For the face of the man holding the telephone wasn't a face she knew. It was the face of a stranger, twisted and flawed with fear.

In the mirror their eyes met. It was more of a shock to her, somehow, seeing his fear by reflection. It gave the incident a touch of furtiveness: as though she'd surprised him in some secret vice by peeping through a keyhole.

He swung away so that she couldn't see his face.

"Kenneth!" She ran down the passage and into the hall. "What is it?"

By the time she'd rounded the corner, his mask of self-sufficiency was back in place. "It's all right," he said. "I just had a bit of a shock."

"But what is it?"

"Ellis. He's got peritonitis."

"Oh!" She wasn't sure what she'd expected, but not that. She tried to collect her wits. "Is it serious?"

"He's in hospital."

His hands, she noticed, were trembling. She stared at him. And the penny suddenly dropped.

"Does this mean," she said, "you and Jim'll be flying the Bat?"

She wouldn't have noticed it if she hadn't been watching for it: the sudden resurgence of fear which flickered for a moment into his eyes and was quickly suppressed. "It'll either be us," he said, "or Robinshaw and Taylor."

He was regaining his composure fast now, and by the time Jim and Jennifer came in from the garden he was able to pass on the news almost matter-of-factly.

Jim was as upset as Oakman had been—but for a different reason.

"Poor old Ellis! I thought he'd been looking sick. When are they going to operate?"

"I expect tonight."

"You don't know for sure?"

"No."

"Hmmm!" Jim looked at his watch. "We've more than an hour till take-off. If we leave right now, we'll have time to call at the hospital."

92

A few minutes later the three of them were on their way to Farnborough.

In the back of the car Christabel was silent. How differently, she thought—and how unexpectedly—the two men had reacted to the news about Ellis. Staring at the back of Oakman's neck, she sighed. She'd been building up, lately, a nice comforting image in her mind: the image of a handsome and fearless pilot with whom she was falling in love. And now, it seemed, her image was flawed: her hero wasn't fearless at all. It did occur to her that perhaps she was judging him overharshly. But her work and upbringing had made her a perfectionist; anything with the slightest flaw she rejected. It was a sort of arrogance, this rejection of anything short of the perfect—her sharpest weapon as a scientist, her Achilles heel when it came to a personal relationship. And it was this arrogance which made her, now, see things from her viewpoint rather than his. And so instead of wondering how she could help him she sighed and thought that things between them could never be quite the same again.

11

The Bat flew north toward her practice rendezvous off the Faeroes, her course 330° magnetic, her speed 550 knots, her height 150 feet.

It was the sort of night that poets and lovers dream of: no cloud, no wind, and a great three-quarter moon bathing the Atlantic in a sheen of silver. After they'd been airborne about an hour they passed the Hebrides: jet-black outcrops of rock ringed by breaking waves as if by fire. A lovelier sight it would have been hard to imagine. But Oakman hardly gave the Hebrides a glance. His mind was on other things.

To start with, the physical demands of flying had kept him occupied. But after a while he found conditions so easy—no wind, no turbulence and first-class visibility—that he was able to switch in the automatic pilot. He had nothing to do then but think. And it wasn't long before his thoughts became centered, to the exclusion of everything else, on the flight to Moscow.

Who would be chosen? Robinshaw and Taylor? Or Oakman and Polhill?

It was ironic, wasn't it? When on the taxi track of Culdrose he'd first thought up the idea of using the Bat it had seemed a bit of an inspiration. But then—almost at once—he'd begun to have doubts. And ever since, the doubts had been mounting and he'd been trying to contract out, while all along the line circumstances had conspired to get him more and more deeply involved: Christabel's enthusiasm, Ellis's illness. He sighed, and stared unseeing at the red glow of his instruments. Why, he asked himself, *have* I been trying to contract out? Why else than because I'm afraid. He tried to be objective about it, to view his fear with the same lofty detachment as he'd schooled himself in the last few years to view the affairs of others. But it wasn't easy. He felt uncertain and alone. But maybe, he thought after a while, I'm getting worked up about nothing. After all, Robinshaw and Taylor *are* more experienced *and* more senior; and when it comes to the point, I can't see them being passed over. In fact, aren't there indications already that they'll be the ones to go? Robinshaw and Taylor, he reminded himself, were rendezvousing that night in the Baltic—"It's a good idea," Pellew had said, "for you to get a sight of the area we'll use for the real thing"—whereas he and Polhill had been sent up to the North Atlantic. And another thing, Robinshaw's standoff bomb had been launched more accurately than his; and weren't they likely, for the actual flight, to choose the crew who had shaped up best in the trials?

An idea came to him, and his eyes slid sideways to Polhill. Suppose he altered their air speed. Not a big alteration—for that would be noticed. Just enough to make them, say, five or ten minutes late at their rendezvous. Whereas the efficient Robinshaw and Taylor would doubtless arrive dead on time.

Oh, God, he thought, pull yourself together; what a thing to have thought of! He cut out the automatic pilot and forced himself for the next half hour to fly manually.

The Bat whispered north. Once they'd passed the Hebrides there were no landmarks en route. They simply flew on and on, lulled to drowsiness by the sibilant sigh of their jets, drugged to somnolence by the great swaths of moonlight which poured around them into a sea that was motionless as glass.

They were about two hundred miles short of the Faeroes when Polhill yawned, stretched and announced that he was going to get a radio fix.

Oakman looked at him curiously. "What for?"

"Just a check."

"Don't trust my flying, eh?"

Polhill smiled. He tapped the automatic pilot. "I don't trust even George," he said. He tuned in his radio. After a few minutes' adjusting and calculating, he smiled. "Looks like we're spot on."

The Bat, at not far short of the speed of sound, swept on over the North Atlantic. Soon they could see the aurora borealis, flickering like fairy lanterns along the northern horizon, white and purple and apple green.

"With all this light," Polhill said, "refueling should be a piece of cake."

Oakman grunted.

Their rendezvous time was 2250. At 2245 they reduced speed and started to scan the horizon section by section. Visibility was first-rate; but for two aircraft to meet by night at a map reference after navigating blind for nearly eight hundred miles is easier said than done, and Polhill was neither surprised nor unduly perturbed when 2250 came and there was still no sign of the tanker. They circled for a couple of minutes, then started a square search. Things would have been easier, of course, if their rendezvous had been at a visible point—say, over one of the islands. But on the actual operation they'd have to keep clear of land, and Pellew had decided to make the tests as realistic as

96

possible by assuming the same conditions. So they now had only a chart reference from which to start their search. Oakman concentrated on his instruments, flying each leg that was given him with impeccable precision.

On the third leg Polhill said quietly, "I think I've got her. Two o'clock. About a hundred feet up."

Oakman stared through the glass of the cockpit. At first he could see nothing. Then a shadow passed ghostlike over the aurora. His eyes focused on it; and he was able at once to pick out, quite clearly, the gray triangular shape of the Valiant delineated against the stars.

With a grunt of relief he turned toward her. He climbed to three hundred feet and formated on her starboard quarter. For something like a couple of minutes the two aircraft flew side by side, swaying slightly under the stars like ships at anchor rocked by an unseen swell. Then from the tanker's cockpit a light flashed briefly—indicating that the flight refueling operator was in position and the drogue streamed. Oakman throttled back, and the Bat dropped beneath and astern of her companion.

Everything was done in silence—again simulating the flight to Moscow, when radios of course would be taboo. The planes' navigation lights were switched off too—again simulating the real thing—and this meant that Oakman had to call on all his skill as he maneuvered to pick up the drogue.

The drogue swung down from the tanker's belly at the end of a hundred feet of rubber pipeline. Using the Bat's long antenna-like proboscis as a sight, he edged the plane forward, his aim to insert the proboscis into the drogue. But at the first attempt he failed, and in the uncertain moonlight the pipeline swung back at them, dangerously close. He cursed. He was too proud of his reputation as a pilot not to feel thoroughly annoyed with himself. And to add to his annoyance, he knew *why* he'd missed the drogue. He hadn't been concentrating. At the back of his mind had been the thought, What does it matter if I do make a hash of things? It'll all go down in the log: it'll all be a bit more evidence to prove that Robinshaw is the man for Moscow rather than me. But now it came to the point, he knew he couldn't make a hash of things a second time. His integrity as a pilot was something he just wasn't prepared to throw away. He concentrated on flying the Bat with pinpoint accuracy, and at the second attempt the steel-tipped proboscis struck home. It was gripped at once by a ring of claws inside the drogue, and the two planes were united.

In the tanker's cockpit a light on the instrument panel flashed green. "Fuel on," the engineer called to his pilot. He turned the refueling cock to "full," and the Bat started to suck in kerosene at the rate of three hundred gallons a minute.

Fuel poured silently down the hose. There were no hitches, no snags, as the two aircraft, joined in gargantuan mating, flew steadily on, one beneath the other, under a backdrop of stars and the great gold disc of the moon.

At the end of ten minutes the light on the Valiant's instrument panel changed from green to yellow. "Fuel cock closed," the operator called. And a moment later, "Drogue disconnected. Refueling complete."

The aircraft broke apart.

The Valiant, her job done, waggled her wings and set course for Iceland. And the Bat, too, headed for home. They'd proved it practicable to rendezvous at a chart reference and refuel without lights at zero feet.

The flight back, inevitably, was something of an anticlimax. On the way out they'd been keyed up by the need to make an accurate rendezvous with the tanker—if they'd missed her altogether they'd have been in trouble—while the actual refueling had been difficult enough to keep

98

them on the *qui vive*. But no such sense of urgency disturbed the even tenor of the flight back; however carelessly or inaccurately they flew, they could hardly miss the whole of the British Isles, with its thousand and one airfields, beacons and homing aids! They settled for a course of 142, an air speed of 550, and George. And once again, for over an hour, they had nothing to do but think.

After a while Polhill looked at his watch. "They'll have operated on Ellis by now."

"Hmmm."

"Guess I'll call in after debriefing. Make sure he's O.K."

"Suit yourself," Oakman grunted. "I'm for bed." He was shorter than he'd meant to be. For he was thinking, again, of the flight to Moscow.

He thought about the flight to Moscow a great deal as they headed south. And the more he thought about it the more certain he became that in the end Robinshaw and Taylor would be the crew to be chosen. And it wasn't wishful thinking that brought him to this conclusion; it was simply that after twelve years in the R.A.F. he knew how these things were decided, and he just couldn't see the powers-that-be passing over a crew who were both senior and more experienced. So you can stop worrying, he told himself as they started their run-in to Farnborough. Everything's going to be all right.

The three Bats were due back from their practice refueling at much the same time. Pellew had therefore decided to lay on a meal for the air crews as soon as they landed, and then debrief them together.

When Oakman and Polhill came into the mess one crew (the stand-ins for Ellis and Maynard) were already down and tucking in to their coffee and ham and eggs. But there was no sign yet of Robinshaw and Taylor.

By the time the four of them had finished their meal

99

and chatted about this and that for the best part of twenty minutes, they were getting a bit impatient; so Oakman decided to go across to Control and see if they had news of how long Robinshaw and Taylor were likely to be.

He felt a bit tired as he climbed the stairs, but not particularly anxious. Certainly he had no sense of foreboding and no premonition of disaster.

He found the control room in a flap, with staff officers and radio operators bustling about with coded reports and long faces.

"No, sir," the duty officer said shortly. "We've no news at all."

Oakman didn't like the way he said it—like a V.I.P. with plenty to hide being quizzed by the press.

"You can't say where they are?"

"Afraid not, sir."

He felt the stir of anxiety now. He stood uncertainly in the doorway, watching the bustling, preoccupied figures. I'll get nothing out of this lot, he thought. I'll try Pellew.

Pellew's office adjoined the control room. Its door was ajar. As he raised his hand to knock, Oakman could hear the group captain's voice quite clearly. He was on the telephone.

"Of course, sir," he was saying, "they can't *really* have violated Soviet air space . . . No, they were far too experienced a crew to get off course . . ."

Oakman's hand fell from the doorknob. He began to tremble. It can't be true, he told himself. I just won't believe it's true. Yet he felt no surprise, only a wave of numb, uncontrollable fear, when Pellew, seeing him in the doorway, called him in and told him that a couple of hours ago Robinshaw and Taylor had been shot down in flames somewhere to the north of Gotska Sandön.

12

It was 10:30 A.M. on the fourth day, and Cabinet and Chiefs of Staff were again in session. Again the news was bad. And time was running out.

The Prime Minister didn't pull his punches. The country, he said, was on the verge of panic. The man in the street had trusted both government and Forces at first; but now, with the ultimatum period more than half expired and a reply still not landed, he was having second thoughts. There'd been petitions, strikes and riots—some Communist-inspired, others sparked off by spontaneous fear. The Afro-Asian bloc were bringing pressure on the West to negotiate. And Russian sabotage was assuming serious proportions. "Only last night," the Prime Minister said, "the Atlantic cable was cut in three places."

He went on to speak of two especially grave developments. The Polaris submarine which had set out under the icecap had failed to report its position at the last check time. "We must face up to the fact that she may be lost. . . . And even more serious, our low-level bomber project has run into trouble. Basil!" He turned to the air marshal. "Perhaps you'll give us the facts on this."

Sir Basil Timperley was as blunt as the Prime Minister

had been. "The fact is," he told his audience, "we've had a setback. In the past the Baltic has always been a 'safe' area, unscreened by Russian radar or fighters. But it's a different story now. Last night we sent a Bat and a tanker to rendezvous for practice refueling off Gotska Sandön—that's an island in mid-Baltic. And both were shot down." He paused, letting the implications sink in. "Now the first thing we asked ourselves was how were the planes spotted when they should have gone in under the radar screens? Well, we know the answer to that one. The Foreign Office have just had a note from the Swedish attaché, to complain that last night our military aircraft violated their air space. It's true, of course. You can't get into the Baltic wihout violating *somebody's* air space. We routed the planes as best we could—over uninhabited country. Yet they were picked up, *and* news of their approach got through to the Russians. We can draw only one conclusion from that. There's a ring of Soviet-controlled listening posts, probably a lot of them, in subs and fishing boats the length of the Scandinavian coast. And we can't get into the Baltic."

He paused again. He looked at the semicircle of anxious, slightly puzzled faces. They were worried, of course—apart from anything else, a share of his own anxiety had communicated itself to them. Yet they hadn't, he could tell, grasped the full significance of what he was saying: they hadn't enough technical know-how for the implications really to strike home.

"So we can't," he repeated, "get into the Baltic. You ask why that's so serious? It's a matter of fuel consumption. The maximum range of a Bat is 1,100 miles. And it's 550 miles from mid-Baltic to Moscow. In other words, even refueling in mid-Baltic is cutting it fine. And if we can't refuel as far east as the middle of the Baltic our Bat won't have enough kerosene to get to Moscow and back. Somewhere, over Soviet territory, she'll run out of fuel. And that, for the crew, will be that."

They could see how the land lay now. What had started off as a reasonable risk had become, quite suddenly, a suicide mission: a "kamikaze."

They were shocked. Yet they were unwilling to give up the project.

And this was for several reasons. At the back of their minds was the thought that now was no time for sentimentality, that it was justifiable to sacrifice one crew to try to preserve the heritage of the West. At the back of their minds, too, was the thought that R.A.F. air crew were professionals, men whose sense of duty should have inured them to the thought of making even the ultimate sacrifice. They were influenced also by the vague expectation that maybe something would turn up which would give the air crew a chance. Perhaps the Bat's range could be increased? Perhaps she could reach Moscow by another route? Perhaps the crew could parachute to safety? And there was one other reason, too, for their clinging to the idea of a low-level bomber. The idea might not look so good at the moment. It might have had the bottom pretty well knocked out of it. But it was still something they understood, something they felt they could cope with. For the fact was this. Every man jack of them at the meeting that morning was over forty-five and had served in World War II. Some of them were over sixty-five and had served in World War I as well. Courage and low-flying airplanes were things they understood—not like rockets and missiles and all the paraphernalia of push-button warfare which they had to take on trust from the scientists. And it seemed to them that the scientists, in their hour of need, had proved a broken reed. Ballistic theorists might reassure them that the settings on their rocket computers were accurate to the thousandth part of a degree. But their rockets

103

still weren't able, it seemed, to land in Red Square; and there was nothing which they, the Cabinet, could do about it. With the scheme for using the Bat, on the other hand, they were back on ground they understood. The problems involved might be semi-technical; but they were the sort of problems which they felt they might themselves, with ingenuity, solve. And so, although the scheme looked as if it were about to founder beneath them, they continued to clutch at it, desperately, irrationally, as drowning men at a straw.

And the man who clutched the straw most fiercely of all was Timperley.

Sir Basil Timperley was one of the last of the old guard. For years younger and more gifted men in the service had been advocating a switch over to guided weapons—manned aircraft, they had argued, were as useless in the sixties as cavalry had been in 1939. Yet Sir Basil, swimming against the tide, had continued to champion piloted planes. Some people thought him a Blimp (it was a pose he deliberately cultivated at times). But there was a great deal more to him than that. Beneath his bluff exterior was a shrewd, cautious and eminently practical brain. He had, for example, been one of the few people in the service to see the potential of the Bat, a plane which he had sedulously fathered from blueprint to operational prototype. And now, it seemed, there had arisen a situation tailor-made to prove the point he'd been trying to hammer home to his clever young subordinates for years: the point that although the age of push-button warfare was undoubtedly around the corner it hadn't arrived yet, and that at least one conventional piloted plane, the Bat, was still an integral part of the service.

So he was thankful, now, that the Cabinet still seemed to have faith in the Bat. It made his task of reassuring them so much the easier.

104

He reassured them not by minimizing the difficulties—he was too honest for that—but by emphasizing the scale and urgency with which the difficulties were being faced up to. He told them about the two teams—"which include the finest brains in the country"; about the special equipment—"some of which has already been tested and found first-rate"; and finally about the crew—"we've settled now for the fellow who thought the idea up, Squadron Leader Oakman, one of our most brilliant pilots, a young man who's already made a name for himself in the service and who I'm sure is the best possible choice . . ."

The Cabinet were impressed.

There was a short silence. Then the Leader of the House said diffidently, "I suppose the crew know they can't refuel? And are still willing to go?"

Sir Basil looked down his nose. "Of course," he said.

They went on to talk of other things: of security measures, anti-riot precautions and a press campaign to minimize the effects of Soviet propaganda—although all of them knew in their hearts that one thing and one thing only would now sponge away, in a single stroke, the rising tide of fear which was threatening to engulf the nations of the West: the landing of a return message in Red Square.

It was midday before the meeting broke up.

As the ministers filed out of the committee room, the Prime Minister drew Sir Basil aside.

"One question. And I want a straight answer."

"Very well."

"The other day you gave the Bat a better than fifty–fifty chance. What chance do you give it now?"

For a long time Sir Basil was silent. And when he spoke it was hesitantly and with none of his usual brusqueness. "That's a *very* difficult question, Prime Minister . . . I reckon we'll solve the refueling problem, at least partially—

in fact, we've the germ of an idea already. But if we can't get into the Baltic, navigation's going to be very, very difficult. . . . Still"—he squared his shoulders—"I reckon we'll think of something. I reckon I'd still give us odds not far short of fifty–fifty."

"And the crew?"

"Frankly, they've very little chance."

"One in ten?"

"No. Not one in a hundred."

They paced the room, their shoes making no sound on the thick-piled carpet.

"Not nice," the Prime Minister said at last.

"Not nice at all. But better two men should die, sir, than two million. Or twenty million."

"I don't believe it would come to that."

"But we can't be certain, can we?"

It all comes back to that, the Prime Minister thought. We can't be certain. He sighed. And his mind went back to Passchendaele and a headquarters dugout behind the lines and a brigadier with tears astream his face because his regiments were going over the top and getting themselves mowed down in cross fire while he was condemned to sit on his arse in a nice, safe sandbagged shelter. He felt very tired and very old. "I want the crew given every possible chance," he said. "And before they take off I want to see them."

Another person to feel tired and old that morning was Mrs. Harley.

She was sitting in Jennifer Polhill's kitchen, watching the preparations for elevenses; and her voice was indignant.

"Then there's that cheeky milk boy. He's going too!"

Oh dear, Jennifer thought, I must go easy on today's milk.

"That's three people not delivering." Mrs. Harley sniffed,

and ticked the defaulters off on her fingers. "No milk. No laundry. No papers."

"No papers?"

"My dear! I called at Whitelaw's on my way here. Young Ian's going to a protest meeting tonight. In Trafalgar Square. And he told his father not to expect him back. Just like that!"

Things are slowing down, Jennifer thought. It needs so few people to walk out on their jobs, and all the little things we've taken for granted for years are suddenly cut off.

And if people are running on the fourth day, she thought, God knows what they'll be doing on the seventh.

She glanced at Mrs. Harley, more in hope than expectation. "Had *you* thought of evacuating? You've no ties here."

Mrs. Harley sniffed. "It'll take more than a few Russian rockets to frighten me!" she said.

But her hands, Jennifer noticed, kept twisting and twining around her handkerchief; and when, an hour later, she set off home, she looked very tired and very old.

13

At about the time the cabinet meeting broke up and Mrs. Harley was walking out through the Polhills' lich gate, the members of another committee were settling themselves into chairs in the operations room at Farnborough. S.A.S.O. was there, together with Pellew, an operations officer from Bomber Command, the Director of Intelligence from the Air Ministry, the head of the Instrument Department and the Deputy Director of the R.A.E.; also two other civilians, an enigmatic character from the Foreign Office, and a diffident little man with horn-rimmed glasses who was chairman of the independent company, Midair Refueling. They were the operational team. And they'd met to try to find a way out of the difficulties now facing the flight of the Bat.

S.A.S.O. was in the chair. It was clear, he told his team, that the Russians had extended their protected zone. They now had evidence of this, over and above last night's shooting down of the Valiant and the Bat. A submarine had tried to get into the Kattegat, but had found it sealed off; recce planes approaching the Baltic had picked up evidence of extensive new radar cover; Intelligence had reported a chain of listening posts down the east Scandinavian coast, and both Finland and Sweden (under obvious pressure) had warned Western military aircraft to keep clear of their territory. It all added up to two very unpleasant facts: there seemed to be no hope now of refueling in the Baltic, and no hope of getting into the Baltic undetected.

They discussed alternatives.

But the alternatives just weren't practical. It was impossible to get a low-level bomber to Moscow from the north, south or east because of the vast distances involved. Which meant they were left with the prospect of having to refuel somewhere west of the Baltic—say, in the Kattegat. Yet this would leave the Bat with barely sufficient kerosene to reach Moscow. There'd be absolutely no margin for error, no hope of return; and the Russians would have warning of their approach.

It began to look as if the scheme would have to be shelved.

For the first part of the meeting the four R.A.F. officers had done most of the talking. The civilians, conscious of the fact that they were swimming in unaccustomed waters, had had little to say for themselves. But as a last resort S.A.S.O. now turned to the little man with glasses from Midair Refueling. He turned to him more in courtesy than expectation, for he thought it unlikely that a civilian could solve an operational problem which was stumping the best brains of the R.A.F.

"Have you any ideas, sir?"

The little man blinked nervously. He spoke very fast. "Well, I have an idea of sorts. Probably not much use to you gentlemen." He coughed apologetically, pulled out a sheaf of exceedingly grubby notes and adjusted his glasses. "Here we are now. BEA Viscount flights, London Airport to Stockholm, every Monday, Wednesday and Friday: take off London 1735, arrive Stockholm 2020. Friday night would be the night for us. . . . I thought of Helsinki first, but I

109

gather the Russians are buzzing airliners close to their fron-
tier." He paused for breath and looked at the semicircle of
uncomprehending faces. "Afraid I'm not explaining this
very well. But I thought perhaps we could fly a tanker and a
Bat along the BEA route to Stockholm. If two planes are in
close formation, you know, ground radar can pick up only
the single echo."

S.A.S.O.'s face lit up. "I see what you're getting at. We
substitute a tanker for a BEA Viscount, fly her on the BEA
route to Stockholm, and close-formate a Bat on her." He
looked at the little man with sudden interest. "That's a
damned good idea."

"Well, of course, there's rather more to it than that." The
little man thumbed through his notes. "The real fun is
working out details. Like making sure the pilot of the tanker
uses the same radio patter as the pilot of a Viscount."

They got the scheme out of him piecemeal and none too
coherently. As the bits fell into position their enthusiasm
grew, until at the end they realized it wasn't just an answer
of sorts he'd given them. It was the perfect answer, worked
out with ingenuity and the most painstaking attention to
detail. What it boiled down to was this.

At 1735 on Friday evening a BEA Viscount would take
off as usual from London Airport on the routine flight to
Stockholm. There would be nothing in the least suspicious
about this; it was a scheduled run of the sort BEA had been
making every Friday night for the last fifteen years. The
Viscount would climb to its normal height and set course
along its normal track for the Swedish capital. Soon after
it crossed the East Anglian coast—and long before it could
be picked up by continental radar—the airliner would be
joined by a tanker (an R.A.F. Valiant). This Valiant would
be decked out with BEA markings and would carry civil
navigation lights; in other words, seen at night from the

110

ground, it would look very like a civil airliner. At an agreed spot over the North Sea the two planes would part company, the real airliner to start orbiting southern England and the fake one to continue on course for Stockholm.

From that moment the BEA aircraft would fade out of the picture. Her passengers would be told they'd developed some minor mechanical fault and were using up fuel before returning to London to make a precautionary landing. By the time their fuel had been reduced to the required level, the flight of the Bat—one way or the other—would be over.

The Valiant meanwhile, her navigation lights ablaze, would be following the BEA route to Stockholm. Over the North Sea she'd be joined by Oakman and Polhill in the Bat. The Bat would formate on her. Closely. So closely that on the continental radar screens which would soon be picking them up and following their progress the two planes would appear as one. And while formating, the Bat would refuel, leaving her final suck to the last possible moment.

So far, so easy. But once over Stockholm how could they detach the Bat without her being spotted? How could they get her past the coastal listening posts? And what could they do with the Valiant?

Throughout the small hours of the night the little man had paced his room, chain-smoking and drinking cup after cup of hot, sweet tea. He had the basis of a first-class idea; what he needed now was a bit of a brain wave to make it click. But the hours passed; this scheme and that scheme (which seemed so promising when they first came into his head) turned out to be flawed; and the link which would complete his chain eluded him. He had almost given up hope when the inspiration came.

As the Valiant approached Scandinavia her radio operator would call up Stockholm control. "We've got undercarriage trouble," he'd say, or words to that effect, "but we think we

111

can right it, so we're holding course." Nothing suspicious would be read into this. Later, as the Valiant approached Stockholm Airport, following the usual BEA route at the usual BEA height, she'd again call Control. She'd say the trouble wasn't rectified yet, but they thought the landing gear might be iced up and they proposed to let down to the warmer air stream of, say, a thousand feet to try to unfreeze it. This was fairly standard procedure, and would be unlikely to arouse suspicion. Now in the case of Stockholm (as the director of Midair Refueling knew) the letdown zone lies due east of the capital, over the approach to the harbor. So Valiant and Bat would now have an excuse to let down over the eastern Swedish coast. It would look highly suspicious, of course, if the pseudo airliner at once went rushing into the Baltic at zero feet. But on the other hand, she could now very well go a *little* way into the Baltic at a height of say eight or nine hundred feet. At the moment the two planes were clear of the land and the listening posts, the Bat would detach itself, plummet to sea level and set course for Moscow.

She'd have got into the Baltic undetected and full of fuel.

As for the Valiant, she'd climb back to ten thousand feet, report her undercarriage still sticking and say she was returning to London to carry out a belly landing.

It was logical and foolproof.

They spent the best part of an hour trying to fault the scheme, but they could find no flaw in it. They had been presented with the complete answer, all neatly tied up.

The little man was a bit embarrassed by their enthusiasm.

"I'm only sorry," he said, "you can't refuel farther east. Because this idea, you know, won't be much help to your crew."

That was a fact. They had all worked it out for themselves as soon as they'd got the gist of what the little man

112

was getting at. If the Bat refueled over Stockholm she'd have enough kerosene to reach Moscow and fly *part* of the way back. But only part. On the return flight, somewhere close to the Russian coast, she'd run out of fuel. There was no hope of her meeting up with a tanker that far east, and little hope of her crew surviving an ejection.

The little man's brain wave, in other words, had saved the scheme but not the crew.

This was something the team regretted. Some of them regretted it passionately—the thought that they were condemning two men to almost certain death made them feel physically sick; others regretted it objectively, writing off the air crew as inevitable casualties of a cold war which had already claimed hundreds of thousands of unknown victims in almost every country of the world; still others simply shut their minds to the human issue, telling themselves that the cause was more important than the men. And this, of course, was true. The team had been given the opportunity of salvaging that which mattered most: the scheme. They took it. And wrote the crew off.

After a while they began to talk of the one big problem which still remained: navigation.

The Bat came back from the approaches to the Channel at zero feet. Her launching trials had gone smoothly. Flying at the same height, course and air speed as they would use on the actual operation, Oakman and Polhill had launched their standoff bomb without difficulty, and had watched its canister parachute into the sea close to the target buoy. So the final stage of their mission, it seemed, would present no difficulty . . . if only they could get to the firing point.

The sea, that morning, was as blue as gentian and as calm as a dew pond, for an anti-cyclone off Iceland was bringing an Indian summer to the countries of the Atlantic seaboard.

As they came up-Channel the white beaches of the Côtes-du-Nord sparkled like quartz in the sun; a chain of cotton wool clouds floated like smoke rings above the Scilly Isles; and the world, it seemed to Polhill, had never looked so beautiful. Almost too beautiful, he thought—like a full-blown rose, too perfect to last. He sighed and thought of how lovely Jennifer had looked the night before he'd left, five years ago, for his tour of duty with SAC and had known he wouldn't be seeing her for a good many months. And it came to him that love reached full flowering only when it grew in the shadow of transience.

As they climbed to cross the coast not far from Lyme Regis, Oakman said suddenly, "I reckon they'll call the whole thing off."

"You think so?"

"If the Baltic's sealed, we'd not stand a chance."

"Hmmm."

He knew what Oakman wanted. Reassurance. Reassurance that the powers-that-be would find the technical difficulties so great that they'd give the idea up. But this reassurance he didn't feel able to give. For it seemed to him that with time running out, the powers-that-be would clutch at any idea, no matter how intransigent the snags. And Oakman would hardly be reassured if he told him that.

Soon they were nearing Farnborough: the long straight ridge of the Hog's Back to the east, the even lines of Aldershot's barracks and playing fields to the south, and beneath them the blue rotating circle of Frensham Pond. They turned onto their final approach.

They'd expected, on landing, to have a few hours' rest; but they had barely parked and climbed out of the Bat when a messenger came bustling up. Pellew, they were told, wanted to see them at once, in Flying Control.

In the quiet of his office the group captain gave them the

114

outline of the scheme to refuel over Stockholm. He didn't go into detail, partly for security reasons and partly because the crew had been promised a complete flight plan would be handed them on a plate, and the exact tracks and times of the amended scheme hadn't yet been worked out. He did, however, tell them enough for them to realize, very clearly, what was the big difference between refueling off Gotska Sandön and refueling off Stockholm.

When he'd finished, neither pilot nor navigator had much to say. Polhill asked a couple of technical questions on navigation, and Oakman asked what chance they'd stand of survival if they ejected over Russia. Pellew told them his two teams had their heads together at the moment and were working out a detailed flight plan—"including survival drill"—and that he hoped to be able, later in the evening, to brief them for a full-scale rehearsal. In the meanwhile he didn't think they ought to leave the airfield. . . .

They walked out of his office, down one flight of stairs and into the operations room, which was about the one place on the airfield where they knew they'd be undisturbed.

Oakman's face was white. "A fine mess," he muttered, "we're in now."

Polhill nodded. Too wrapped up in his thoughts to feel like talking, he walked across to the mock-up model of the Gulf of Finland which had been built along one wall of the operations room.

The model was a work of art: eighteen feet long, with beautifully molded contours, and every detail—lakes, roads, towns and forests—accurately pinpointed; there was even a thread of silver wire marking the line of a network of overhead cables. I wonder, Polhill thought, if we'll come down in the forest or the steppe. Or maybe the sea? Or maybe we'll buy it from the ack-ack over Moscow. Oh, Jennifer, he thought, what will happen to you and the children now?

He looked at his pilot and, for a moment, hated him because he had so much less to lose. Then it came to him that he was giving up too easily, that the people who gave up easily were the ones with little to lose. And he had so much. So he looked again at the model of the Gulf of Finland, and told himself that while there was life there was hope.

After a while Oakman came and stood beside him. "No Doppler. No radio. No beacons. Navigation's going to be a sod."

"You're telling me!"

"Can we make it by dead reckoning?"

"After three hundred miles' blind flying over the Baltic! Not a hope."

"What's the answer then?"

"Maybe one of the teams'll think of something."

Oakman drew on his ciagrette. "If they *don't*, I reckon there's no point in our going."

"I wouldn't count on that."

They talked of technicalities: of likely errors in the inertial navigator, of compass anomalies and chart inaccuracies. Then Oakman said slowly, "I wonder if Christabel's got any bright ideas."

"She's working on navigation. She'll certainly know the setup."

"Think I'll have a word with her."

Polhill was loath to leave the operations room for a while. So they agreed Oakman should contact her first, and that Polhill should join the pair of them in something like half an hour—which would, he said, give him the chance to study their new route from Stockholm up the Gulf of Finland.

As the door of the operations room closed behind his pilot, Polhill settled down to study the model methodically, section by section. Now I mustn't, he told himself, worry

116

about Kenneth (he'll be O.K. when it comes to the point), and I mustn't worry about the flight plan (that'll be handed us with the details all cut and dried). What I *must* worry about is memorizing the route—in case something goes wrong with the navigation and we have to fall back on visual flying. He knew which part of the route would be especially vital: where they left the Baltic and crossed the Russian coast, somewhere between Tallinn and Leningrad. For they had, he knew, to pinpoint their position *exactly* as they crossed the coast, so that their moving map could be accurately reset—otherwise they'd quickly become lost in the vast expanse of plain and marshland which stretched for three hundred and fifty featureless miles between the Gulf of Finland and the Russian capital. He studied the coast and its hinterland, searching for points he could memorize. He noticed the plethora of estuaries—the Narva, Vasavere, Luga, Plyussa, Pyarnu and Nerva—and the random scattering of lakes. They'll show up best, he thought. Rivers and lakes: especially—if the night's fine and the ground's powdered with snow—the lakes. He shut his eyes, memorizing their configuration: the diamond-shaped Narvskoya Vdkhr, the unnamed chain which necklaced down from Guba Bay, and (farther inland) the almost perfect circle of the Ozero Samro. Then he turned his attention to the photographs. There were about a hundred of them. Most of them were aerial photographs, taken from very high altitude, and these were of little use. But there were also a couple of dozen which had been taken from the ground. Now, Jim Polhill, he told himself, look carefully at these. People have risked their lives to take them, knowing they might be invaluable on just such a flight as this. He peered at them one by one: a timber yard in Kingisepp, peat-cutting fields on the outskirts of Gatchina, marshaling yards on the line between Narva and Tapa, and a hydroelectric scheme on the

117

lower reaches of the Luga. He screwed up his eyes and wished he'd taken a course in Pelmanism.

When he glanced at his watch he was surprised at how quickly half an hour had slipped by.

He pushed the photos back into their file and left the operations room, carefully (as a routine security measure) locking the door and handing the key to the guard. He collected his car and drove around the taxi track to Dispersal.

He had arranged, somewhat vaguely, to meet Kenneth and Christabel "across at Dispersal"; and at the back of his mind was the expectation that he'd find them walking, hand in hand, somewhere on the great tarmac parking area behind the catapult ramps. But he drove twice around the parking area and failed to spot them. He looked in each of the three hangars, but the hangars were empty. Feeling slightly put out, he parked his car and walked around to the back of the dispersal pens. This was the wildest and most unkept part of the airfield: a wilderness of long grass, thorn scrub and the occasional boggy pool. And it was there he saw her, sitting on her mackintosh at the edge of a sheet of brackish water. He walked across to her.

"Where's Kenneth?"

"I don't know." Her voice was lifeless.

"What's going on, Christabel?"

She didn't answer.

He sat down beside her, wanting to help but not quite knowing how. "You two had a lovers' tiff?"

"We're not lovers," she said. "Or ever likely to be."

"But you have had a tiff?"

She said nothing. She sat staring at the pool of brackish water, swishing it with a broken reed.

"Christabel," he said, "I *want* to help. Won't you tell me what's wrong?"

118

She shivered, and looking at him for the first time, "Oh, Jim," she said, "haven't you enough on your plate?"

"Look. I'll say it again, for the last time. I *want* to help."

"Well, if you must know, I'd say we've had more than a tiff. More like a flaming row."

"Tell me."

"I daresay," she said slowly and without much conviction, "it was partly my fault. He rang at a bad time. We've been working flat out, you know, on the Bat's navigation. And getting nowhere. Then, just as we start a promising new line, Ken rings up and says he wants to talk to me." She spread her hands in a little disclaimer of responsibility. "I wouldn't have minded if he'd had something important to say. But he dragged me all the way here for nothing. Absolutely nothing." Her voice trailed away in puzzled diminuendo.

"He must have had something to say."

She shrugged.

"What *did* he say?"

"Well, it was the same old stuff we went over days ago, at Culdrose. Was it really right to be going to Moscow? What would happen if we sat tight and did nothing? Would it be the end of the world if we *did* kowtow to the Russians? As if any sane person could doubt it!"

"Well, obviously Ken doubts it."

She looked at him very straight. "I'm sorry," she said, "but I don't think he does. I think he's just plain scared."

He rubbed his chin. "Now let's be adult about this, Christabel. Of course he's scared. Wouldn't you be if you thought you had only three days to live?"

She looked away. "Oh, Jim! I'm sorry . . . Of course you're both scared. But I mean . . . well, you're not giving way to it like he is."

"I don't want," he said slowly, "to sound priggish. But

perhaps in a way it's easier for me than it is for Ken. You see, I've made up my mind that what we're trying to do is mighty important and very much worthwhile."

"And you think he has doubts?"

"I think, my dear, he wants someone to talk things over with—someone to help him, someone to lean on."

He knew by the vehemence of her reaction that his point had got home.

"But what an attitude for a man! I want a man *I* can lean on. Not a man who wants to lean on me."

"If I sound like Miss Lonelyhearts giving advice, you asked for it. . . . When two people love each other, the leaning isn't all one way. There's leaning *and* propping, on both sides."

She was silent for a long time. And when she spoke it was without her usual assurance. "You think he wanted help? And I let him down?"

"I think it's possible."

"But, Jim! How *can* he have doubts? Over something so obviously good and right, something—you said it yourself— so important and worthwhile?"

It was some time before he answered; then he said slowly, "You're lucky. You're a very positive person, with positive views. Ken's a bit of a drifter, you know. He's un-committed. He sees the other side of every argument. And be fair to him: it's a bit hard to expect him to give his life for a cause he's not sure he believes in."

She trailed her reed across the surface of the pond. For a long time there was silence, and when she did speak her voice was puzzled. "How long have you been flying with Ken?"

"About eighteen months."

"You must know him well."

"Pretty well, I'd say."

120

"Tell me, Jim. What sort of man is he?"

Polhill shifted uneasily. "Don't believe I want to try and dissect my pilot's character."

"Oh, for God's sake!" Her hands clenched. "In a couple of days we may all be radioactive dust. What a time for schoolboy scruples!"

She was trembling, and her face was pale and drawn. And it came to him how much she'd had to cope with in the last few days. If I don't help her, he thought, *she* could be the one to crack up. He sighed.

"Well, I'm no psychologist, Christabel. But it could be like this." He paused, collecting his thoughts, then choosing his words with care. "Take his life. It's been a success story, hasn't it? all the way through, with success coming easy? Only son of rich parents, no hardships in the war, his father giving him an allowance through your cadet college at Cranwell, and it all so very easy—the flying, the ground subjects, the luck, the girls. So he's a success. But at heart I think Ken's a diffident sort of person; none too sure of himself, maybe a bit surprised at his own success, and feeling all the time he's got to live up to his reputation. Oh, I know what you're going to say. He *seems* self-assured—almost self-centered, in fact. But I think that's only skin-deep: like a cloak to hide behind." He smiled. "But I'm getting into deep water."

She didn't return his smile. "You men have an unfair advantage," she said slowly. "I mean, a man and a woman can't have the same sort of relationship that you and Ken have: at least not applied to something worthwhile, like flying a plane or doing something physically dangerous."

"In the relationship between a man and a woman," he said, "I'd have thought there were compensations!"

"Oh yes! Ken and I are physically attracted to each other.

121

But you *know* him better than I do. I just haven't a clue to what makes him tick."

It seemed to Polhill that the conversation was getting a bit out of hand. "At any rate," he said, "on the practical level, he's a damn fine pilot."

"Hmmm!"

"And that, you know, takes some sort of guts."

"I suppose so"—slowly—"but he's so up in the air, so uncommitted. I just don't know what's important to him, or what he believes in."

"Perhaps he doesn't know himself."

An even longer silence. He was about to suggest they return to the car, when she said suddenly, "*You're* not uncommitted, are you, Jim?"

"On this issue, no."

She swirled the reed around the brackish pool at her feet, and a water bug came swimming to the surface. She watched it twisting and twining inconsequential patterns across the water.

"And Jennifer?"

"She feels the way I do. Somebody *has* to get through. It's just bad luck for us the somebody happens to be me."

She nodded and stared at the water bug. It was crossing and recrossing the pool in random darts; now fast, now slow, now straight, now in a series of curves.

"Jim," she said, "what's the water bug doing?"

He wasn't put out by her sudden change of ground. He regarded the water bug with due attention, for a long time. "I don't really know," he said at last.

"All that coming and going. Do you think there's any point to it?"

"I seem to remember," he said slowly, "that some old philosopher with a beard once asked the same question."

"And?"

"He looked at the water bug and asked it, 'Oh, you twisting and turning water thing, what are you doing down there with your small black waistcoat on?' And the water bug answered, 'I write and rewrite everlastingly the word of God.' "

"Oh, Jim," she said, "that's what I wanted to hear. You'll never know how much."

For a while they sat in silence; then she got up, smiling and tucking her mackintosh under her arm. "Will you take me back to my instruments?"

He looked at her, noting the pallor of her skin and the dark circles under her eyes. "Why not give your instruments a rest?"

"I'd rather go back. Please."

They set off around the taxi track. For a while neither of them spoke; then Christabel said simply, "Don't worry about the navigation, Jim. Everything's going to be all right."

He was surprised at her certainty. "You sure?"

For a moment her hand rested on his. "I promise you, Jim," she repeated, "everything's going to be all right."

14

She tossed her mackintosh on a table and collapsed into the one more or less comfortable chair in her office. She was dog-tired. For she had left the Instrument Department only four times in the last forty-eight hours—twice for conferences, once for supper with the Polhills, and once to meet Kenneth at Dispersal. The rest of the time she'd been working.

And the work hadn't been going well.

She looked around her room at the plethora of maps, charts, reference almanacs and notes, at the sheafs of calculations of frequencies, at the detailed cross references of astral and visual fixes, and it came to her that she and the people working for her were in very real danger of losing sight of the wood in a confusion of trees. She blew the hair out of her eyes and tried to think straight.

It wasn't hard to see what had happened. To start with, she'd tackled the navigational problem with skill and enthusiasm. Then things had begun to go wrong. First, they'd found they couldn't get into the Baltic; then Kenneth had seemed anxious to contract out—and this attitude of Kenneth's had worried her and had made her doubt the importance of what they were trying to do. Her work, as a result, had suffered. Her talk with Jim, however, had gone a long way toward restoring her faith both in human nature and in the flight of the Bat; and she now had everything nicely worked out. If only she could think up a way of navigating the plane *and* of giving the crew a hope of survival, then everything in the garden would be lovely. She'd have helped them both.

"Everything's going to be all right," she had said to Jim on the airfield. She had believed it at the time. But she had believed it, she realized now, because she had wanted to, rather than on the strength of the facts. However, she had made her promise. Now she must try to keep it.

She set to work, recalculating the maximum error (due to magnetic anomalies, etc.) likely to have built up in their navigation by the time they passed over the Russian coast.

After a while she realized she'd made a mistake, the sort of mistake that would never have occurred if she hadn't been so tired. She tossed the calculations aside. She lit a cigarette, and noticed that her hands were trembling. Christabel Barlow, she told herself, you're no damn use to anyone in your present state; you need a good sleep, a good meal and a new face; and then perhaps you'll think straight instead of in ever decreasing circles. But how can I eat and sleep, she thought, when so much is at stake and time's running out, not only for Ken and Jim but maybe for hundreds of thousands of others, all over the world? Her eyes strayed to the top drawer of her desk and the little tube of tablets which she had already delved into twice. I know, she thought, I'll be like the gals in the pulp magazines: I'll have a Benzedrine and a bath.

They didn't go in for baths in the Instrument Department. So she walked across to her quarters, collected the necessary bits and pieces, and shut herself thankfully in the anonymous white-tiled room with its stereotyped layout of built-in bath, basin and towel rail. As she ran the water and took off her clothes, she kept her mind deliberately blank. I'll think of nothing more important, she told herself, than the temperature of the water and the fresh, clean scent of the soap. She made a great ritual of getting her bath very full and exactly the right temperature. Yet all the while, without her realizing it, her mind was on other things; and before she subsided into the water she opened her bag, took out her little tube, and swallowed another Benzedrine.

The water was warm and comforting, and she soon began to relax. It was as though a spring inside her had been released, and she unwound, thankfully, like a clockwork doll that has been screwed to breaking point, then suddenly freed. She didn't think of megaton bombs, or suicide flights to Moscow, or beacons or navigation inaccuracies. She didn't think of anything. She simply luxuriated in the warmth of the water and the sensuous slide of soapsuds over her body. And after a while her mind became empty and clear, like a finely tuned instrument waiting to be played on.

She stayed in the bath for the best part of half an hour. Then she dressed slowly, made up carefully and walked across to the mess and ordered an early tea. She was surprised how hungry she was. She drank three cups of tea and ate an indecent number of cakes, all in a strange preoccupied unawareness of what was going on around her. Then she walked back to her office in the Instrument Department. She locked the door and disconnected the telephone. She knew exactly what she was going to do. Think.

Now I must think of two things, she told herself: a way of navigating the Bat, and a way of saving the crew. She knew very well that a great many people had been trying to do just this for days—and had failed. But she told herself that *she* wasn't going to fail; that she was in the unique position of having both the technical know-how and a personal interest in the fate of the crew. She leaned back in her chair and shut her eyes.

Navigation first, she told herself. Now just what *was* the problem?

It all stemmed, she could see, from their need to use the moving map.

Now, Christabel Barlow, she thought, go right back to the very beginning: just why do we have to use this moving map?

She'd done enough test flying in the Bat to know the answer from personal experience. When one flies low by night at supersonic speeds one can see only a very short distance ahead—one's view of the ground is limited to a narrow belt flashing immediately beneath one incredibly fast; one can't in fact see far enough ahead with the naked eye to be able to avoid obstacles. (Suppose, for example, a plane is flying toward a range of hills at a height of two hundred feet and a speed of a thousand miles an hour. By the time the pilot's eye has registered the fact that the ground ahead is rising and he has pulled back on the stick and the controls have taken effect, it is too late: the plane will have buried itself in the hillside.) In other words, it is essential for a pilot to have some sort of artificial aid to warn him of what hazards are coming up ahead.

And the only effective artificial aid for the flight to Moscow would be the moving map. Christabel had to admit this. For a long time she sat quite motionless, her eyes shut, trying to think of alternatives. But always in the end she was driven back to the same conclusion: no other aid would do—it had to be the moving map.

And the moving map, of course, was possessed of one great disadvantage. It needed, every so often, to be reset.

She'd done enough work on the map equipment to be

able to see the position quite clearly. The Bat would take off with its map accurately set, and for the first part of the flight all would be well. But after leaving Stockholm the plane would be faced with three hundred miles' blind flying over the sea. And by the end of this three hundred miles the crew would find that the map was inaccurate; that their recorded position under the cross wires didn't coincide with their actual position—i.e., with the ground they were passing over. So the map would have to be reset.

And how could they do this?

This was the crux of the matter.

This was the rock upon which the whole operation seemed likely to come to grief. For unless the map *could* be reset as they approached the Russian shore it would be no use to them for the run-in to Moscow.

Christabel screwed up her eyes. On a normal flight, she knew, a plane could check its position easily enough, with the help of such navigational aids as Doppler, radar or radio, or even by dead-reckoning navigation or visual fixing. But in the case of the flight of the Bat each of these methods had some insuperable snag.

Take Doppler. The Doppler was a sort of electronic eye, able to scan the ground beneath them and feed back information into the plane's navigational computers. But it had two drawbacks. It didn't work over smooth water, and its radiations would be picked up by the Russians. So Doppler was out.

So, for obvious reasons, was any type of forward-looking radar. The Russians would pick up the radiations. And the vital element of surprise would be lost.

Nor was their radio of any use. A single transmission and the Russians would be on to them in a flash. While all normal beacons and transmitting stations in the area would certainly be either switched off or jammed.

Which left navigation by means of visual pinpointing or by dead reckoning.

Visual pinpointing when you're flying at high speed at zero feet is difficult enough by day. By night it is virtually impossible. And in the case of the Bat, Christabel reflected, there was an added difficulty. The obvious way for a plane to pinpoint its position in the Baltic would be to fly close to land—say, over one of the numerous islands or some prominent stretch of coast. Yet this was exactly what the Bat *mustn't* do. It must steer clear of land—or else it'd be spotted and reported during its run-in. In other words, flying by visual aids was out of the question.

That left dead reckoning: the old, time-honored technique of a navigator laying off course, wind speed and magnetic variant, then calculating a track. But this sort of navigation was none too accurate when flying a long distance—an error of one degree and at the end of the Baltic crossing the Bat could be anywhere inside an area of twenty-five square miles. And on this particular flight there'd be two additional difficulties. The wind would be hard to assess—for the Russians were hardly likely to broadcast weather reports, and wind-finding by night from a low-flying aircraft is at the best of times a rough-and-ready business; also the northern part of the Baltic is prone to local magnetic anomalies—due to the presence of iron ore. In other words, no matter how carefully Polhill calculated a course, and no matter how carefully Oakman flew it, they'd be exceedingly lucky if they hit the Russian coast at exactly a preselected spot.

Yet unless they did just that, they stood little chance of resetting their map and getting to Moscow.

It was a problem, a problem to which there just didn't seem any answer. For a couple of days now teams of specialists from Farnborough and Bomber Command had been working on it. A number of ingenious suggestions had been put forward. But in every scheme there'd been a serious element of risk of the Bat's being detected. And lack of detection, of course, was a prerequisite of success. What was needed, Christabel decided, was a fresh approach to the problem, a complete breakaway from the line of thought being followed at the moment. She lit a cigarette, pulled out pencil and paper and carefully summarized the basic facts.

1. The Bat must somehow fix its position accurately as it approaches the Russian coast.

2. The Bat can't do this by using its own navigational aids (such as radar or radio), since any transmission it makes will be picked up by the Russians.

3. The plane must therefore rely on an *outside* aid: something extraneous to its own equipment.

4. This outside aid must be incapable of detection by the Russians (which rules out radio beacons, flashing lights, etc.).

5. Since the Baltic is effectively sealed off and there is no hope of getting anything in to drop, say, a marker beacon, the Bat must rely on *something already there*.

"Something already there." It sounded hopeless. For what was there, she asked herself, at the approaches to the Russian coast except a lot of islands, the occasional lighthouse, and maybe the even more occasional fishing boat?

Her pencil dropped to the floor. She sat very still, her mind all of a sudden wonderfully clear. And the answer came clicking out—as if on a ticker tape, just like that. So simple that the experts with their abstruse calculations had overlooked it; so unexpected that if she hadn't worked for six months with a marine navigation company she'd very likely have overlooked it too.

The wonderful thing was that it solved the navigation issue. *And* it gave hope to the crew.

For several minutes she basked in a haze of slightly smug self-congratulation. Then the doubts began to seep in.

130

Quickly she picked up her pencil and started to make a list of every conceivable snag. Then, when the list was complete, she went through it, item by item, penciling in how each difficulty could be overcome. Until only two remained: two problems which had to be resolved before her scheme was foolproof. One she might need help with, but the other she could sort out herself. Now.

She pulled out her diary and thumbed through the address section. On the last page she found the name she was looking for: Ted Benson (Mecca Marine Navigation) Richmond 6645, Extension 7. She reconnected the telephone and reached for the receiver. I only hope, she thought, he's in.

It seemed to take a very long time to get through to Mecca Marine, and an even longer time to locate Ted Benson—his extension number, she found, had been changed. But at last his voice came through, distant and none too clear. "Benson speaking."

"Ted! This is Christabel."

"Good grief! A voice from my past. How are you, darling?"

"Fine. Now listen, Ted. This isn't a personal call. This is business. And terribly important."

"I'm desolate, but listening."

"Remember those marine radar sets we worked on? The ones wanted for ice detection?"

"Yes."

"They were going to Finland, weren't they?"

"Yes."

"I want to know if they're in use yet. It's terribly important. Find out for me right away, would you?"

"Same old Christabel. 'Do this, do that. And at the double.'"

"Please, Ted!"

"On one condition."

131

"Which is?"

"That you have dinner with me one day next week."

"Same old Ted. Always an eye for the main chance!"

"That's a date then. Shall I ring you back?"

"No," she said, "I'll hold."

She waited for what seemed an eternity, but was in fact less than five minutes. Then Benson came back with exactly the information she'd prayed for. The radar sets, he told her, had been sold nine months ago to Juhani Kallela. They'd been installed in the dozen most modern trawlers of his fishing fleet, based on Lovisa. And he knew for certain the sets were in use, because only a couple of weeks ago the Mecca representative in Finland had sent in a servicing report.

Relief flooded over her. For a while she flirted quite light-headedly with Benson, agreeing to meet him next Thursday at Le Coq d'Or. Then she remembered that one other point—albeit a minor one—had still to be sorted out; so she said her thank you and her look forward to seeing you on Thursday, and rang off. Then she set to wondering how she could find out the state of the ice in the Gulf of Finland.

She remembered from school geography lessons that the northern and eastern reaches of the Baltic froze up in winter. She *thought* that in late October the ice wouldn't have started to form yet along the Russian coast. But she had to be sure. Several ways of finding out occurred to her—such as ringing Finland House or the Air Ministry Meteorological Office. But both these involved a security risk. She frowned and tapped her teeth with the end of her pencil, and after a while it struck her that maybe it was silly to go on playing her hand alone, and that her scheme was sufficiently tied up now for her to put it to higher authority. She reached again for the telephone.

"Group Captain Pellew, please," she said.

Pellew was skeptical at first; he'd listened to so many schemes in the last forty-eight hours that he'd become inured to disappointment. But this, he had to admit, was something new. His interest was caught. He asked two or three technical questions. Then for several minutes he sat quite still, staring out at the darkening airfield.

"Yes," he said suddenly, "you've got it—provided there's no ice. But we'll have to check on the ice."

Ten minutes later Christabel was on her way to London, leaning back against the leather upholstery of Pellew's staff car and watching the rush-hour traffic streaming past.

It had seemed at first rather like taking a sledge hammer to crack a nut, this rushing up to the Royal Geographical Society to check the state of the ice. But on reflection she saw the sense of it. The Royal Geographical Society were likely to have the most comprehensive data in England on such a subject. Also the chances of a security leak were reduced to a minimum, for the library of the R.G.S. was about the least likely place in London to harbor a Russian microphone.

The staff car turned into the cramped little courtyard in Kensington Gore. Another few minutes, she thought, and we'll know where we stand. For some unaccountable reason she had felt certain up to now that everything was going to be all right, that she'd find the ice hadn't yet started to form. But now the matter was about to be put to the test her confidence suddenly deserted her. She ran up the broad stone steps which led to the entrance hall. She signed the visitors' book and walked quickly upstairs to the library. From the walls, old prints and explorers' relics looked down at her impassively: Philby's Diaries, Livingstone's chair, a scale model of the *Discovery*, obsidian spearheads from Easter Island. And it came to her that if there *was* ice in the Gulf of Finland, then all these things would very soon be so much radioactive dust or else transferred to a Soviet museum. Her step quickened and she kept on moistening her lips.

"Ice in the Gulf of Finland? We should soon be able to tell you that."

The librarian walked across to the filing cabinets in the center of the room. She pulled out a drawer marked FINLAND and thumbed through the index.

"Agriculture, hydrography, population. Ah, here we are! Climate."

Under the heading of CLIMATE about two dozen books were listed and perhaps twice as many articles. Some were in English. The librarian ran her finger down the list.

"I suggest you try this one first: 'Ice Winter 1959/60 along the Finnish Coast,' by Erkki Palosuo."

In less than two minutes Christabel had the pamphlet in front of her.

Her assurance had vanished completely by this time; her fingers, as she skimmed through the headings, were trembling. So much depended on such a little thing. Did the ice start to form in October or in November?

Palosuo's treatise was detailed, erudite and concise. And yet, maddeningly, she couldn't for some time find what she wanted. There were so many graphs and tables, so many summaries of abstruse statistics, that the simple basic fact she was seeking eluded her. But at last, in the penultimate chapter, she found it . . . "So even in the particularly severe ice winter of 1959/60 the real freezing up of the Gulf of Finland did not begin until November 15; and not until November 23 did the icebreaker *Sisu* have to render assistance to shipping." There followed a table giving just the figures she wanted.

"The average date for the first appearance of sea ice in the Gulf of Finland is November 18.

"The earliest date ever recorded for the first appearance of sea ice is November 9.

"And the average date for the formation of permanent winter ice is November 30."

So everything was going to be all right.

Thankfully she collected a few more facts from Palosuo's treatise—details of the average temperature, humidity and barometric pressure for the last week of October; she said good-bye to the librarian, who seemed almost disappointed that no more facts were needed; then she took her staff car to the Air Ministry and got on the scrambler to Pellew.

"It's all right," she said. "There's no ice in October. The fishing boats'll be out."

She heard his grunt of relief. And he began to tell her of the steps he'd taken, while she'd been away, in anticipation of good news. He'd got hold, he said, of Benson and a team of technicians from Mecca Navigation; they were working on the radar sets now, while other technicians from Farnborough were fitting special radar receiver antennae into a pair of Bats. Things were going smoothly, and if they worked all night and didn't run into unexpected snags they ought to be ready for a test flight at dawn. But they wanted to talk to her, he said, about whom they should have on the fishing boat to operate the radar.

This was far too important and complex a problem to be decided on the phone, so they agreed to meet in the Bat's hangar as soon as she returned to the airfield.

Driving back in the staff car, she had difficulty in staying awake; her head kept lolling against the leather upholstery, and she couldn't stop yawning. She opened both windows and lit a cigarette; but after a while even the draught and the physical act of smoking couldn't dam back her tiredness, and she fell asleep, sprawled awkwardly and uncomfortably across the back seat of the car.

135

She didn't come to until they pulled up at the main gate. Then the police officer's torch flashed over her face, and she sat up, brushing the hair out of her eyes. She felt terrible. Her head ached, her mouth was dry, and she was shivering with cold. She asked to be dropped at the mess.

As she climbed out of the car her legs felt they didn't belong to her. She noticed that the driver was eying her curiously. "You all right, ma'am?"

"Yes, thank you," she said. "It's only pins and needles." She walked as firmly as she could up to the mess. Probably, she reflected, he thinks I've had one over the eight!

When she'd washed and had a cup of tea she felt a little more human: a little, but not much. She told herself that this was no time for feeling under the weather, that things were only just beginning, and that she'd need all her wits about her in the next forty-eight hours. So she opened her bag, took out her little tube of tablets and swallowed another Benzedrine. She knew very well that it was dangerous to take too many in too short a time. But if ever there was an emergency, she thought, this is it. She rested for twenty minutes, then, feeling a great deal better, walked across to the test hangar.

All night long arc lights blazed from the hangar roof, and insect figures crawled over and in and out of two of the Bats. Brackets were made to take the weight of a specially calibrated radar receiver; an aperture was cut into the instrument panel to house a left/right homing indicator; and a small metal strip, ten centimeters long, was fitted into either side of the aircraft's nose. Meanwhile at Mecca a special coding circuit was meticulously designed: a circuit which could be fitted both to the Bat's radar receiver and to Mecca's marine radar sets. And in the small hours of the morning a specially modified Mecca set was flown post-

136

haste to Thorney Island and then by helicopter to a naval frigate on patrol off the Isle of Wight. At dawn a Bat from Farnborough homed onto this frigate straight as a pigeon to cote. And everyone breathed a heartfelt sigh of relief.

Oakman and Polhill, who had flown the test flight, guessed that some new scheme was in process of being worked out. But exactly what the scheme was no one seemed able to tell them. They tried to find Christabel, hoping to pump her. But Christabel Barlow, they were told, had left the establishment; and no one knew where they could find her.

15

It was an old man who took the chair that penultimate morning in the committee room of No. 10. In the six days since he'd received the Russian note the Prime Minister had aged almost beyond belief. And the drive back from his early morning audience at Buckingham Palace, through angry hostile crowds, had filled his cup of disillusion to the full. For the mood of the crowds had been ugly: ugly with fear. Now, as he looked around at the faces of his Cabinet and Chiefs of Staff, he could see the same fear—albeit for the most part decently concealed. I've failed, he thought; I'm still convinced myself that the Russian note is bluff, but I've failed to convince others. And they won't dare take the risk of its *not* being bluff. His eyes strayed to the electric wall clock. The eyes of his Cabinet followed. And he could read their thoughts: maybe less than thirty hours to live. He began his routine summary of what had taken place since their last meeting.

It was a familiar story. Nothing the authorities could do had been able to dam back the tide of fear which was now swelling up, like a comber to breaking point, throughout the West. For there was one thing and one thing only now which would make this fear subside: the landing of a reply in Red Square. And this hadn't been done. The Prime Minister dealt briefly with their catalogue of failures in the past twenty-four hours: four missiles with diversionary satellites had been fired, and all four had been intercepted and destroyed; the Polaris submarine which had set out under the icecap had been given up for lost, and there was no other submarine with harmless warheads able to get to a firing position in time; an effort by Intelligence to set up a short-range launching ramp in Poland had been discovered and liquidated. So it looked, he told them, as if there was only one hope left: the Bat.

He went on to deal with the vicissitudes of their plans for the Bat. It had looked at one stage, he told them, as if the technical difficulties would be insurmountable, but a couple of brilliant improvisations had enabled them to push ahead. The tests were completed now; rehearsals had been satisfactory; the weather was favorable; "And tonight, God willing, the plane will try to get through to Moscow. And I can tell you one thing," he added. "I had a word with the crew this morning. I was *very* impressed. I've every confidence that if it's humanly possible to get through, they'll do it. . . ."

They discussed the flight for quite a while, the Prime Minister and Sir Basil using their powers of persuasion and their specialized knowledge to try to convince the Cabinet that the flight would succeed. But in this they failed. That it *might* succeed was obvious. But what, the Cabinet wanted to know, if it didn't? What was the Prime Minister going to do if, at midnight, it became clear that the Bat *hadn't* got through? Would he sit tight and do nothing? Or would he go to Moscow?

His own inclination was to sit tight and do nothing. But in this he was alone. And he knew it. The strikes and

139

demonstrations, the crowds and riots and protest marches, had shown him that. To the man in the street *anything* was preferable to the risk of a nuclear war.

They went over the old familiar ground which had been covered so often before. Rarely in history, the Prime Minister reminded them, had the Russians started a war; they'd never been the attackers, always the attacked. And again: "I've met the Soviet Chairman. He's a great admirer of strength and a great believer in bluff, but I'm convinced he'd not *really* start a war; remember how he climbed down over Cuba." And the Cabinet took his points and nodded their heads. But it was all, he knew, like water off the backs of so many ducks. For no matter what he did or said, a seed of doubt would remain in their minds: a seed too terrible to be disregarded. At the last analysis, he knew, they'd ask him to go to Moscow. Even as he was speaking he could see that their minds were made up. And so, like the astute politician he was, he shifted ground to give himself room for maneuver.

"But of course," he said blandly, "everything depends on the Bat. If she gets through, then there's no problem. . . . Now she takes off"—he glanced at his notes—"at five thirty this evening. The flight'll take roughly four hours. Which gets us to nine thirty. Add, say, a couple of hours, in case of delays and we're at eleven thirty. So I suggest we have another meeting here, at midnight. We'll know by then where we stand."

They didn't like it—he could sense that. They thought it was leaving the issue of his going to Moscow too long in abeyance. But he wasn't in the mood to argue. He was preparing to cut the meeting short when the Leader of the House exploded his bombshell.

"I've been wondering," he said quietly, "if we'll be much better off even if the Bat *does* get through!"

There was an astonished silence.

It was a plausible theory the Leader of the House went on to expound. The whole object of the Russian challenge, he argued, had been to prove that Soviet weapons were streets ahead of the West's, and to demonstrate this the Russians had landed a rocket in Hyde Park and had challenged the West to land a reply in Red Square. "Now if we land our reply by rocket," he went on, "it'll be clear we really *have* got a deterrent. But I wonder if the Russians will be all that impressed with a reply landed by low-level bomber? . . . What I mean is this: a low-level bomber might get through once with the help of surprise but would it get through a second time without surprise? And think of the time lag if it came to war. A missile could get through in three or four minutes, a bomber would take three or four hours . . . So surely even if we do land a reply by the Bat, the Russians and their missiles will still have the whip hand? And know it?"

Sir Basil levered himself to his feet.

It was almost unheard of for anyone to rise at a cabinet meeting, and the others looked at him curiously. His anger was the more impressive for being held so politely in check. He addressed himself to the Leader of the House.

"In the last five years, sir, many of my 'clever' young subordinates have advanced just the arguments you're advancing now. 'What's the use of planes?' they've cried. 'Planes are finished. The only worthwhile weapons in our day and age are missiles.' Thank God some people in the R.A.F. had the sense not to listen. Because now, at the moment of crisis, the only part of our deterrent that's effective is those very piloted planes that the 'clever' young men despised. And I want to make one thing clear. Low-level bombers are an integral part of our deterrent; they're on a

141

par with Titans and Polaris; they're not—as a lot of people seem to think—a legacy of the past, a throwback to World War II. And this isn't just my opinion. It's the opinion of, among others, the U. S. Navy, who're steadily increasing their carrier-borne low-level attack capability." He paused. "And the point's this. U. S. carriers are patrolling the Pacific and Mediterranean this very minute with their A3D Skywarrior nuclear bombers alerted for take-off. They may be shadowed by Russian subs and their aircraft may not have the low-level range to reach Moscow. But there are plenty of places in Russia on which the A3D's—and plenty of other types—*could* carry out low-level attacks if it came to war. And the Russians'll get the point. If one low-level bomber can get through, so can others. And low-level bombers, you know, can carry just as big a megaton bomb as missiles."

He sat down.

And before the Leader of the House had had time to spark off a general discussion, the Prime Minister cut the meeting short.

"For more reasons than one," he said briefly, "I'm convinced we'll be all right *if* the Bat get through. The man in the street won't care *how* our reply's landed, so long as it gets there. As for the future—if we meet the Russian challenge this time, they won't dare precipitate another crisis for years. Now our next meeting is here, twelve midnight. . . ."

As the Ministers and Chiefs of Staff filed thoughtfully out of the room, he drew Sir Basil aside. "I'd like," he said, "to have another look at the flight plan."

Sir Basil unbuckled his brief case. "Of course. I've got it here."

142

They bent over the flight plan, studying tracks and graphs of fuel consumption and details of the plan for ejection.

Sir Basil left Downing Street at ten forty-five; about the time that Jennifer Polhill was usually brewing up coffee for elevenses with Mrs. Harley. But there was no milk for elevenses that penultimate morning. And no Mrs. Harley.

Mrs. Harley had gone the way of the milkman, the post-man, the laundryman and Jennifer's odd-job gardener: she'd left the built-up area of Greater London and was head-ing for the Atlantic seaboard.

Jennifer could picture her—the average not very intel-ligent person who'd been brave at first but who now was beginning to panic—queuing disgruntledly for the west-bound trains, grumbling about how the services had let them down and ending up in some overcrowded Cornish village, exhausted, short of food and not one iota safer than if she'd stayed at home. Jennifer didn't blame her—she'd have taken the children to Wales or Cornwall herself if she had thought it would do the least bit of good. But this is something there's no escape from, she thought; it's like the wrath of God; there's no point in trying to hide.

She heated Anne's beef broth and carried it upstairs. She didn't think she was especially upset that morning, but as she was feeding Anne she suddenly found that her face was wet with tears. And the tears just wouldn't stop: they went on and on. She wondered how many other mothers, all over the world, were feeding their babies that morning, and weeping.

It doesn't matter what happens to Jim and me, she thought. But, oh, God, didn't you tell us to bring the little children to you?

143

16

After seeing the Prime Minister, Oakman and Polhill were driven back to Farnborough. They were then bundled aboard a Transport Command Comet and flown, quickly and secretly, to Lossiemouth, a naval air station at the mouth of the Moray Firth.

After six days of planning and preparing, things had come to a head, and events moved fast.

At Lossiemouth they were met by S.A.S.O. They were told they had an hour for lunch; then they were wanted in the operations room for final briefing. It was a bit of a rush—but a rush, they were quick to note, that was controlled and purposeful and geared to a preplanned tempo.

They'd expected to find a lot of top brass at the briefing. But much to their relief, there turned out to be only themselves, a stand-by crew and Pellew; with S.A.S.O. himself to do the talking. But for all its atmosphere of almost cozy informality, the briefing was lucid, concise and worked out literally to the last second and the last degree.

Oakman and Polhill had known for the last twenty-four hours that a new scheme was afoot. They'd practiced a series of homing runs with their specially coded receiver onto a naval frigate, they'd rehearsed ejection procedure and dinghy drill and they'd memorized a particular stretch of the Russian coast; also Christabel had disappeared, leaving only an enigmatic message with Jennifer Polhill to say, "Don't worry, everything's going to be all right." But the details of the scheme they hadn't, for security reasons, been told.

S.A.S.O. told them now.

"I've good news," he began. "We've thought up a way of getting you to Moscow, *and* of getting you back. . . ."

Polhill's face lit up. But Oakman showed little sign of emotion; he had withdrawn more than ever in the last twenty-four hours into a private world of his own: a world of fatalistic solitude, impervious, it seemed, to either hope or fear.

S.A.S.O. told them he'd run through the broad outline of the scheme first; then he'd go into detail, giving them their exact times and courses, etc.; and finally, if they wanted advice on any particular aspect they could have it—he'd arranged for specialists on every conceivable subject (from radar coding to dinghy survival) to be on call in an adjoining room.

"Now you take off from here at 1740"—he glanced at his watch—"in just over three hours. The Navy have laid on a scheme for getting you off undetected, in case there're Russian agents about—I'll give you details later. After take-off you'll fly due east and then southeast at zero feet for roughly an hour. Then, in position 54°00' North, 04°00' East, you'll climb to 11,000 feet and rendezvous with a tanker. This tanker will be a Valiant decked out as a BEA airliner, with BEA markings, etc. It'll be lit up like a Christmas tree with full navigation lights, so you should have no trouble spotting it. You'll formate on it, and connect to the refueling drogue. You'll then fly with the Valiant, in close formation, to Stockholm. You're to stay plugged in, and top

145

up with fuel every half hour, leaving the last suck till you're above the airfield . . . And over Stockholm, Polhill, you can check and reset instruments . . . Now you know the drill for letting down. You rehearsed it last night; so did the Valiant. As soon as you're both down to eight hundred feet and clear of land, slip your drogue and drop to zero feet. And get down fast, or the radar'll pick you up. Once in the Baltic, you're on your own. We've worked out tracks for you, and these include a couple of weaves to avoid islands. Steer clear of shipping as far as you can, and take no notice of lighthouses and beacons—we think the Russians are rigging 'em."

He paused. "And now for the surprise, the idea that's made the whole thing possible and is going to save your lives. At the end of the Gulf of Finland there'll be a fishing trawler. How it got there you needn't worry your heads over. But it'll be there, in position 59°39′ North, 27°30′ East, exactly fourteen miles off the Russian coast. Now this trawler'll be using ordinary marine radar. The Russians are used to trawlers using radar, so they'll not be suspicious. But this particular radar set will have a specially built-in coding circuit. In the nose of the Bat, as you know, there's a directional radar receiver. And the point's this: this receiver will have the *same coding circuit,* so that only the Bat, you see, can pick up the trawler. And as an added precaution the trawler's radar will be rigged so that the coded transmissions go out only in the sector you'll be approaching from: i.e., away from Russia. Now the drill's this. You'll fly up the Gulf of Finland by dead reckoning. When you think you're fifty miles short of position 59°39′ North, 27°30′ East, you'll switch on your radar receiver. And you'll use your left/right indicator to home on the trawler. You'll fly slap over the top of the trawler at a height of a hundred feet. And this'll enable you to fix your position *exactly*. In other words,

146

you'll approach the Russian coast at a known spot, *and* with your instruments precisely checked and reset."

Polhill nodded. The trial runs they'd been making off the Isle of Wight made sense now. It all added up.

S.A.S.O. went on to deal with the flight to Moscow, the release of the message, and the passing back of the coded report to say the operation had been successful. Then he came to the flight back.

"If you cut your speed coming back, you'll have *just* sufficient fuel to get to the Gulf of Finland. When you're approaching the coast, switch on your radar receiver again and use it to home on the trawler. When you're half a mile short of her, eject. The trawler crew'll be standing by to pick you up. They'll take you to Lovisa, in Finland. And by this time tomorrow you'll be back safe and sound in Farnborough. And," he added dryly, "I daresay one or two people'll be offering to buy you a drink. . . ."

It gave them a chance.

There were still a lot of things that could go wrong. They might miss their rendezvous with the tanker; they might snarl up the refueling; Stockholm Control might refuse to clear them for descent; they might be picked up by the listening posts as they broke away; they might be picked up by Soviet warships as they crossed the Baltic; they could fail to locate the trawler; they could lose their way on the run-in to Moscow; they could hit an uncharted hazard such as a newly built radio mast; they could be shot down by the Soviet defenses; they mightn't survive the ejection; they mightn't survive the shock of landing in water that was within a couple of degrees of solidifying to ice. But they had a chance now, a chance not only of success but of survival. And that—and not the difficulties—was what they grasped at. Even Oakman came out of his trance and took heart.

S.A.S.O. handed them a meticulously prepared brief, with details of tracks and rendezvous points and graphs of fuel consumption. He then went on to deal in detail with different aspects of the flight. First, weather.

This was everything they could have hoped for. The big anti-cyclone which had been building up in the central Atlantic had drifted now to the North Sea and was bringing settled conditions, with light winds and good visibility, to the whole area. There was a full moon; and at the approaches to Moscow the ground was covered by a sprinkling of snow, harbinger of the Russian winter. So conditions for visual flying were pretty well ideal. The only trouble they might run into, S.A.S.O. said, was a bit of low cloud over the Russian coast; but this was thought to be local and well broken.

Second, diversions. Not much was possible, he told them, in the way of creating a diversion. But at 2115 hours, as the Bat ought to be starting her run-in, the Americans were planning to lob a Thor into the area east of Moscow. This, it was hoped, might distract the Russian defenses.

On the question of radio, S.A.S.O. emphasized the need for silence—until the standoff bomb was actually launched.

"Then," he said, "you must pass an 'Operation successful' message right away—the second the bomb's clear. Because it's not enough simply to land the message; we must *know* you've landed it, so we can tell the world. . . . Now we've given you an operational call sign. It's been suggested you take the code name that's being used this week by Lossiemouth's Buccaneers. That seems to make sense—good for security. Their call sign is 'Mockingbird.' So your personal call sign—not that we expect you to use it—is Mockingbird O for Orange. And the moment your bomb is launched, we want you to radio back the signal 'Mockingbird nested.'

148

Is that clear? Simply 'Mockingbird nested.' When we hear that, we'll know everything's gone according to plan."

S.A.S.O. then went on to deal with each stage of the flight in meticulous detail: from their kitting up, right through to their dinghy survival drill. And finally he asked if they had any questions.

Polhill said he'd like another look at the Russian coast where they expected to make their landfall; he wanted, he said, to be sure he could visualize the rivers and lakes—"just in case something goes wrong with the navigation." He was taken to an adjoining room and shown the model of the Gulf of Finland which had been transported bodily from Farnborough.

While he was studying it, Oakman ran through ejection and dinghy drill with a squadron leader from the Institute of Aviation Medicine.

"Let's take it," the squadron leader said, "you're coming up to the trawler at 500 knots, height 200 feet. First, get your speed down to something like 250, then pull up your nose. Drop the visor over your face, and reach up and pull the ejector lever with both hands—you may not be able to release it, remember, with one hand. And another thing: pilot and navigator have to eject within a couple of seconds of each other, because once you pull the pilot's lever, the control column's broken and knocked forward to avoid snapping off the pilot's legs as he's shot out, so the plane of course dives straight in. . . . Once you're clear, everything's automatic. You're shot up 450 feet. The parachute opens. The seat drops clear. And the second you hit the water, your dinghy and Mae West inflate. In the dinghy remember to release your harness to avoid parachute drag. And don't forget that if you use Sarah, the trawler may be able to home on you, but so will a flock of Russian patrol boats. . . ."

The briefing and the answering of questions took the

149

best part of a couple of hours; which meant they were left with a bare hour and a half for tea and kitting up. It wasn't long. But it was enough. For as S.A.S.O. knew, the less time they had for thinking, the better.

Both of them had a few last-minute things they wanted to attend to. Oakman strolled across to the hangar with a member of S.A.S.O.'s staff; he was anxious to make a last-minute check on the Bat. While Polhill went first to the station chapel, then to his cabin to be sure that his "just-in-case" letter to Jennifer had been left where it was sure to be found.

At 1630 they had a snack tea brought them in the operations room.

At 1650 a safety-equipment officer brought in their kit, and they began, methodically and unhurriedly, to put on warm underclothes, immersion suits and lightweight flying overalls.

And at 1715 they walked out to where the Bat lay like a great white moth on the hard standing, her standoff bomb slung snugly under her belly and her anti-radiation paint glowing faintly beneath the stars.

17

As they walked to the waiting plane, the moon was rising out of the sea and the stars shone gemlike from a sky that was clear and cold. For a moment they paused, touched by the beauty of the night; then the "Halt!" of a security guard jerked them back to reality.

There were two guards—marine corporals—and they took a very close look at Oakman and Polhill before they let them through. It was comforting, in a way, to know that Security, right up to the last moment, was so meticulous.

Beside the Bat, making, he said, a last-minute check on their equipment, was Pellew. He wished them luck. "I'll buy you a drink in the mess tomorrow night," he called as they settled into their seats. Then the cockpit canopy was pulled to, and they were on their own.

For the last hour they'd been, to say the least, on edge—sweat on their hands, and thoughts running amok into channels that were taboo. But now they had something to do which called for both mental and physical alertness, they pushed their fears into the background and got on, thankfully, with the job of preparing for take-off.

They settled into their seats. They strapped themselves in. They took out the little red safety pins from the side of their ejector mechanism. They adjusted their bone domes. They checked their oxygen, their intercom and their instruments. And at the end of a couple of minutes they were ready to start up. Oakman flickered his navigation lights. He waited for the ground crew to give him the go-ahead, then pressed the starter buttons, one at a time. With a couple of muffled explosions the engines fired, idled for a moment, then revved up into a steady pulsating whine. Polhill pulled out his check list.

"Fuel?"

"Contents and pressures O.K. Booster pumps on."

"Hydraulic pressure?"

"Three thousand pounds."

"Air brakes?"

"In."

"Flaps?"

"One third down."

"Controls?"

"Controls free. Trims set. Autopilot out."

In the soft red glow of their instruments the litany continued until each of its thirty-seven items had been carefully checked. Then Polhill checked their three chronometers (there's no point in an aircraft's carrying only two, since if they read differently there's no telling which is right and which is wrong). The chronometers agreed to the nearest second: it was coming up to 1736. Oakman flickered his lights again, and the ground crew ran under his wings and jerked away the chocks. He started then to taxi out to the end of runway zero five, the Bat, without lights, gliding ghostlike over the gray tarmac. At the end of the runway he throttled back.

"Sixty seconds," Polhill said.

He lined up carefully, dead center between the double row of sodiums, their mile-long springboard into the night.

152

He eased open the throttles; and the pent-up power of their jets made the plane vibrate and tremble against its brakes.

Polhill was watching his chronometer. "Fifteen seconds," he said, "to go."

Oakman released the brakes, at the same time easing the throttles right forward against their stops. And they began to roll: slowly at first, then faster and faster. As they gathered speed down the runway he glanced up, and saw above him the navigation lights of a pair of Buccaneers sweeping low overhead, the noise of their jets drowning the sound of his take-off—so that anyone watching the airfield would never realize that a Bat had left the ground. (They were taking no risks of a last-minute security leak.) The sodiums streamed by, faster and faster. The lead-out lights ahead grew brighter. The drum-drum-drum of their wheels on the tarmac diminished, and the control column first stiffened, then "bit." Oakman glanced at their air speed: 160 knots. He waited a couple of seconds, then eased back on the stick, and the Bat rose cleanly and sweetly into the night.

They went through the routine drill. "Speed, 180 knots, wheels in and locked . . . 200 knots, flaps coming up. . . ." To start with, Oakman concentrated on his instruments. Then, when they were on course, the trim was set and the Bat throttled back to normal cruising, he looked outside.

They were flying low down the Moray Firth, parallel to the shore. Behind them the individual lights of Lossiemouth were already merging into a single diminishing glow. To their right the land lay black and sleeping, save for a cluster of lights around Buckie and Banff and the occasional flare of a car's headlamps questing the narrow coastal road. To their left as they cleared the Firth and turned into the North Sea an enormous blood-red moon, hazed faintly with mist, was hoisting itself out of the water. And ahead was darkness: four hundred miles of open sea rolling everlastingly

153

on to the far Norwegian shore. There was no cloud and little wind, so conditions for low flying were near ideal. Soon they banked to starboard and settled on course for position X: their rendezvous with the tanker.

As they flew southeast the moon rose higher, and once it was well clear of the horizon they were able to use it to judge their height. For if they gained height, then the gap between them and the moon's reflection widened; and if they lost height, it closed. For quite a while Oakman flew by the moon. Then he realized that conditions were smooth enough to use the autopilot. He set the lower limit to two hundred feet, and the Bat flew steadily and automatically southeast, while the moon rose higher, the stars shifted across the zodiac and the minutes ticked by. Apart from keeping a dead-accurate course and speed, they had nothing to do.

It was all so simple. All so easy. They could hardly believe that this was it: that they were now embarked on the flight on the outcome of which the fate of nations hung in the balance. But as they flew on they realized that the ease and the simplicity were an illusion. For as Sir Basil had said, "All's well if all's well; but the second the slightest thing goes wrong you've had it." That was the crux of the matter. So long as things went well the flight *was* easy. Indeed it *could* be easy all the way to Moscow and back. But they'd only to make the slightest error, one link in their chain had only to reveal the slightest flaw, and the whole scheme would blow up in their faces.

They checked and rechecked their instruments and their course and height and speed. And at the end of an hour they were coming up to their first moment of danger, the first link which looked cast-iron but which might for all that unexpectedly part and precipitate them into a crisis: their rendezvous with the Valiant.

It sounded easy: for two aircraft to fly to the middle of the North Sea and meet over a map reference. And nine times out of ten it *would* be easy. But there was always the possibility of something going wrong: compass error, human error, cloud at the rendezvous point. In this particular case there were added grounds for anxiety. For the Bat couldn't use her radio. And the Valiant was supposed to be flying a BEA route to a BEA schedule, and it would look highly suspicious if she suddenly started to fly in circles in the middle of the North Sea; in other words, if the Bat didn't make the contact dead on time it would jeopardize the whole plan.

At 1835, Polhill checked the chronometers. At 1837 he estimated they were twenty miles short of position X, with a shade over three minutes to go. Acting on a predetermined plan, Oakman swung the Bat briefly off course; then pushed open the throttles and began a wide climbing turn at 5,000 feet a minute. At 1840 he leveled off at 10,200 feet and swung onto the BEA track of 080. This was the moment of truth. He peered anxiously through the windshield. The Valiant ought to be dead ahead, lit up like a Christmas tree, 800 feet above them and flying on the same course.

But he could see nothing.

He was about to start weaving either side of their track in search of her, when he saw what looked like an extra-bright star flashing away on their port bow. And the second he focused on it, the Valiant came into view, so sharply delineated that he could only wonder he hadn't spotted her before.

He wiped the sweat off his forehead and turned toward her. The first hurdle had been cleared. He formated beside her starboard wing, while Polhill and the Valiant navigator exchanged a series of prearranged signals by Aldis.

When the tanker had unwound her pipeline and indicated

155

she was ready to pass fuel, Oakman dropped below and astern of her; then he crept up underneath her, like a calf to its mother. The pipeline hung motionless from the Valiant's belly, its aperture outlined by a trio of guide lights. Using the probe on his nose as a sight, Oakman inched the Bat forward till with a clunk of steel on rubber the connection was made, and the aircraft were joined one to the other. A cock on the Valiant's control panel was turned to "full," and kerosene began to flow down the pipe and into the Bat's tanks at the rate of three hundred gallons a minute.

Once the aircraft were mated, their intercom circuits became automatically linked, and the crews were able to talk to each other without fear of detection.

"How are you doing, Ken?" The pilot of the Valiant (a squadron leader from Mildenhall) had known Oakman at Cranwell.

"We're fine, Bill, thanks. Never seen *you* so lit up before!"

For a time they chattered of this and that, while kerosene flowed smoothly between them, and their aircraft, moving slightly in relation to each other like vessels in swell, flew steadily east. When the Bat had taken in three hundred and fifty gallons, the stopcock in the Valiant was turned to "closed." But the aircraft stayed together, linked by sixty feet of pipeline.

Staying together had several advantages: the crews were able to talk; the Bat could take in fuel at a second's notice; and the planes were forced to keep close.

And keeping close was important now. For they were coming up to the coast of Denmark, and the radar screens of half a dozen countries would soon be picking them up.

Keeping close formation wasn't difficult. It did call for concentration and a never ending series of minor adjust-

156

ments on control column and throttles. But Oakman didn't mind. In fact he was glad to have something to occupy his attention.

At 1930 they passed over the Kattegat. The inshore waters were dotted with pinheads of gold: the lights of the Scandinavian fishing fleets. As they came up to the coast of Sweden they took in another hundred and fifty gallons, filling up to capacity, knowing their lives depended upon how much kerosene they could squeeze into their tanks.

They flew on and on, one beneath the other, at the BEA cruising speed (330 knots), and the BEA height (11,000 feet) and on the BEA route (up airway Amber 7 and onto corridor Red 4). The pilot of the Valiant, using a BEA call sign and BEA patter, made routine checks with Gothenburg and Copenhagen. He checked the weather at Stockholm—getting, incidentally, the exact barometric pressure, which he passed on to Oakman so that the Bat's altimeter could be accurately set. And at 1945—by which time Oakman and Polhill had been airborne a shade over two hours—the pilot of the Valiant called up Stockholm Control and told them he was having trouble with his undercarriage.

This was the second moment of crisis. How would the controller react?

The odds were that he'd simply acknowledge the call and leave it to the pilot to advise him how serious the defect was before he took action. But here again things *could* go wrong. The controller might be officious; he might smell a rat; he might insist on diverting them.

Oakman and Polhill listened anxiously to the one-sided conversation—they could hear the Valiant but not Stockholm. At first they were none too sure that things were working out right, for the controller seemed to be asking a great many questions; then much to their relief, they heard their pilot say, "Right. I'll call you again as we approach the

157

airfield," and a moment later he was telling them that Stockholm had agreed they should keep on course. The second link, it seemed, was holding. They were over the forests and lakes of Skaraborg and Ostergotland now, a dark wilderness of swampland, mountain and pine, broken by only the occasional glimmer of light from village or town.

At 2000 they turned onto airway Green 3 at the approaches to Stockholm.

When they were ten miles short of the capital, the Valiant pilot spoke on his radio again to the Airport Control, and once again Oakman and Polhill listened anxiously to a one-sided conversation. This, they knew, was a ticklish moment: if things went wrong now they were in trouble. But it became clear almost at once that Stockholm Control were being co-operative. And as they approached the airfield the Valiant began to lose height.

"We're O.K.," the pilot told them. "We're cleared to let-down."

It was almost too easy, almost too good to be true.

They were on schedule, with everything going according to plan.

The Valiant passed over the center of Stockholm at 8,000 feet, giving Polhill a position check and the chance to reset his instruments. He reset them with meticulous accuracy, knowing he wouldn't get another chance in the next three hundred miles: the inertial navigator, the altimeter and the all-important moving map. And soon they were letting down over the coast.

The weather in the Baltic was pretty well perfect: a full moon, first-class visibility and only a few infrequent wisps of cloud. From 6,000 feet they could see the offshore islands almost as clearly as if it were day. Instinctively Oakman formated even more closely to the Valiant; so closely that on the coastal radar screens they gave only the single echo;

so closely that far below them only a single shadow was reflected on the moonlit sea. Their altimeters unwound: 5,000 feet, 4,000, 3,000. And soon they were clear of land. They sucked in a last-second drop of kerosene. They exchanged a last word with the crew of the Valiant.

"Thanks for your company. Here's where we love you and leave you."

"Good luck, Kenneth."

"Thanks . . . Breaking away . . . Now."

Oakman throttled back, and the pipeline parted. He pressed down the Bat's nose, and the sea came rushing toward them—nearer and nearer, till the gap between moon and reflection was pared to a hairline and it seemed to Polhill as though they were flying straight into the water. Then at the last second they leveled off. Oakman eased open the throttles, and the Bat went hurtling east. At six hundred knots. At zero feet. Alone.

And the moment they were over the Baltic the atmosphere changed.

On the first stage of their flight they hadn't really believed what was happening to them; they'd expected any second to hear the voice of the Farnborough controller recalling them as if from a NATO exercise. When they sighted Stockholm they'd felt a stir of excitement, but the full import of what they were doing still hadn't struck home. But when the pipeline parted and the Valiant climbed away and the blink and flash of her navigation lights had faded into the stars, then the truth hit them. They were alone. And they were afraid.

They were afraid because they were faced now with the unknown. Who could tell what Soviet defenses mightn't be waiting to ensnare them—as they'd already ensnared Robinshaw and Taylor? Perhaps the night fighters were already

159

alerted? Perhaps the homing missiles, even now, were lining up on them?

They hugged the water, knowing the lower they kept the less the chance of their being detected, while the moon climbed higher, lacquering the surface of the Baltic with a sheen of gold, and the needles of compass and altimeter stayed as steady as rocks, and the miles were eaten away—at the rate of one every six seconds.

After a while the air in the cockpit began to get unpleasantly hot, for at the speed they were flying the skin of the Bat was hotter than boiling water. But they couldn't reduce speed. They had a schedule to keep to. So they flew on, with the sweat beginning to form under their bone domes and trickle perversely into their eyes, and the water content of the wisps of cloud they passed through evaporating with a little hiss to steam as it touched the heated surface of their fuselage and wings.

At 2030 they turned into the Gulf of Finland. Once again they seemed to be dead on ETA; dead, too, as far as they could tell, on course.

As far as they could tell . . . That was the crux of it. Since leaving Stockholm they had had to rely solely on compass and navigational plot. They had already flown without check for a hundred and fifty miles; they had another hundred and fifty to go. As far as they could tell, they'd flown accurately. But wind change or magnetic anomaly could already have thrown them substantially off course; and this error, by the end of another hundred and fifty miles, could easily be increased to fatal proportions. So they could only hope to God the trawler would be waiting for them and their receiver wouldn't go temperamental.

As they altered course to pass—they hoped—midway between the Finnish and the Estonian shore, Polhill searched for the lighthouses which might, in normal times, have given them a navigational check: the flashing group of the Tah-kuna or the occulting beam of the Apollomadalik. But the lighthouses—as they'd been given to expect—were no longer in use. The approaches to Russia were as dead as a nuclear-contaminated desert: devoid of light, sound or any trace of life. More in hope than expectation Polhill tried to pick up a bearing from one of the Russian radio beacons. But the beacons were either silent or jammed. Even the Narva commercial network on frequency 585 was silent. They could only fly blindly on.

There was a bit more low-level cloud in the Gulf of Finland. Not enough to be troublesome, but enough to make them thankful it wasn't thicker. They passed through a couple of belts of poor visibility and turbulence, with the hiss and crack of snow particles as they hit the Bat sounding like boiling water poured on ice. Oakman eased back on the throttles and their speed dropped; better, he thought, to be a few minutes late for the rendezvous than to have our wing tips colandered by the snow. Then, once again, they were in the clear, streaking at zero feet over a dead-calm moonlit sea.

At 2040 they made a last-minute check on everything that conceivably *could* be checked: altimeter, fuel consumption, oil pressures and temperatures, and the controls for releasing their standoff bomb. Then, at 2050, they switched on their special receiver.

Moistening their lips, they peered at the light at the base of their left/right indicator: the light which told them whether or not they were picking up the trawler's transmissions.

And the light glowed green, and the needle of the indicator began to tremble.

A wave of thankfulness engulfed them. So once again everything was going according to plan. The trawler was

161

in position; her radar was transmitting; they were picking it up; in less than ten minutes they'd have homed onto her, passed over the top of her, reset their instruments and made an accurate landfall over the Russian coast. But first they must correct their course so as to pass directly over the trawler. Polhill was waiting for the needle to steady and tell him which way to turn—when the green light went out and the needle quietly subsided.

They stared at the indicator in disbelief. One second it had been their lifeline; the next, it was a slab of inanimate metal—lifeless, useless, devoid of substance or meaning.

They waited for the light to come on again.

But it didn't.

Clumsy with anxiety, Polhill checked power supply and circuit. He changed the bulb.

But the light still didn't come on. The needle lay limp.

And the Bat went hurtling toward the unknown shore; blind, lost, at a thousand feet a second.

"My God!" Oakman's voice was harsh with fear. "We've had it!"

Even as he spoke, a belt of cloud came rushing toward them out of the night. One moment they were in the clear. The next a pearl-gray opaqueness had blotted out horizon and stars. And the cloud belt, this time, was full of turbulence. The Bat reeled and shuddered, struck as though by a flurry of blows from a giant celestial hammer. Their straps cut into and bruised their shoulders. On the instrument panel their needles flickered into a meaningless blur.

It was the moment they'd dreaded. The moment when things went wrong, and the whole scheme blew up in their faces.

"It's no good," Oakman shouted. "I'm turning back."

Then, suddenly as it had come, the cloud was gone. They were in air that was still and unbelievably clear. And ahead of them, so bright that it hurt their eyes, was the vast expanse of the Soviet Union, dead white under a mantle of powdery snow.

"Keep her down." Polhill's voice was sharp. "Don't alter course. There's still a chance."

He stared at the wilderness of white now rushing beneath their wings, so fast that every outline was blurred and so close that it seemed he had only to trail his hand out of the Bat to pick up fistfuls of the powdery snow. Oh, God, he thought, if only we could hit a river, an estuary, a lake— something I could recognize.

But the featureless carpet of snow remained unbroken. And the Bat, with Oakman frozen stiff with terror onto the controls, went hurtling blind at zero feet into the unknown.

18

Christabel had had no end of a job persuading Pellew to let her go.

When he had asked her advice, that evening in the test hangar, about whom they should send to operate the trawler's radar, she'd had too much *savoir-faire* to suggest herself right away.

"Well," she'd said, "it must be someone who can install the coding circuit, *and* who knows enough about aircraft to help the Bat if things go wrong."

"Not a technician from Mecca?"

"Oh no, sir. That wouldn't do at all." She launched into a complex and highly technical explanation of how the operator would have to adjust the transmissions so that only the Bat would receive the coded signals, while normal signals were sent out in other directions.

Pellew scratched his head. "So it had better be someone from the Instrument Department?"

"Yes. And someone who's been security-screened."

"Hmmm!"

She let the implications sink home. She wanted *him* to suggest her going; but when it became clear that his thoughts just weren't running that way, she said simply:

164

"You know, I'm the obvious person."

He had been adamant at first. It was quite out of the question, he'd said. And even if he approved the idea—and he certainly didn't—the Air Ministry would never wear it.

She had been hard put to hold on to her temper—for she was determined to be the one to go—but she had managed it; and she'd played her cards exactly right. Arguments alone, she'd realized, would never convince him; nor would pleading. But a combination of banter and an appeal to his sense of the romantic was something he'd find hard to resist.

"But, sir," she said, "girls do all sorts of things nowadays."

"More's the pity."

"But there's no actual danger. Why shouldn't a woman go?"

"Things might go wrong."

"For the crew of the Bat, yes. But not for the crew of the trawler. And after all, sir"—she played her strongest card—"you know I *have* got a personal reason for wanting to go."

He thought it over. He had old-fashioned ideas about women. The magazine pictures he'd seen in recent years of teen-aged girls drilling with rifles and flame throwers appalled him. Yet this, he told himself, *was* a bit different; this wouldn't, for the crew of the trawler, develop into a shooting war. The crew of the trawler would simply be fishing—and well outside Russian waters; so they'd hardly be likely, would they, to run into trouble? (This way of thinking didn't in fact hold water. Pellew ought to have known that the cold war recognizes neither international rules—such as the sanctity of fishing rights—nor ethical rules—such as the sanctity of women. But, in his blindness, he drew comfort from the belief that there'd be little chance of the girl's running into physical danger.) He looked at her thoughtfully. In a way she *was* the obvious person to go. The idea had been hers in the first place; she'd need no

165

special training to operate the radar; she was one of the few people accustomed to work with both aircraft and marine equipment, so if anything went wrong she'd have the technical know-how to put it right; she'd been screened by Security; and, as she'd said, she had a personal reason for seeing the job through—wasn't she supposed to be keen on the blue-eyed Squadron Leader Oakman? Pellew was shrewd enough not to underestimate the importance of a personal tie-up; for there was a world of difference, he knew, between doing a job because it mattered to mankind with a capital M and doing it because it mattered to someone one loved. Yet a residue of doubt lingered on.

"My dear," he said, "this'll be a tough assignment. You've been working flat out: day and night. We can't risk a crackup."

She laid a hand on his arm; she smiled her most dazzling smile. "Do I look," she said, "as if I'd crack up?"

He stared at her for a long time, but her gaze didn't drop. "Hmmm!" He rubbed his chin. "I'll think it over."

She had the good sense not to press her advantage too hard.

They had walked twice around the hangar and checked for the umpteenth time that the receiver was being correctly installed, when Pellew said suddenly, "Tell me how this radar equipment works."

Now careful, Christabel, she thought. Make it too simple and he'll think any fool can work it. Make it too complex and he'll think you're muddleheaded.

"Well, sir, you see those two strips of metal either side of the Bat's nose?"

"Yes."

"They're like two ears tuned in to a preset frequency. When the Bat's pointing straight at the trawler's radar, both ears pick up the same amount of transmission; but if one ear's pointing a bit away from the radar it picks up less. The amount of transmission that's picked up is relayed to the left/right indicator in the nose of the plane; and this indicator tells the pilot which way to turn to get both ears hearing the same: i.e., to be heading straight for the radar set."

"I see. So once the radar is installed, you don't need any special skill to operate it?"

"It's not as simple as that, sir. The installing itself calls for a good bit of skill. You see, unless things are done just right, the Russians may pick our transmissions up. So we've got to limit them to a fifty-mile range, *and* channel them into a sort of funnel pointing along the Bat's approach track: away from Russia."

"Hmmm!"

"And another thing. The person working the radar *must* be *au fait* with aircraft procedure. Suppose the weather clamps down and the Bat has to switch in its responder beacon. Or suppose we want to use our walkie-talkie to home the plane down: these are things you can't do unless you're clued up on the drill."

"Hmmm!"

They walked twice more around the hangar; then Pellew seemed suddenly to make up his mind. Telling Christabel to wait, he hurried across to his room in Flying Control. For a moment he stood by the window, staring out at the buttery glow of the sodiums. Then he got on the scrambler to the Air Ministry.

While he was phoning, Christabel kicked her heels—none too patiently—in the hangar. She'd got Pellew on her side, she was almost certain of that; she only hoped the powers-that-be wouldn't now prove recalcitrant.

For it was terribly important to her that she should be the one to go.

Polhill had accused her of failing to help Kenneth at the time he needed help most, and there had been enough truth in his accusation to hurt. But she could put that right now. If she went on the trawler, not only would it be her idea that would save Kenneth's life; she would actually take part with him in the operation itself. It isn't often, she thought, a woman has the chance to do something like this for the man she loves: something so wonderfully worthwhile. They *must* let me go.

The minutes ticked by. Soon Pellew had been gone a quarter of an hour. She wasn't especially anxious at first. She told herself that delay was a good sign: that at least they couldn't have turned down the idea flat, that they must be talking it over and going into ways and means. But when the quarter of an hour lengthened first into half an hour and then three quarters, her restlessness increased. After a while she began to pace the hangar, biting her nails.

She'd been pacing the hangar and biting her nails for very nearly an hour before Pellew came back and told her, quite simply, that it was all arranged: that the Air Ministry had agreed she could go.

Relief flooded over her.

She hardly listened to Pellew as he told her that she was to "disappear" from the establishment first thing in the morning and report for briefing to New Scotland Yard.

"Now I'll fix an early call," he added, "and transport. You get all the sleep you can."

She laid a hand on his arm. "Thank you," she said. "I won't let you down."

He watched her walking away: small and frail against a backdrop of hangars and arc lights. I only hope to God, he thought, I've done the right thing.

His doubts wouldn't have been assuaged if he could have watched her during the next few minutes.

168

For by the time she'd walked back to her quarters, reaction had set in. Now that she was no longer keyed up, mentally or physically, the effect of the Benzedrine began to wear off; and quite suddenly she was so tired that she could hardly keep open her eyes. She undressed as if she were drunk, her mind blank and her movements unco-ordinated. She half fell, half climbed, into bed; and was asleep, quite literally, as soon as her head touched the pillow.

Nine hours passed, as quickly, it seemed to her, as nine seconds. At first she just couldn't believe the voice that was saying, over and over again, "Ma'am! Wake up. It's seven o'clock." Then she opened her eyes, and the mess orderly and the familiar cup of canteen-brewed tea swam into focus.

She felt none too good—Benzedrine has a depressing aftermath. But there's always a price tag, she thought, and I couldn't have done without it. She sat up reluctantly and sipped her tea and tried to collect her thoughts.

So much had happened so quickly in the previous twenty-four hours that she was glad now of the chance quietly to sort things out. It was funny, wasn't it, she reflected, how she'd got so involved with the flight of the Bat? She'd been in at the scheme's conception—that evening on the taxi track at Culdrose; and soon she'd be in at its grand finale—somewhere hundreds of miles away, off the Russian shore. And there was a rightness about this, she told herself, because from the very start she'd championed the scheme with all her heart and all her mind and all her strength.

As she sipped her tea, she asked herself why she'd championed it so fiercely. It was partly, of course, because of its supreme importance. But there was more to it than that. She'd championed it, she had to admit, partly because of her relationship with Kenneth.

169

Their relationship was neither easy nor simple. She was on the threshold of love. But no farther than the threshold because he was so infuriatingly uncommitted, so vague in his beliefs, so self-contained, so apparently self-sufficient. He was the sort of man it was terribly hard to get through to. His attitude over the Bat, she reflected, was typical. No sooner had he thought the idea up than he'd begun to have doubts; no sooner had the idea become a practical reality than he'd tried to back out. And this back-pedaling, this seeing two sides of every question and the world in shades of gray, seemed to Christabel a weakness. If he backs out of this, she thought, he'll back out of other things. I'll never know where I stand. So it had become terribly important to her that he *didn't* back out. At one stage it had looked as though he'd have an excuse to. Then she'd hit on her bright idea. And that had solved everything, in the happiest possible way. It had made the flight possible; it had made his survival a likelihood rather than a pious hope; and it had given her the chance to help him in the most positive and practical way of all—by joining with him in the actual operation. She wasn't blind to the dangers. She was too intelligent to be blind to them. But she discounted them in view of the possible rewards. And—as was perhaps only human— she preened herself a little at the thought that it was *her* idea that was going to save both the world and the man she loved.

She sipped her tea. And it was stone-cold. She came to with a start and scrabbled for her watch: Seven twenty. In three quarters of an hour the staff car would be waiting to take her to London. She jumped out of bed, washed and dressed quickly and hurried across to the mess.

She was gulping down her coffee and toast when she heard the sound of an aircraft taking off. Looking out of the window, she saw a Bat disappearing to southward over the hangar roofs. It was Oakman and Polhill, she guessed, test-

170

ing the special receiver and indicator which had been installed during the night. Her lips tightened. She'd wanted to talk to them before she left the airfield; she'd wanted them to know that everything was going to be all right. Her fingers drummed on the window sill. She didn't like being thwarted. She thought of getting Control to pass them a message, but time and Security were against her. Then she thought of Polhill's wife.

She shut herself in a telephone booth and got the number out of a local directory. Jennifer Polhill answered almost at once.

"It's Christabel here, Mrs. Polhill."

"Oh, hello, Christabel."

"I've wonderful news for you. Everything's going to be all right."

"You mean"—breathlessly—"he's not going?"

"No, he's still going. But we can get him back."

"Oh!" It was an expressive "Oh": slightly incredulous, but filled with sudden hope. "Can you tell me?"

"Not on the phone."

"No, of course. Shall I come to the airfield?"

"I'm sorry, Mrs. Polhill. Truth is I'm off to London in a moment, and I shan't be back for some days. I just wanted to tell you the good news."

"I see . . . No, I don't see. Doesn't Jim know?"

"We only thought of this scheme last night. I was going to tell him about it this morning. But he's flying."

"I see . . . And this scheme for getting him back—is it really going to work?"

"Yes."

"You're sure, Christabel? I'd far rather know the truth."

"I *promise* you," she said, "we'll get him back."

An unidentifiable sound came over the wires, a sort of cross between a sob and a long-drawn sigh. There followed

171

a moment's silence; then Jennifer Polhill's voice, curiously muffled, as though she were holding a hand over the mouthpiece: "Nicola, go back and finish your breakfast."

A pause, then: "Yes, it is the lady with the pretty hair."

Another pause, then, more clearly: "Christabel! Would you mind saying hello to Nicola?"

"Hello, Nicola," she said.

"Hello."

A pause while Christabel searched for something to say. Little girls of five weren't her line of country. "Are you having a nice breakfast?" she ventured at last.

"Yes."

Another pause, then: "When's my daddy coming home?"

"Quite soon, Nicola."

"Will he come home tonight?"

"Not tonight, and not tomorrow night. But the night after that."

"You promise me!"

"I promise you," she said, "your daddy'll be back in three nights."

"All right. Bye for now."

"Bye-bye, Nicola."

"Thanks," Jennifer Polhill said, "for everything."

"That's O.K. And you can stop worrying now. Ye gods, I must fly! Bye, Jennifer."

"Bye for now."

As she put down the receiver she saw Pellew's staff car drawn up outside the mess, and the corporal driver was looking pointedly at his watch.

She couldn't make out at first what was so odd about the drive to London. Then she got it. The traffic was going the wrong way. At 8 A.M. cars should have been flowing *toward* the city, but the flow now was in the opposite direction.

She knew why. She'd heard about the exodus which had been gathering momentum in the last twenty-four hours: of the tens of thousands of families who were fleeing the big towns to squat like migratory sea birds along the coast of Cornwall, southwest of Scotland and Wales. But she hadn't quite realized what the exodus meant in terms of human hardship and suffering: the overloaded cars, the crowded trailers, the schools of bicyclists, and the families of hitch-hikers (for public transport was proving unable to cope with the stampede west). And there were other eye openers, too: the anti-government slogans chalked on roadways and walls, the plethora of posters and placards, the posses of demon-strators, all urging the Prime Minister to go to Moscow rather than risk the holocaust of a nuclear war. And it came to her how lucky she had been these last few days to be leading a cloistered life inside the R.A.E. and to have plenty to occupy her mind.

At the approaches to Whitehall the staff car was routed through side streets; big demonstrations, the police told them, were blocking Parliament and Trafalgar Squares. But the detour didn't involve much loss of time, and it still needed a few minutes to nine o'clock as they drew up at the entrance to New Scotland Yard. She climbed out of the car, tossed back her head and walked up the broad stone steps with a confidence far more apparent than real.

Her first impression of New Scotland Yard was of brisk efficiency. She was expected, and there were no formalities or delays. A messenger led her at once down a tiled cor-ridor and into a small but pleasantly furnished room.

There were a couple of Parker Knoll chairs in the room, a filing cabinet, a flat-topped contemporary desk, three Tretchikoff prints and a man who looked like a successful business executive: heavily built, forty-fivish and getting a little thin on top. The man got up and held out his hand.

173

"Christabel Barlow?"

She nodded.

"You and I," he said, "are flying to Helsinki this afternoon. So I'd better introduce myself: Iain Mackinnon."

She noticed the expensive cut of his lightweight tweeds, the sapphire cuff links and his silk hand-woven tie. "I've always wanted," she said, "to fly first-class in a Comet."

He smiled. "You've got there in one. V.I.P. company director and his confidential secretary."

She gave him an old-fashioned look. "Hmmm!" she said.

Well, at least, he thought, she's got a sense of humor. He pulled up a chair. "Have a seat, Christabel," he said, "and I'll put you in the picture."

He didn't sit himself. He offered her a cigarette, then started to pace the room.

"Briefly," he said, "the setup's this. A Finnair Caravelle—not a Comet, I'm afraid—leaves for Helsinki at one thirty this afternoon. We'll be aboard. Seats and passports are fixed, and two coded radar circuits'll be hidden in our luggage. The Caravelle gets to Helsinki at six o'clock—that's eight o'clock local time. We've been promised a quick clearance through the customs. We'll book in at a hotel—that's to allay suspicion in case passengers arriving by air are being watched. We'll have dinner; then we'll collect a car and drive to Lovisa—a port about eighty kilometers east of Helsinki. We should get there soon after midnight—in time, with any luck, for a few hours' sleep. First thing next morning we board a trawler, put to sea and head southeast for the Neugrund—the fishing grounds nearest the Russian coast. Trawler and crew are all laid on, of course; so there'll be no trouble getting the special coders aboard.

"Now it's about eighty miles from Lovisa to the Neugrund: say, ten hours' steaming at eight knots. That means you'll have bags of time—all day tomorrow, in fact—to get your radar equipment rigged up and tested. Once we're in the fishing grounds we'll start trawling. And we'll time the trawl to take us slap over the rendezvous point—both when the Bat's going in and coming out. Sound O.K. to you?"

"Sounds fine," she said, "except for one thing. Won't we look a bit silly if the Helsinki customs fish a pair of radar coders out of our bags?"

Mackinnon picked up his desk phone. "Bring in Miss Barlow's radio," he said.

A moment later she was examining a neat-looking transistor. She flicked it on and was rewarded with John Anthony's friendly patter on "Housewives' Choice." She looked at the back, but could find no trace of anything out of the ordinary.

"It is really in here?"

He nodded. "We're taking two coding circuits. Just in case. Mine's even better hidden, I think. But the great thing about yours is you should be able to find an excuse for hanging on to it all the time."

She smiled. "I'll stop asking silly questions. I'm sure you've thought of everything."

He didn't contradict her. "That's fine," he said. "Because we've a lot to do and less than three hours to do it in. Now first I'll brief you on your background." He pulled out a sheaf of notes. "You're my secretary, remember. But there's a bit more to our relationship than that. . . ."

At the end of a couple of hours she was as limp as a rag doll. And very considerably shaken.

She was limp because of all she'd been told to memorize. Details of her background; details of Mackinnon's background; and details of every stage of their journey, and of just what to do in the event of things going wrong. And she was shaken because of the tiny phial that had been

175

screwed into her signet ring. "If you have to use it, put the finger well into your mouth," Mackinnon had told her, "and bite with your back teeth. That lessens the chance of any dribbling out. It takes effect in six to eight seconds. And it's quite painless." She rather wished Pellew could have heard that. It would have brought him up to date on the cold war.

They left New Scotland Yard at midday, hailed a taxi and were driven to London Airport. They could talk and relax in the taxi, Mackinnon told her—the driver was a plain-clothes man—but the moment they set foot in the terminal building they'd need to be on the *qui vive*. "On a job like this," he added, "you never know when you're being watched."

She was suitably impressed.

At London Airport they went through the usual routine: the search for their departure bay, the wait while flights were called to every part of the world except Finland, the perfunctory check by emigration, the walk to their plane, the finding of their seats, their air hostess's concern that everyone was strapped in, then the long haul around to the end of the duty runway. Christabel had done enough flying to be more than a little blasé about the business of getting an aircraft into the air, and the mechanics of taking off and setting course left her cold. But she was anything but blasé about their fellow passengers. As the Caravelle lifted effort-lessly into a bright blue sky, she looked them over. Was it possible, she asked herself, that one of them was a Russian agent? That typically English-looking spinster, perhaps, with the sensible shoes and the silly hat? Or the meek and mild junior-grade civil servant with the apology of a mustache? Instinctively her eyes slid around to her transistor, perched on the luggage rack over their table.

"Christabel! A drink?"

Iain Mackinnon was smiling at her, reminding her of the role they'd agreed upon and rehearsed in Scotland Yard.

"Oh, that would be lovely," she said.

As the Caravelle headed east nobody appeared to take much interest in the prosperous-looking executive and his attractive secretary who were clearly intent on combining business with pleasure. But if anyone *had* been interested he would probably have been more envious than suspicious as he watched what looked like the opening gambits for a weekend on the expense account.

Christabel rather enjoyed going through the motions of a flirtation with Iain Mackinnon. He wasn't quite what she'd expected—in a rough-and-tumble with James Bond she wouldn't have fancied his chances—but he was not unattractive, he had a nice sense of humor and he was attentive and considerate—though that, of course, she reminded herself, would be because he was playing a part.

Mackinnon in point of fact, after initial qualms, *was* quite enjoying himself. He'd been furious at first to be saddled with a woman on a mission of such importance. But he'd been coming gradually to the conclusion that things might have been worse. She seemed a sensible, pleasant enough kid, though there was no telling, of course, how she'd measure up to an emergency, and she was very much an amateur— look at the way she kept glancing up at the transistor! He must stop that. He asked her, after a while, if she knew why the notice "Beware of Pickpockets" had been removed from all the restaurants and pubs in central London. She said, "No, why?"

"Because," he told her, "as soon as anyone sees the notice, their hand instinctively goes to their wallet and their eyes to the bag with the valuables."

He raised his glass. He waited for her to raise hers. And when their glasses had clinked and their heads were very

177

close together, he whispered, "So keep your eyes off that Pandora's box on the luggage rack."

"Sorry," she said.

She looked so miserable and crestfallen that he couldn't help smiling. "Don't take it so hard, Christabel," he said. "We're all like that at first."

"I know," she said. "It's not that. Just don't call it Pandora's box."

"No?"

"No. It brings back memories. Out of my unhappy past."

Oh, why, she thought, out of all the names he could have chosen for the transistor-cum-coding circuit did he have to pick on Pandora's box? It brought back memories, didn't it? Memories of that night—was it really less than a week ago?—in the cabin at Culdrose. Memories of the dream that she'd thought forgotten and done with.

He refilled her glass. "Forget the past," he said. "Think of the present."

She tried. And to all outward appearances, she succeeded. Yet a little of the zest had somehow gone out of her play-acting; and a little cloud of fear, blown up from an unexpected quarter, cast a shadow over the rest of their flight.

Soon the blood-red disc of the sun dipped into the Baltic. Outlines first softened, then faded. By the time they were letting down over Helsinki it was quite dark.

The Helsinki customs were a bit of an anticlimax. Christabel had been afraid that incoming visitors might be searched with unpleasant thoroughness. But her fears proved groundless. Their bags were opened, it's true; but their clothing was hardly disturbed. The number of her transistor was noted (to facilitate re-exportation, the customs officer explained); but the set itself was given no more than a cursory glance. Then they were out of the airport building and hailing one of the orange-number-plated cabs. They

178

drove down brightly lit streets to a hotel just off the Esplanaad-ikatu.

It was a small, exclusive hotel: very comfortable, very discreet and, Christabel felt sure, very expensive. Mackinnon seemed quite at home in it. He chattered in fluent Finnish to the porter and introduced "my new secretary, Miss Barlow," to the receptionist. Then they were shown to their rooms: two adjoining single rooms on the second floor, pleasantly furnished in contemporary style.

Left alone, she washed and unpacked. She knew just what to do: just how many clothes, for example, to leave lying about to create the impression that she was spending the night. When she'd done everything that had to be done, she sat on the edge of her bed and lit a cigarette. Things, she told herself, seemed to be going well.

After a few minutes Mackinnon joined her. He looked approvingly around the room, then asked if she was ready for dinner.

"O.K.," she said. "But I'm disappointed. I hoped to see you doing your stuff."

"What stuff?"

"You know. Finding the microphone in the doorknob. Defusing the time bomb. Hauling Ivan from under the bed."

"That was all done," he said briefly, "before we got here."

"Oh!" She felt suddenly rather foolish. "Sorry for the second time."

He eyed her speculatively. "I wouldn't take things too lightly, Christabel. Especially as we were followed back to the hotel."

"Oh!"

"Now come down for dinner. And keep your wits about you."

For the first time, he didn't look a bit like a prosperous executive. There was a watchfulness about him now—the watchfulness of a man who was no stranger to physical danger. She followed him into the dining room in a mixed-up state of mind, part apprehensive, part reassured.

Dinner was a strange meal. There were the trappings of luxury—good food and wine, soft lights and courteous service; there was the aura of romance—they were supposed, weren't they, to be on the threshold of a clandestine affair; and there was the background of fear. "We were followed back to the hotel," he'd said. "Keep your wits about you." So what might happen? A grenade through the window? Strychnine in the coffee? A call from the Finnish police? It sounded all so melodramatic, the sort of thing that could happen only in storybooks or to other people, never to oneself. She took her cue from Mackinnon, eating what he ate, drinking as much as he drank (which wasn't much), matching her conversation to his and observing her fellow residents with the same apparently casual interest.

And absolutely nothing happened—except that they had a first-class meal.

After coffee he suggested a stroll before they turned in. It was their cue to clear the hotel. They went upstairs. They put on coats, he an Aquascutum gabardine, she a Wetherall reversible. Out of his case he pulled what looked like a king-size electric shaver; he slipped it into the pocket of his gabardine—it made a bit of a bulge, but no more than might have been caused by a pair of gloves; he then went to Christabel's room. He picked up her transistor. He looked at it carefully. Then, using the aerial pin as a key, he unlocked the back. He pulled out the coding circuit and passed it to Christabel, who slipped it into the big casual handbag which matched her Wetherall. Then they went downstairs, hand in hand, and out through the swing doors and into the brightly lit street. And what could have been more natural?

Although it was after ten, there were still a fair number of people about. They walked slowly down the Esplanaad-ikatu, admiring the window displays: the cut glass, the ryijy-rugs and the classically simple furniture. After a while they came to the Havis Amanda fountain: a naked sea nymph, surrounded by seals, aglow in the gold of the street lamps. They walked around the fountain slowly—three times.

Christabel giggled. "Which angle do you like her best from?"

"I'm trying," he said, "to seee if we're being followed."

Her hand tightened on his. "And are we?"

"I just don't know. It's possible all passengers from the Caravelle are being watched. . . . Scared?"

"Yes," she said.

"That's good. The dangerous time is when you stop being scared."

They drifted away from the fountain, down toward the fish market, with its quays, waterways and trawler crow's-nests rising like minarets above the warehouse roofs.

They found the Volkswagen exactly where they'd been told they'd find it: at the side of Kalastiain Oy's refrigeration unit. At the edge of the quay an old man with black sea boots and a pipe was leaning against a pile of fish crates. As they passed, Mackinnon said something in Finnish, and the old man handed him a key ring and spat.

"All clear," Mackinnon muttered to Christabel. "Hop in quick."

Ten seconds later they were driving out of the fish market.

Mackinnon drove fast; not so fast as to draw attention to the Volkswagen, but fast enough to make life difficult for anyone trying to follow. For perhaps ten minutes they twisted and turned and doubled back through a maze of side streets, until Christabel was completely lost. Then, suddenly, they debouched onto the Porvoo–Lovisa highway:

181

a ribbon of white, slashing the darkness like the cut of a sword. The purr of the Volkswagen's engine increased in tempo and pitch. The needle of the speedometer crept up to ninety kilometers. And it wasn't long before the houses were left behind, a scent of wood and resin was in the air and they were streaking fast through blue-black forests of conifers.

There wasn't much traffic about, but what little there was made it difficult for them to decide whether or not they were being followed. There *were* headlights behind them; and when Mackinnon slowed down, a Volvo and a long-distance truck went rumbling past; but other lights, it seemed to Christabel, slowed to keep pace with them. Or was it her imagination?

They increased speed to a hundred and ten, then dropped back to ninety again. And still the headlights tailed them—sometimes a little nearer, sometimes a little farther away, but never leaving them, as though on a tow of long, invisible elastic.

"I think," Christabel said after a while, "we're being followed."

"We are."

"But *how,* Iain? How have they got on to us?"

"The Russians, my dear, have been preparing this thing for years. You can bet they've overlooked nothing either in defense or in security. And their agents are everywhere. Maybe we were tailed from the Yard, maybe from the plane, maybe from the hotel. But not to worry. We rather expected this. We've made arrangements."

"Oh!"

Mackinnon glanced at his speedometer. "Another five miles," he said, "and there'll be a roadblock. We'll get through. But the car following won't."

On a long, straight and deserted stretch of road, flanked

182

to the left by water and to the right by forest, a red light swung to and fro. As they slowed down they could make out the vague outline of vehicles: a truck over on its side, a tow crane drawn up behind it, an ambulance and a police car with its winking light. All very realistic. As they came to a stop beside the man swinging the lamp, Christabel could see every detail as sharp and clear as at the climax of a dream: the skid marks, the pile of broken glass swept into the side of the road and the policeman making notes in his car. What she didn't see was the two men with their heavy long-barreled guns crouched in the lee of the overturned truck.

Mackinnon spoke briefly to the man with the lamp. The man nodded. He turned toward the truck and grunted an order, and as he turned Christabel could see his face quite clearly in the blood-red glow of his lamp. He was smiling.

Mackinnon pulled out to the center of the road to avoid the truck. "Don't look back," he said.

Behind them the headlights grew larger and brighter; then they came to a halt. For perhaps a couple of seconds there was absolute silence. Even the wind in the conifers seemed to have died. Then everything happened at once.

There was a tinkle of glass, a searing eruption of light and a scream of such unbelievable agony that sweat broke out on Christabel's face. She spun around.

The scene was framed in the rear window, like an obscene etching: the flame throwers pouring great banners of gold over the car, the petrol tank exploding, the metal melting to liquid and lying in blazing pools on the road, and the white-hot disintegrating figures which squirmed and twitched and then lay mercifully still.

Mackinnon slipped into gear and the Volkswagen gathered speed. After a while he said, "I'm sorry, Christabel. But it had to be done."

She was trembling and damp with sweat. She wanted desperately to cry, but she wasn't going to. For some time she couldn't trust herself to speak; then she whispered, "Why did they have to use flame throwers?"

"They shouldn't have."

"But why did they?"

"It was a cruel war for the Finns. They've long memories. And they don't often have a chance to hit back."

She shivered. "You can make excuses for them?"

"I can understand. I can even sympathize."

She stared at him. The urbane company-director mask had been stripped away, and his expression was cold and without mercy. I know nothing about him, she thought. I kidded myself that we spoke the same language and played to the same set of rules, but I was wrong. I don't even begin to understand him. For a while she said nothing. But in the silence her thoughts kept creeping back to the white-hot, twitching figures; and what she couldn't forget she felt she wanted to try to understand. She did her best to be objective.

"You say you can sympathize. You're not Finnish, are you?"

"Only by adoption."

She asked what he meant by that. And as the Volkswagen ate up the miles along the road to Lovisa, he explained.

"My brother and I first came to Finland, Christabel, before you were born. We came to fight in a war you've probably never heard of: the Russo-Finnish War of 1939–40. We didn't come because we liked war. Or because we hated Communism. It was just that the Finns had been attacked. They were putting up a heroic fight against impossible odds; and although a lot of people were *talking* about help, no one was *doing* much. So we worked our passage to Finland. We were both, as it happened, goodish skiers; and we

184

were Territorial-trained. The Finns were glad of us. And pretty soon we were in the thick of it: first in Karelia, then in the Mannerheim Line."

He paused, and in the soft reflected glow from the dashboard Christabel could see the set of his mouth. It wasn't pretty.

"It was like a boxing match, Christabel—a heavyweight fighting a flyweight. And the heavyweight throwing punch after punch. And the punches landing. And the flyweight being bludgeoned to his knees. And getting up. And being knocked down again. And keeping on getting up, though his nose was broken, his teeth knocked down his throat and his eyes punched blind. Just think of the odds: four million men against eighty thousand. It ought to have been over in days—like Holland, or Czechoslovakia. But it went on for four months. And it didn't end until the cream of Finland's manhood had been wiped out: one out of every nine of them dead in woodland or lake, like 'the flowers of the forest.' It was Thermopylae without the happy ending. It makes the Somme and Okinawa and Stalingrad all look like a Sunday school picnic." His voice trailed away.

She sighed. "And it *was* a war I'd never heard of. It's a terrifying world, isn't it?"

"Yes. So forget, Christabel, even if you can't forgive."

She shivered. Maybe I'll forget in time, she thought. But not yet—not with the heat of the flame throwers still on my face.

"And your brother?" she asked.

"He survived the hot war, but not the cold."

"Oh! I'm sorry."

"As a matter of fact, he was killed just five days ago. At a rocket site at Murmansk."

"Oh!"

She saw how it was. His brother's death had served as a

185

whetstone to Iain Mackinnon's hate. It had been a long time (more than twenty years) since he and his brother had lain in their snow hide and listened to the Russian shells crumping down on the Mannerheim Line above Vyborg at the rate of fifty thousand a day. Memories had begun to fade. But his brother's death had revived them. And that, of course, was why he was here now on the road to Lovisa. And that was why the flame throwers hadn't appalled him. Vendettas aren't fought to the Queensberry rules. That she could understand.

It was striking midnight as they crossed the river at the approaches to Porvoo.

Mackinnon kept to the waterfront, avoiding the center of the town, then cutting back to the Lovisa highway through a maze of side streets. He didn't get lost. And Christabel marveled, not for the first time, at the meticulous planning which was giving their mission an air of deceptive simplicity. Once back on the highway, they were able to average a steady eighty. And half an hour later they were nearing Lovisa.

Lovisa lies at the head of one of the many inlets which bite deep into the coast of southern Finland. It is a prosperous town—saw milling, wood pulping, light industries; and its port of Valkom was the headquarters of Juhani Kallela's trawlers.

Juhani Kallela had twenty-two trawlers, of which roughly half were prewar and half postwar. The postwar ones were fine vessels, not large according to international standards—for they fished most of the time in restricted waters close to their ports—but strongly built and equipped with every conceivable aid: asdic, radar, ice cutters and deep-freeze refrigeration. At one time Kallela had kept a pretty tight rein on his fleet; but since the war (in which his three sons had been killed) he'd let things slide a bit, giving his

186

skippers a good deal of freedom—provided they continued to bring in results. Carl Ekolf was his favorite skipper. And if Carl and his vessel, the *Ladoga Star,* sometimes did other things than trawling, it suited Kallela well enough to turn a blind eye. That was why he saw no occasion, now, to ask what the *Ladoga Star* was doing moored to a quay at Valkom.

The Volkswagen drew up to the water's edge a shade after twelve thirty. It was a perfect night: full moon and a galaxy of stars, the sea dark and motionless, and the cottages rising in tiers like the backdrop to a stage. It seemed at first as if there were no one about. Then a fisherman and his girl came strolling down to the quay. Mackinnon spoke to them. To anyone watching, it would all have seemed perfectly innocent: the tourists who'd got themselves lost, the hotels that were closed, the couple who happened to live close at hand, the invitation to "come and spend the night with us."

Five minutes later Christabel and Mackinnon were drinking hot black coffee and mesimarja in Carl Ekolf's kitchen.

Ten minutes later they were dossed down for the night, she clutching her casual handbag, he with what looked like an electric razor tied to his wrist.

"We've less than five hours," he said. "So don't waste time talking."

"Right," she said. She was too tired to be witty.

She was tired, and her sleeping bag was warm and comfortable; but she couldn't sleep. For a long time she lay awake, her eyes open. Whenever she closed them she saw flames: white-hot, searing flames and bodies that twisted and jerked like marionettes; some of the flames lapped a roadway, others the sea. She heard the whisper of waves on a nearby shore, the muted creaking of boats swung by the

187

tide, the complaint of sea birds, and Mackinnon's snores. After a while she heard a clock strike two.

She shut her eyes—resolutely. Let the flames burn, she thought; why should I care who's in them? She was about to drop off when she heard Mackinnon say in his sleep, quite distinctly, "I'll be with you in a second, Jamie." She was still trying to puzzle that one out when she, too, fell into a deep, exhausted sleep.

They had no difficulty next morning in boarding the *Ladoga Star*.

They were wakened at five. They breakfasted. Mrs. Ekolf close-cropped Christabel's hair. They dressed in full fisherman's kit, including oilskins. They hid their coding circuits in tins of bait. Then they walked out with Carl into the cool, crisp morning, across the quay and onto the trawler. It was as simple as that.

The *Ladoga Star* was waiting to put to sea. Though the sun had not yet risen, a handful of gulls were already wheeling about her mast; the chug-chug-chug of her Diesels vibrated softly over the water, and her navigation lamps gleamed pale and incongruous in the gathering light. With a minimum of fuss they cast off. An engine-room bell tinkled briefly; the thresh of their screws increased in tempo, and they stood seaward at a sedate four knots.

It was too early for many people to be about. But the harbormaster gave them a wave as they cleared the breakwater, and a little later they passed a couple of crayfish and pike boats coming in on the flood tide. Then they were working their way through the maze of islands and shallows which led to the open sea.

Their plans were cut and dried. They'd do nothing until they were well clear of land. Then—surprisingly—the first thing they'd do would be to start to trawl. They'd trawl

188

because they wanted fish in their hold: fresh Baltic herring to provide cover in emergency for the radar operator and for their bits and pieces of special equipment (the walkie-talkie, the spare coder and a mysterious bundle wrapped up in oilskins which belonged to Mackinnon). And it was typical of the thoroughness of their plans, Christabel reflected, that the Baltic herring would be fresh, caught that morning, not fish which might arouse suspicion in the event of their being boarded by being several days old.

Keeping to their prearranged schedule, Christabel stayed below while the trawl was in progress. For on deck she'd have been more hindrance than help; also they were still within telescope range of the shore. So she sat on the bunk in Carl Ekolf's cabin, unpacked the coding circuits and checked—as far as she could without current—that they'd come to no harm in transit.

As she worked she could hear a strange cacophony of sound: the hiss of water against the trawl, the background throb of the engines, the occasional thump of sea boots on the deck above, a noisy hammering from the hold as the crew got busy knocking up a "hide" into which she and the special equipment could be bundled in emergency, and the sound of men's voices from the bridge immediately over her head. She could recognize the voices—Carl's and Iain's. But not what they were saying. For they spoke in Finnish.

It was twenty-three years since Carl and Iain had met. But there are some memories that the years distill rather than blur, and they talked from the start as old friends. They talked first of the month they'd spent together in the Mannerheim Line. Then they talked of their families and friends.

"And your brother Jamie?" Carl asked after a while. "How is he?"

"They got him a week ago. In Murmansk."

189

"Ah! I am sorry, Iain. Always the best ones that go."

"He was a fool to go back."

"But we always do. Like dogs to our vomit."

For some minutes they stood in silence; then Carl struck the deck rail a great blow with his hand. "But we get maudlin! Let us talk of more cheerful things. That girl you've brought with you. She is pretty, eh? What would your wife think?"

"I didn't ask to bring her. She was foisted on me."

"But you don't complain!"

"No. She may be an amateur at intelligence work. But she knows her job."

"What made them give you a woman?"

"Good cover for the trip to Helsinki. I think she's got some tie-up with the pilot flying the Bat. And she knows her radar—I'm told she's *the* expert on this particular aircraft's aids."

"Ah, you British! To trust an amateur with a job like this."

A seaman came clambering up to the bridge and asked if they could raise the trawl.

Carl looked at his watch. "So soon?"

"Waldi thinks we're running into a shoal."

"Right then." He swung the engine pointer to "dead slow." "Hoist the trawl."

The winches took up the strain; and the nets came inboard, slowly, slopping little pools of water onto the deck. They seemed at first to be empty. Then, all of a sudden, they were filled with fish: little squirming six-to-eight-inch Baltic herring, iridescent, agleam with rainbow hues—black, purple, indigo and violet; cobalt, sapphire, aquamarine and turquoise; and all the range of greens, from deepest emerald to palest olive. The sunlight glinted on them as they cascaded into the hold.

190

By the time the trawl had been emptied, the inverted crates of Christabel's "hide" were knee-deep in a shimmering morass of fish.

"You can get cracking now on the radar," Mackinnon called down to her.

As the *Ladoga Star* headed southeast for the Neugrund, she set to work modifying the radar set on the bridge. It wasn't difficult, especially as she had at her disposal the Mecca representative's set of servicing tools. Once again she marveled at the meticulous planning which had led to the tools being left aboard the trawler at just the right time. She worked slowly and methodically: first incorporating a switching device into the existing mechanism, then inserting special coding gates into both the transmitting and receiving circuits. Every move she made she treble-checked. She knew there was no hurry, but the result had to be perfect.

While she worked, Carl Ekolf kept his crew—and that included Mackinnon—off the bridge. It would be no help to the girl, he knew, to have her every move anxiously and critically watched. He spoke only once, in his thick guttural English:

"All things O.K.?"

"Yes, thanks."

"If anything you vant, you say."

She nodded, smiled absent-mindedly and got on with the job.

It was past midday before she finally straightened up, blew the hair out of her eyes, and said briefly:

"Finished."

Then came the dilemma: to test or not to test?

This was the one point on which their briefing hadn't been a hundred per cent explicit. The difficulty was this. It would have been reassuring to know that their special transmissions were now correctly coded and operating at the right power; but this was something that couldn't very well be checked from the trawler itself, since the transmissions could be picked up only by a receiver which was some distance away and in the right sector. Also there was the possibility— albeit a remote one—that if they did a series of tests, their transmissions might somehow be picked up and investigated by the Russians. And they'd look pretty silly, wouldn't they, if they tested their gear before the Bat was due and were hauled off to Kronstadt for their pains! In the end Christabel decided to switch in the coding circuits for a few seconds only, and to direct them toward the nearby island of Kulema.

They checked from crow's-nest and radar screen that no other vessels were in the vicinity. Then she flicked down the switch.

And to her, and everyone else's, relief the transmissions pulsated out and were reflected back from Kulema. All, as far as they could judge, was well. Thankfully she cut the current.

Once the radar was fixed they had nothing to do but hold course for their rendezvous in the Neugrund, now less than thirty-five miles to the south.

They had lunch. They made brief alterations of course to avoid the islands of Gogland and Bolshoy Tyuters. And at three o'clock, to fill in time, they again started to trawl.

They had just finished lowering their nets when a lookout spotted the helicopter. It was low on the water, and coming straight for them.

Christabel scrambled below, ready to crawl, if the need arose, into her hide. The rest of the crew got on with their jobs.

Carl Ekolf recognized the helicopter at once: a Mil MI-4 of the Red fleet. It passed slap over the top of them, fast, at a height of about a hundred feet. Then it came back

192

to investigate. With a great roaring of rotors it hovered over their masthead. They could see the pilot quite clearly, peering down at them, scribbling notes on his kneepad. They could guess what the notes were: details of the *Ladoga Star* and her position, course and speed. After about five minutes the pilot seemed satisfied. He waved briefly. And the Mil flew away to the north.

"A routine inspection," Carl Ekolf said. "It's happened before."

Mackinnon nodded, but he was shaken. They were all shaken. The Mil had been a reminder that for all the sea's apparent emptiness, they were not alone.

By five o'clock they were coming up to the Neugrund, and Mackinnon called a conference in Carl Ekolf's cabin to run, for the last time, over their plans.

They checked and double-checked every stage. They went over the drill for every eventuality: when to switch in the coders, what to do if the Bat seemed unable to pick them up, what to do if they were disturbed during transmission. This last was their recurrent nightmare. It wasn't likely to happen, but there was always the chance that by sheer bad luck it might.

"Now then, Christabel!" Mackinnon was very business-like. "Suppose we're boarded. What do you do?"

"Well, I come down here. I pull out the drawer from under Carl's bunk, and I crawl through to the fish hold. I check that everything's hidden that ought to be hidden—the walkie-talkie, the spare coder and your bundle of oilskins. Then I pull the drawer to and sit tight till you give me the all clear."

"Right. Let's see you do it."

She pulled out the drawer, slid aside a panel of the bulkhead which had been specially loosened and crawled into her hide. Then, reaching back, she carefully replaced panel and drawer.

"O.K.!" she shouted. "I'm in."

"Is the stuff all hidden?"

"Yes."

"Hmmm! Out you come then."

As she crawled back into the cabin she screwed up her nose. "Ugh! Cold and smelly! Don't leave me in there too long or I'll deep-freeze!"

The prospect didn't seem to worry him. "Now, Carl! If the worst comes to the worst, you know what I'll do?"

"If you have to . . . yes."

"Good. So don't try getting onto the gunboat yourself. I'll be better equipped."

Christabel looked from one to the other. "What are you two talking about?"

"It doesn't concern you, Christabel. I'd tell you if it did."

"But of course it concerns me. We're a partnership."

There was a slightly awkward silence. Then Mackinnon said briefly, "Well, if we *are* boarded, odds are it'll be by a Russian gunboat. And if worst comes to worst, I'll try to get across to her."

"And?"

"And blow her up."

"Oh!" She moistened her lips. She didn't know quite what to say. In the end she decided she'd better be matter-of-fact and practical. "How?"

"You know that bundle wrapped up in oilskins? Inside, there's a frogman's kit and a couple of limpet mines."

"Oh!" It was like the phial in her signet ring: more than she'd bargained for. Not for the first time she had the feeling that things were getting out of control, that she'd become involved in something too big for her to cope with. For the rest of the conference she was unusually quiet.

194

By the time they'd gone through their plans, it was dark, and the *Ladoga Star* was moving slowly over a dead-calm sea, her navigation and trawl lights glinting red, green and white on water as motionless as glass. The three of them climbed on deck and stood for a while by the rail. Faintly, away in the southeast, they could make out the flashing beam of a lighthouse.

"Kir'yamo," Carl Ekolf said. "On the Russian coast. Flashing corrupt."

Christabel shivered. She looked at her watch: a little after six o'clock.

The Bat would be airborne now.

Excitement stirred in her. God knows, she thought, I've had enough excitement, shock and fear in the last twenty-four hours. But this, it seemed to her, was something more than excitement. It was a sort of fulfillment, a sense of rightness that the strands were at long last coming together to a preordained climax. The Bat'll be over the North Sea now, she thought. She could picture them: Jim doing whatever had to be done efficiently and without the slightest fuss; Ken tensed up and afraid, but hiding his fear under a cloak of disinterest. And you'll both be all right, she thought. I promised you'd be all right, and that's the way it's going to be.

After a while Ekolf went up to the bridge. According to the dead-reckoning plot, they were less than a couple of miles now from their rendezvous. But dead reckoning in the Baltic, with currents and magnetic anomalies, is tricky; and as a check Ekolf switched on their radar—taking care of course not to make the special contact which would trigger off their coders. The radar confirmed their position: 59°38′ North, 27°29′ East. They were almost alongside their rendezvous, with an hour to spare. He rang for "dead slow."

The hiss of their bow and trawl waves faded to a barely

195

audible sigh, and the *Ladoga Star* lost way, moving over the sea so slowly that she left behind her not even a trace of wake. The moonlight poured down, drugging them with its somnolent beauty, making the trawler glow like a dream ship, hove to in a newly created world.

Then came the serpent into Arcady. A little after seven thirty a pear-shaped blip appeared at the bottom left-hand corner of the radar screen.

Carl's lips tightened. He called Mackinnon and Christabel to the bridge, and the three of them peered at the echo. Its position was due south of them. Its range eleven miles. It seemed to be zigzagging along a patrol line at right angles to the *Ladoga Star*. Its speed was fifteen knots.

"Moving some, for a trawler!" Mackinnon's voice was grave.

"And too near the Russian coast."

"You think it's a gunboat?"

"Yes."

There was nothing they could do about it. And even if it *is* a gunboat, Mackinnon thought, and even if it *does* come to investigate us, it needn't be the end of the world. Christabel can hide in the hold. We can switch in the coding circuits. And, if we have to, we can transmit to the Bat with the Russians right alongside. So long as we're able to keep on using our radar . . .

The blip moved slowly across the screen. At one stage it was less than five miles away. But it made no effort to close with them. It showed no interest in them. And soon its greater speed was drawing it farther away from them with every passing minute. Eventually it disappeared.

The moment the gunboat was out of sight Carl and Mackinnon were prepared to put it out of mind. But Christabel's anxiety died harder.

196

"If they hold that course," she muttered, "they'll be slap between us and the Bat when we want to transmit."

Mackinnon frowned. "Will it matter? I thought only the Bat could pick our transmissions up."

"That's what we *thought*. But we didn't bargain for a Russian receiving set slap between us at a range of a dozen miles." She ran a hand through her hair. "I'm pretty sure they won't be able to monitor the transmissions, but I'm afraid there's a chance they'll spot our radar pattern's a bit odd."

"And board us to have a look?"

"I just don't know, Iain. I don't think it's likely. But it *could* be."

She was anxious. What was it S.A.S.O. had said to the air crew? "All's well if all's well, but the moment things go wrong you've had it." That of course had been said about the flight of the Bat. But it applied equally well to what went on on the trawler. And the frustrating thing was there wasn't a damn thing they could do about the gunboat. They couldn't postpone their transmissions; they couldn't shift their rendezvous. When the time came—and it was coming very soon—they could only switch in their coders and wait.

About twenty minutes after the gunboat had vanished, Carl made a last check on their position. "Stop engines," he ordered. "Raise the trawl."

The *Ladoga Star* hove to, her lights cutting great swaths of white across the deck and spotlighting the tens of thousands of herring cascading into the hold. As the rendezvous time drew near, their trawl was lowered again, and the ship and all aboard her became very quiet.

At the agreed time, fifteen minutes before zero hour, Christabel switched in the coding circuits.

She peered eagerly at the screen. But it was empty—unless the Bat was early, she reminded herself, it wasn't likely to be in range for at least another five minutes. She felt keyed up and nervous. The radar screen flickered and danced in front of her eyes; it kept blurring and slipping out of focus. Watching it minute after minute was more than she could bear. She walked to the deck rail and stared out at the sea, ruffled now by a sudden breeze from the north.

Beside her, Carl Ekolf drew in his breath. The hiss, like a sudden oath, was as shocking as a douche of cold water. She spun around.

He was staring at the radar screen. And his face was gray.

For the pear-shaped blip of the gunboat was back. And coming toward them. Fast.

They stood in a little circle in front of the screen. For a moment they were too shocked to speak; then Carl leaned forward, measuring the speed of the blip against a calibrated ruler. Again he drew in his breath. "Over forty knots! In five minutes she'll be alongside."

"Christabel!" Mackinnon's voice was sharp. "Into the hold."

"For God's sake," she whispered, "keep the radar on. The Bat'll pick us up any minute."

She scrambled down the companionway, through Carl Ekolf's cabin, under his bunk and into the hold. As she slid aside the bulkhead, the stench of fish and the cold of the refrigerated air struck her like a physical blow. She took great care to square off the bulkhead; then, having checked that the walkie-talkie, spare coder and frogman's gear were in place, she shone the torch on her wrist watch: ten minutes to zero hour. If the Bat's on time, she thought, we'll be picking her up any second. Or perhaps we've picked her up already; perhaps even now her reflection is bright on the radar screen.

It was hard to sit there, longing to know what was happening, anxious to help, but ostracized at the moment of crisis.

198

She crouched beneath the inverted crates, with the fish close-packed around her. If she shone her torch upward she could see, through cracks in the wood, the myriads of cold, wet bodies wedged nose to tail. Their rainbow colors had faded now, their suppleness had given way to a frozen rigidity. And their eyes were glazed with a veneer of newly formed ice. She shivered—not only with cold.

After a while she began to try to work out what was going on from the noises that came through to her. She could hear quite a lot, especially from the bridge, which was immediately above and behind her: the restless pace of sea boots, the murmur of voices—but in Finnish of course, so that she had no idea what they were saying—and the rhythmic purr of their radar scanner. The last brought her comfort. All's well, she thought, as long as the radar scanner keeps on rotating.

After she had been in the hold three or four minutes she became conscious of a high-pitched whine which started softly then grew steadily louder. It didn't come from the bridge; it seemed to come from somewhere beyond the trawler's keel. Perhaps, she thought, it's the motors of the approaching gunboat.

The noise cut dead. Then came a great deal of shouting—angry shouting, it seemed to Christabel—in Finnish.

A moment later the sliding panel was wrenched aside and Mackinnon came squirming into the hold.

"My kit. At the double, Christabel."

She hauled over his bundle of oilskins. "What's happening?"

"They're sending a boarding party."

"Oh, God! Do they know we're transmitting on radar?"

"I doubt it, or they'd have sunk us on the spot." He began to climb into his frogman's kit.

She helped him strap on the cylinder of compressed air

and the black-horned limpet mine. "Have we picked up the Bat?"

"No. When we pick it up Carl'll stamp three times on the deck, to let you know."

Quickly he checked his immersion suit, from flippers to breathing tube. He was adjusting the mine's preset fuse when there came from the deck above three clear and unmistakable stamps.

They looked at each other. Christabel wasn't what you'd call a religious person—she wore a crucifix around her neck, it's true; but the crucifix had been her father's, and since his death she had worn it more out of filial than Christian piety. But her hand went up to it now, and she shut her eyes and gave thanks to God. When she opened her eyes she saw Mackinnon was looking at her curiously.

"You know," he said, "we're not out of the wood yet."

"But in five minutes the Bat'll be overhead."

"We mayn't get five minutes. The Russians'll be aboard any second."

Fear swept over her as she realized what he was getting at. The Russians were obviously suspicious of the *Ladoga Star*'s radar—for they'd come to investigate her the moment the coders had been switched in. Now she was pretty sure they wouldn't have been able to monitor the actual transmissions; but on the other hand, if it was the radar they were suspicious of, one of the first things they'd look at would obviously be the radar screen. And the first thing they'd see on the screen would be the bright blip of the approaching Bat.

She realized then that Iain Mackinnon hadn't put on his frogman's kit as a mere precaution.

"Iain," she whispered as he slid out of the hold, "be careful."

He nodded. And for the first time since he'd come crawl-

200

ing into the hide, she saw his face clearly, outlined for a second against the light from Carl Ekolf's cabin. She caught her breath. For his skin was gray and pallid, little beads of sweat were standing out on his temples and his eyes were glazed. It was a face she'd seen before: Ken's face, in the Polhills' L-shaped hall—the face of fear.

"Good luck," she whispered.

He tried, not very successfully, to smile. Then the panel was pulled to, and she was alone.

She crouched down in her hide, uncertain and afraid. Things were going wrong, and she couldn't do anything to help. For a while she rocked to and fro, like a child trying to comfort itself. Then the purr of the radar scanner got through to her, and she took heart. After all, she thought, so long as the radar's on, the Bat'll be homing on us. And it's that that matters. Provided the Bat gets through, it isn't all that important, is it, what happens to Iain, or the *Ladoga Star* or me?

She could hear a good deal of noise going on from beyond the bulkheads: men's voices and the tramp of sea boots. But she paid no attention to them. She concentrated on that which mattered most: the scanner.

As she listened to it rotating, she could picture what would be happening, some twenty or thirty miles away, in the Bat. They'll have switched on their radar receiver by now, she thought. They'll have picked us up. They'll be turning toward us.

The purr of the scanner faded and died, and everything, quite suddenly, was very quiet.

She didn't believe it at first. She tried to tell herself that the scanner had stopped because of some unimportant temporary fault: Carl was retuning the set, perhaps, or there'd been a short circuit or a cut cable? But in her heart she knew that none of these reasons would hold water. One

201

thing and one thing only could have brought the scanner to a stop. The Russians had told them to switch off their radar.

She looked at her watch. It needed less than five minutes to the time of their rendezvous.

Once again she could picture the scene in the Bat. Oakman and Polhill's relief at picking the transmissions up; their amazement and consternation when they suddenly stopped; Polhill frantically checking his instruments; the seconds ticking away, and the left/right indicator limp and motionless; their gradual realization that at the vital moment the trawler had let them down, that they were going to fail, that they were lost, alone, hurtling at a thousand feet a second toward an unknown shore.

So her bright idea had led to this.

She just couldn't believe it.

But the minutes passed, and the radar scanner made neither movement nor sound.

She knelt on the ice-covered boards of the fish crate and prayed. Oh, God, she prayed, send the Russians away—just for five minutes; just for one minute. Give us just one minute, God, to transmit in, and the Bat'll get through, and Ken and Jim will be safe, and there'll be no nuclear war. Doesn't that weigh with you, God? Think of the children who'll be killed in a nuclear war, the hundred of thousands of children burned, blinded and maimed; all for the sake of a minute.

The tears ran warm and salt into her mouth. But there was no miracle from overhead: only the sound of footsteps and guttural voices.

She rocked to and fro. And suddenly all the tiredness, strain and heartache of the last six days welled up inside her in a spate of bitter resentment. She wanted to scream. She wanted to rush out of the hold and claw at the Russians' eyes. But she was impotent. And she knew it. Only one way

202

of venting her fury was left her, and she took it. She wrenched off her crucifix and flung it against the side of the fish crate.

"So much," she sobbed, "for Your mercy!"

The clink of the crucifix as it hit the side of the crate sobered her up, and her fury turned suddenly to fear. No good, she thought, will come of blasphemy.

From overhead came a vibrating roar, and a blinding light poured suddenly into the hide.

She was terrified. For a second she really thought that God was coming in fire and wrath to punish her. Then she realized what had happened. The tarpaulin covering the fish had been flung back, and the trawl lights were flooding into the hold. She froze. She felt very naked, and very afraid.

She heard voices, ordinary conversational voices; they might have been discussing the weather. The voices went on for some time. Then—sharp and unexpected—came the crack of a revolver, and a bullet thudded into the fish hold a little to the left of her hide.

This is what comes, she thought, of blasphemy.

A second bullet thumped into the fish away to her right.

But this can't be happening to me, she thought. This can't be me, Christabel Barlow, crouched in a fish hold in the middle of the Baltic, being shot at by the Russians.

She heard the third bullet splinter into the fish crate above her head. Pain knifed through her. She put her hand to her scalp, and her fingers came away red and wet. Oh, Ken, she thought, who'll work the radar for you now? Her knees buckled. And she slumped face down to the deck and lay still, her eyes as glazed as the eyes of the Baltic herring which stared down at her incuriously.

As the girl scrambled down from the bridge, Mackinnon had grabbed Ekolf's arm.

"Carl! Can we run for it?"

"No. They've treble our speed. If we run, they'll open fire."

He was racked by indecision. He hadn't the weapons to fight. His heart urged him to run. But his head told him they'd not get far, that their only hope was to stay put and bluff. "I'm afraid," he said, "we'll be having visitors."

"What went wrong?"

"Damn gunboat must have been slap in the path we transmitted in. Sheer bad luck."

"Will they know the transmissions came from our radar?"

"Maybe."

Carl pursed his lips. "I hope your girl has hidden her bits and pieces."

"She'll have done that. What she can't hide is the Bat's reflection, once we pick her up."

They turned to the radar screen, half expecting already to see the giveaway reflection. But the radar screen, apart from the fast-approaching blip of the gunboat, was blank.

"When we pick the Bat up," Mackinnon said slowly, "stamp three times, if you can, to let the girl know."

"Right."

Away in the south a streamer of white flickered over the sea. The gunboat had switched on her searchlights. She was coming straight at them, fast. The light increased in intensity till the *Ladoga Star* was bathed in a harsh white brilliance which hurt the fishermen's eyes and made them feel naked and without defense. And soon, mixed up with the lights, was the whine of high-powered engines. The searchlights grew suddenly larger, brighter, rushing toward them as fast as headlamps on an autobahn. Then, at the last second, the gunboat cut her engines, swung broadside on and hove to less than a cable's length from their trawl.

204

"*Ladoga Star!*" A voice from the gunboat's bridge hailed them in Finnish. "We are going to board you."

Mackinnon's hands clenched on the bridge rail. "I'll be getting my kit on."

"Iain! Don't go unless you have to."

Impatiently he shook himself free. You can bet your life, he thought as he hurried below, I don't *want* to risk blowing myself up—you aren't the only one with a wife and family to think of. As he scrambled down the companionway he could hear Carl shouting angrily at the gunboat, "Keep clear. You'll cut our trawl." The gunboat's reply was lost as the door of the cabin swung to behind him. Then he was squirming into the hold and struggling into his frogman's immersion suit, with the girl helping but not, he could tell, really understanding what the panic was all in aid of. When he heard three stamps from the deck above, he knew there was no longer the slightest doubt about what he had to do. His suit on and his mine and air cylinder in place, he peered anxiously through a porthole. The Russian launch was almost alongside now, coming up to their starboard bow. Quickly he slipped through the mess decks and up to the trawler's port quarter. Quietly he lowered himself over the side. The second before he let go, he glanced at his watch. It needed five minutes to zero hour: the worst possible time for things to go wrong. Our one hope, he thought—and it's not much of a hope—is to get rid of the Russians quickly. The last thing he heard as the water closed over his head was Carl Ekolf, all outraged innocence, arguing with the lieutenant in charge of the boarding party.

It was a first-class impersonation Carl Ekolf gave of a fisherman peaceably trawling in territorial waters when a gunboat comes charging up, scattering the fish, breaking his trawl, boarding him by force . . .

Lieutenant Peter Kazat of the Baltic Fleet cut him short.

He was a thickset, slow-moving man, shrewd and Orientally impassive. His Finnish was good, if a trifle pedantic.

"For one who is innocent, old man, you protest too much. We wish to inspect your radar and search your ship. At once, please."

"I have no option."

"The radar first."

Carl Ekolf was helpless. He could only keep up his pretense. "Radar's on the bridge," he grumbled. "Where it's always been. You nothing better to do than steal fishermen's radar sets?"

Lieutenant Kazat smiled. "If your radar is of the normal type," he said, "we shall not wish to steal it." He ordered three of his men to search the trawler; the fourth followed him onto the bridge.

The *Ladoga Star*'s radar was in the usual place, set back a little from the wheel. The Russians had a good close look at it. And when they came to the screen, the first thing to catch their eye, inevitably, was the reflection of the Bat.

Lieutenant Kazat grunted. He peered at the reflection, whispering excitedly in Russian to the seaman who had come onto the bridge with him, and keeping the while an extremely wary eye on the trawler crew. Leaning forward, he estimated the blip's range—twenty-five miles. Then abruptly he turned to Carl Ekolf.

"Switch off your radar. At once."

There's nothing to be gained, Carl thought, by acting stupid. And nothing to be gained by violence—even if we did manage to kill the boarding party, the gunboat would sink us out of hand. He pushed up the contact switch, and the purr of the scanner faded and died. "Perhaps," he said, "you'll tell me what this is all about?"

Kazat nodded. "First, you must understand, Captain, that these are anxious times for our country. And we can afford

206

to take no chances. . . . Now a few minutes ago we detected a change in the pattern of your radar transmissions. We come to investigate. And on your radar screen we find a strange blip. And I ask myself, Is there any connection between the two? Now your radar *looks* of the normal type. But we must be sure. I therefore offer you two alternatives. You must transfer your radar set to us—we shall give you a receipt for it, and in due course you will be fully compensated. Or you must follow us to Kronstadt, where our technicians will dismantle the set in your ship and in your presence."

"But this is an outrage. My owners—"

Kazat raised his hand. "Which is it to be? Quickly."

Once the set's gone, Carl Ekolf thought, we've no hope of *ever* transmitting; if we keep it, we keep some sort of hope.

"Get your men off my ship," he grunted, "and I'll follow you to Kronstadt."

Kazat looked at him thoughtfully. "Very well," he said. "But no tricks. Take station three cables off our port quarter. We shall train our guns on you, and if you move out of position we shall sink you."

He had just clambered down from the bridge, followed by Ekolf, when his three seamen reported back from their search. They had gone carefully through the trawler, they said, except for the fish hold, and had found nothing.

"Except for the fish hold . . .?"

"The fish hold, Lieutenant, is full of fish."

Kazat turned to Ekolf. He was studiously polite. "You understand what we've been saying?"

"That the hold's full of fish. What do you expect it to be full of? Vodka?"

"Will you show me the fish, please?"

As they crossed the deck, little flurries of wind were darkening the sea. The dead calm of the night had broken; away in the north was a faint suggestion of mist and cloud, and little waves were beginning to slap at the vessels' hulls.

Kazat leaned over the hold. "Switch on the trawl lights," he said. "Throw back the tarpaulin."

He stared at the morass of fish. He was tugged two ways. He was anxious to return to the gunboat, to report what he'd seen and to get on course for Kronstadt. But he was anxious, too, to take back if he could some proof of the *Ladoga Star*'s guilt. His instinct told him that the trawler was up to no good—he could sense the nervousness and hostility of the crew—but on the other hand, he had no concrete proof that she wasn't in fact perfectly bona fide. He'd look pretty silly if his instinct turned out to be wrong. He peered at the fish. He was almost certain they were hiding something in the hold. But how to be sure?

An idea came to him. He pulled out his revolver and handed it to Ekolf. "Have you ever used one of these?"

"No. I prefer the rifle I used in the Mannerheim Line. Its bullets know the way to their target."

Kazat smiled. "It's lucky for you I'm not a vindictive man. What happened between your nation and mine is in the past, and best forgotten. Let us concern ourselves with the present. Take this revolver. It has six bullets in it. Fire three into the hold."

"What!"

"You heard me."

Carl Ekolf took the revolver. He wants to provoke me, he thought. He wants me to do something silly. But I'll not oblige him. His finger was about to tighten on the trigger when he realized there was more to it than that. "Fire three times," the lieutenant had said. And who was going to fire the other three times? Who else but the lieutenant himself; and the lieutenant, of course, would fire at places in the

208

hold where Carl *hadn't*. He saw suddenly, in a moment of fear, what he had to do. He had to aim forward, close to the girl; then, God willing, the Russian would aim his shots aft. He moistened his lips. Come on, he told himself, fire carefully and get it over with. His finger tightened on the trigger, and the first bullet thudded wetly into the fish. And the second. But as his finger tightened for the third time, the *Ladoga Star* rolled slightly in the rising sea, and his bullet flew straight at the hide.

I've killed her, he thought. I've killed plenty of men before. But never a woman.

The revolver clattered noisily to the deck.

Kazat picked it up. "You are clumsy, Captain. Or perhaps nervous?" He leaned over the hold. "I notice you didn't fire aft. I wonder why." He fired three times into the stern section of the fish hold. After each shot he paused, very deliberately, and listened, and studied the faces of the crew. But without the hoped-for result.

He was disappointed. But his suspicions were too deeply ingrained to be weakened by lack of proof.

He was the last of the boarding party to leave. As he swung over the rail, he took a long last look around the deck of the *Ladoga Star,* as though even at the eleventh hour he expected to spot some evidence of guilt. But whatever secrets the trawler had, she kept.

"Three cables," he said briefly. "And no tricks."

He swung down the falls, and the launch went chugging away.

Carl Ekolf watched it butting awkwardly through a rising sea toward the gunboat. He gave no sign of what he was thinking, but against the darkness of the deck rail his knuckles glinted white. After a while he beckoned to one of the crew.

209

"Raise the trawl," he said. "Prepare to get under way. And tell Waldi to look to the girl."

The bullet had ricocheted; and a splinter of wood had plowed a neat little furrow, some eighth of an inch deep, across the crown of Christabel Barlow's head. If she had been holding her head at a different angle or if she had been two inches taller, she might well have been killed. As it was, she passed out largely through shock.

She came to within a few minutes. Her head ached. Her hair was sticky with blood. There was a glassy veneer over her eyes where their moisture content had started to freeze. And she was shivering violently. But she was very much alive.

She felt her head. Memories of little-heeded first-aid lectures didn't exactly reassure her: "Injuries in the neighborhood of the brain should always be treated as serious. . . . Keep the patient still and warm." But the lecturer hadn't, of course, dealt with patients careless enough to get their head injuries in an icebox! Her first impulse was to crawl to the warmth of Ekolf's cabin. Then she remembered the Russians. They must still be aboard; otherwise Iain or Carl would have come to find her. She had just resigned herself to a cold, uncomfortable wait when Waldi pulled back the panel.

It would be hard to say who was the more shocked. She, in her befuddled state, thought he was a Russian. He thought she was dying—for she was blue with cold and her face was a mask of congealed blood. He half dragged, half carried her out of the hold. Since she could speak no Finnish and he no English, it was some time before he realized she wasn't seriously hurt. He turned on the electric wall heater; he washed her face; he stuck plaster over the

210

furrow across her head, which had begun to bleed again in the warmth; then he tried to make her lie down.

Christabel, however, had other ideas. "What happened to the radar? Where's Iain?"

Waldi spread his hands.

"Where's Carl? Your skipper, Carl Ekolf?"

Waldi pointed to the bridge.

She slid gingerly off the bunk and worked her way around the cabin toward the companionway. She found that so long as she moved slowly and kept hanging on to something, she could manage quite well. Waldi followed her, making disapproving noises, but she took no notice of him.

She found Carl Ekolf leaning against the deck rail.

"What's happening?"

He turned. And for a moment his face broke into the most wonderful smile. "So! You are not dead!"

"No. Very much alive. Where's Iain?"

The smile vanished, and a chill of premonition swept over her.

"Is he—" She gestured to the Russian gunboat, now about to get under way.

"You go." He gestured below. "It is best."

"No!" She grabbed the deck rail. "Oh no," she whispered. "Oh no, no, no!" Her eyes were fixed on the gunboat in a glassy, unseeing stare.

Carl Ekolf took her hand. But she just wasn't with him; she was back in the little white-walled room in Lovisa, and Mackinnon in his sleep was saying quite clearly, "I'll be with you in a moment, Jamie." She knew something terrible was going to happen, but she couldn't take her eyes off the gunboat.

Kazat's launch had returned and was being hoisted aboard when a sudden shout rang out from the gunboat's bridge. Searchlights flickered over the sea. And there, midway between the two vessels, caught in their chalk-white glare, was the figure of a man. In his frogman's immersion suit he looked grotesque and evil—like some alien creature dredged up from the depths of the sea. (Hours later, when Christabel and Ekolf were able to piece events together, it was possible to work out what must have happened. Iain Mackinnon had fixed his limpet mine to the gunboat's keel; he had been about to swim back to the *Ladoga Star* when he'd seen Kazat's launch returning—returning, for him, at exactly the wrong moment. For his mine was fused—fused to explode in two and a half to three minutes—and he couldn't now move out from under the gunboat for fear of being spotted by the men in the launch. What his thoughts must have been as he waited quietly beside the mine it is best not to imagine, but he'd not have been human if he hadn't been tempted to defuse. But whatever temptations he'd had, he'd not succumbed. He'd waited until the launch was being hoisted, then made a desperate last-minute dash for the *Ladoga Star*. "But why," Christabel asked, "did he surface? Surely he'd have been all right if he'd stayed down?" Ekolf knew enough about underwater explosions to guess the answer. By the time Mackinnon had got away from the gunboat, he must have known the mine would go up in something less than a minute, and that if he stayed deep the force of the underwater explosion would degut him clean as a fish knife. So his only hope was to surface, to where the underwater pressure would be comparatively low; to risk being spotted in the seconds before the explosion.

And the risk hadn't paid off.)

He was seen. The searchlights swung onto him. Caught in their glare, he was naked—without defense. Before he could dive, the bullets thudded into him—burst after burst of gunfire, churning up the sea, shattering the grotesque frogman's body, turning the green of the Baltic red.

212

It happened so fast that Christabel had time only to put a hand to her mouth and give a queer little half-choked sob; then the searchlights had leaped from Mackinnon's body to the *Ladoga Star.*

She felt as Mackinnon had felt—naked and defenseless. So it's our turn next, she thought.

The glare of the searchlights was too bright for her to look straight into; so she looked a shade to one side, to the gunboat's bow. And there in the bow she saw the muzzle of a gun swiveling purposefully toward them. She watched it, fascinated—turning, turning, till the muzzle, like a blankly staring eye, was pointing straight at her stomach. Say your good-byes, she thought. This is it.

For a second everything seemed to hang motionless: moon and stars, trawler and gunboat. Then with a reverberating roar the gunboat split in two. A moment later the blast from the mine got through to her magazines. There was another and more terrible explosion; a blast of hot air swept the *Ladoga Star;* and the gunboat vanished. By the time the crew of the trawler had picked themselves up, all that remained of the Russian was a cloud of fine dust settling noiselessly onto the sea.

For perhaps ten seconds nobody spoke. Then Ekolf began to shout orders. "Put out the lights. Full speed ahead. Course 030°."

Christabel plucked at his arm. "Please!" she said faintly. "What is it?" His face was masklike.

He hates me, she thought, because Iain was his friend; he thinks his death was my fault, and I daresay he's right. But she didn't care. They had a chance now. It was a pretty slender chance, she knew, for it was long past the time of their rendezvous. But the Bat *could* have been delayed. Or it could, even, have got through to Moscow and be on its way back. So they still had a chance of saving the crew. She

213

licked her lips. She hoped she could make Carl Ekolf understand.

"The plane may be lost. Or it may even be coming back. I want to transmit to them."

She was steeling herself for a showdown—she only hoped she didn't faint in the middle of it—when, to her surprise, he took her arm. He spoke very gently.

"I know vat has to be done. We leave the Neugrund. Then I let you transmit."

"Thank you," she whispered.

She held tightly on to the bridge rail and stared at the sea, now patterned with the shadow of passing cloud. There's still a chance, she thought. It may be no more than a chance in a thousand; but if only it pays off, then everything—even Iain Mackinnon's death—will have been worthwhile.

19

"Keep down," Polhill had said. "There's still a chance." But the coast had come and gone in a flash; they had recognized nothing; and now ahead and on either side lay the same vast wilderness of white, as featureless as the eyes of a man who is blind. If they flew on, they'd hit the hills of the hinterland. If they climbed, they'd be shot to bits by the Russian ack-ack.

So they had to turn. Polhill wished to God he knew which way. At the speed they were flying a turn in the wrong direction would take them another thirty miles off course, and into all sorts of trouble: hills, defense posts, populated areas. Oakman was no help; he was staring fixedly ahead, frozen onto the controls. So the decision was his. He was about to yell at Oakman to turn to port when he saw the river: the thread of black unfrozen water cutting like a weal across the virgin white of the snow. If only, he thought, I could recognize it; it's a thousand-to-one chance, but miracles happen.

The river was in sight for something less than two seconds. It had almost disappeared beneath them when he saw the man-made scars: the paddocks and reservoirs, the canals and gates, and the great horseshoe arc of the dam. And one of the photographs he'd memorized in the operations room at Farnborough leaped to his mind; he could have fitted it detail for detail onto the scene below.

"Ken!" he shouted. "The hydroelectric scheme. We're over the Luga."

Quickly he adjusted the map under the central cross wires. By the time he'd got it fixed, their position was recorded none too accurately. But at least they knew *roughly* where they were.

"Starboard," he said sharply to Oakman. "Turn ninety degrees to starboard."

Oakman shuddered. He moistened his lips. His eyes lost their vacant stare and began to flicker this way and that in fright. But he banked the Bat into an accurate enough turn. His skill as a pilot didn't, in the moment of crisis, desert him.

Polhill peered at the wilderness of snow. It was featureless again. But not so terrifying now that it wasn't completely unknown. His eyes darted from the map to the terrain unfolding ahead.

"Safety height three hundred feet," he said. "In ten seconds we ought to cross the Narva–Leningrad railway."

They stared through the windshield, praying the railway line would be there. And it was: dead straight, a single track standing out darkly against the snow. Then they saw something else, away to their left: the lights of a town. Kingisepp, Polhill thought; we're too far to the north. They swung away. But not before they'd passed unpleasantly close to a cluster of factory chimneys, their stacks rising skyward like accusing fingers, each lit from beneath by the glow of its blast furnace and each with its plume of smoke aglow with refracted light. In the upcurrents of heated air the Bat juddered violently. Instinctively Oakman eased back on the stick.

216

"Keep down," Polhill said sharply. "Safety height's three hundred."

Oakman did as he was told. His fear had thawed a little by this time, but he was still only too glad to have someone to tell him what to do.

They were heading southwest now; no longer lost, but cutting back onto their original track. They weren't certain *exactly* where they were, but they could tell to within two or three miles. And, what was more, Polhill was able to get a rough idea from their moving map of what was coming up ahead.

"We should pass the tip of a lake soon—the Narvskoya Vdkhr."

Oakman nodded.

A quarter of a minute later a sheet of black came rushing toward them out of the west. And now, once again, Polhill reaped the reward for his study of the operations-room model. For he was able to recognize the diamond shape of the Vdkhr, foreshortened and blurred but unmistakable. They didn't in fact pass over the tip of it. They missed it by more than a mile. But they came close enough to give Polhill the chance to reset his map a little more accurately. One more decent check point, he thought, and we'll be spot on: as happy as if we'd homed on the trawler.

The trawler . . . For a moment his attention wandered. If she was lost, of course, they'd stand little chance of survival; for even if they got back to the rendezvous point, there'd be no one to pick them up. But he mustn't think of that; he must think only of what mattered most—getting to Moscow.

He made a series of quick calculations, waited till they'd passed another railway line, then gave Oakman a ninety-degree alteration of course: back onto their original heading, the heading for Moscow. As the Bat straightened out, he peered anxiously ahead.

"Another five degrees to port, Ken; and in sixty seconds we ought to spot a little round lake. Try and go slap over the middle of it. O.K.?"

Oakman nodded.

The terrain had gone featureless again. It was marsh, according to the map: a wilderness of low-lying grassland and swamp; an outpost of the Peipus depression. There were few roads across it, no railway lines and only the very occasional farmstead—nothing for them to check by. They could only hope for the best. They flew on. Polhill was beginning to fear he'd miscalculated, when they saw, almost dead ahead, the silver circle of the Ozero Samro—they'd expected it to be black, but the Ozero Samro, being that much farther inland, was frozen solid, and the moonlight was glinting on it and throwing off great shafts of reflected light. With instinctive skill Oakman eased the control column over and back again, and the Bat weaved slightly and then passed slap over the center of the lake, dead on course. Polhill gave the map a final adjustment, and they'd pinpointed their position: dead accurately.

From now on they could trust the moving map to tell them exactly what was coming up ahead.

"Phew!" Polhill wiped the sweat off his forehead. "Thank God for that!"

Oakman swallowed; his tongue ran over his lips. "Are we O.K.?" He sounded as if he just couldn't believe it.

"Sure, we're O.K. Safety height's still three hundred. Don't get any higher."

"Shall I increase speed?"

Polhill checked their chronometers. They were no more than five or six minutes behind schedule. "No," he said. "Wait till we're past Lake Ilmen."

218

So they'd got back on course, with their instruments set. It was almost too good to be true. The fact was, of course, that they had been lucky. Only some dozen recognizable check points had existed in a thousand square miles, and they'd had the good fortune to fly slap over one of them. As things had turned out, Polhill reflected, they were as well off as if they'd homed straight onto the trawler. Except, of course, for one small thing: they now stood little chance of surviving the flight back.

As if by thought transference, Oakman said slowly, "Wonder what happened to the trawler."

"God knows. She *started* to transmit all right."

"Hmmm! Poor Christabel!"

"Maybe," Polhill said brightly, "they'll be all lined up on the way back. . . . Good God, look out! We're too low!"

Oakman's attention had wandered. The nose of the Bat had dropped. And a belt of conifers was flashing by, less than a dozen feet below their wings. Oakman jerked back on the stick, and they soared out of danger—just in time.

From that moment they neither talked nor thought of anything but the problem of getting to Moscow.

Their saving grace was the moving map. Without it they wouldn't have stood a chance in a million. But now the exact position of the Bat had been pinpointed, they were able to weave this way and that on either side of their track, avoiding obstacles which they could see from the map were coming up ahead. At 2110, for example, they made a detour to avoid the town of Luga (without the map they would have come up to it so fast that they'd have been over the outskirts before they could have swung away) ; a little later they climbed to four hundred feet to avoid a ridge (without the map they'd have flown slap into it, because by the time they saw it visually it would have been too late for the Bat's controls to take effect) ; and later still

219

they let down to a hundred feet over the marshy approaches to Lake Ilmen.

As soon as they reached the lake, Oakman eased the throttles full open, increasing speed for the final run-in to Moscow. In a steady swing the needle of their air speed indicator moved up to Mach 1.34—a thousand miles an hour; fifteen hundred feet a second. In the Bat they noticed the change only in the slightly more muted whine of their jets, and in the increase in heat and vibration. But for anyone on the ground unlucky enough to be in their path, the effect would be catastrophic. For they were beyond the sound barrier now; and in their wake, Polhill knew, they'd be leaving a trail of broken glass, shattered buildings and burst eardrums.

He could picture, all too vividly, the effects of their passage: the devastated homes, the animals driven half mad with terror, the children deafened and maybe shocked to the edge of insanity. It was ironic, wasn't it? The object of their flight was to avoid suffering and war; yet the flight was itself an instrument of suffering. But better, he thought, for a few hundred Russians to be maimed than for countless millions to perish in the holocaust of a nuclear war.

Soon the heat inside the Bat became almost more than they could bear; and although they'd turned their air refrigeration to full they began to have difficulty in breathing, they were sweating like pigs, their instruments danced in a haze of heat and metal surfaces inside the plane became warm to the touch.

"Another fourteen minutes," Polhill muttered.

"Ugh!"

"Should see the decoy soon."

"What decoy?"

"The Thor. Remember? They're lobbing one east of Moscow."

220

"Hope they don't lob the bloody thing short!"

They flew on, hugging the ground—faster than sound—over the Polist marshes; across the rivers with the fairy-tale names—the Pola, the Yavon and the Osuga—until they came to the rising ground of the Smolensk plateau.

"Start climbing, Ken. Rate roughly a hundred feet in thirty seconds."

This, for Oakman, was the trickiest part of the flight. If they gained height too quickly, they'd be detected and shot down; if they gained height too slowly, they'd fly slap into the rising steppe. He flexed his fingers, moistened his lips, inched back on the stick and stared at the snow slopes hurtling toward him like great white combers out of the night.

The steppe didn't rise evenly, at a constant gradient. It rose and fell in a series of wavelike undulations, with the rises, generally speaking, a little longer and steeper than the falls. And the slopes were bathed in moonlight and snow: silent, desolate and unbelievably beautiful. Under happier circumstances, to have flown over them would have been a pilot's joy, like the ecstatic ski run of a dream. And even now, in spite of their appalling responsibility and danger, a residue of exhilaration remained; a sense of grace and daring and wonderfully harnessed power.

Their exhilaration was cut short by a burst of gunfire unpleasantly close to their wing tip.

So they'd been picked up.

Oakman weaved into a valley, and the gunfire was blocked by intervening hills.

They had less than nine minutes to go.

Nine minutes gave the Russians no time to move extra defenses into position. But it did, of course, give them time to alert those already there. Yet what defenses, in fact, were likely to be in a position to stop them? In this case the vastness of Russia (so often her salvation) was likely to prove

221

her bane. For even assuming as many as a million men were employed solely on ack-ack defense, and assuming the defense emplacements were concentrated within an eighty-mile radius of Moscow, this would mean less than one emplacement to every six square miles. And unless the Bat was unlucky enough to fly slap over an emplacement, there would be little chance—at the speed and height she was flying—of her being hit.

They flew on, tensely, bathed in sweat, coaxing the last iota of speed out of their jets, hugging the ground literally for their lives.

The steppes gave them no hint of what might be lying ahead. They lay white and innocent under the moon, apparently asleep. Soon they had topped the Kuvshinovo ridge—1,050 feet—the highest point on their run-in to Moscow.

There was a sudden flash, high in the eastern sky. And a brilliant light, whiter by far than any magnesium arc, blotted out stars, horizon and moon. Both Oakman and Polhill instinctively flung up a hand to shield their eyes. The light flickered, faded and died, leaving only a curious residue of rose pink staining the night. A Soviet nuclear warhead had liquidated the Thor.

It *might* help them. It *might* serve to divert Russian attention to the east of Moscow. It *might* mean that reports of their sonic boom would be put down to either the Thor or the Russian counterweapons. At any rate, it could do them no harm.

Soon they were letting down over the Staritsa-Volga marshes, coming up to the plains at the approaches to Moscow. They were no longer flying a dead-straight course, but were now weaving this way and that, to prevent the defenses throwing up a preset barrage in front of their route. It was tricky flying for both of them. If they got lost, even for a couple of seconds, they might never get back on course. If they misjudged their height, even by a fraction, they'd either soar up into range of the guns or bury themselves in the steppe.

The heat didn't make things easier. Polhill wiped the sweat out of his eyes. "Five minutes," he whispered, "to go. Last check on instruments."

They checked everything that possibly could be checked: their moving map, their engine temperatures, their fuel, their bomb-release mechanism, and their special transmitter for passing back the vital message "Mockingbird nested" the moment their bomb was released. And everything was just as it ought to be. In a moment of mingled incredulity and thankfulness it came to them both that they were on the very edge of success.

A streak of gold, like the "rain" from a child's firework, flashed past their wing tip, lunged into a belt of conifers and exploded into an incandescent pyramid of flame.

The shock of the explosion tipped up their port wing. They fell sideways—straight for the steppe. Desperately Oakman hauled back on the control column, but the snow slopes still came rushing toward them. Then, at the last second, the controls took effect and the Bat leveled up, scraped over a belt of trees and went hurtling off at an angle to her original course.

Polhill slewed around and stared at the sky behind them. But of the night fighter which had attacked them there was no sign. How it had managed to pick them up—a sliver of white streaking at fifteen hundred feet a second over the snow—he couldn't imagine. But it had come unpleasantly close. And it would, he knew, be back.

They swung around onto their original track while Polhill peered at the sky above and behind them. "Get as low as you can," he muttered, "and ready to weave."

They flew on. Tensely. Waiting.

It all happened incredibly fast. One second the sky was empty. The next a streak of silver was hurtling at them out of the night.

"Weave left!" Polhill shouted.

The Bat banked steeply. The rockets flashed past their wing tip and detonated with the most appalling roar against a slope of the steppe. And a second later, with an even more terrifying roar, the night fighter, unable to pull out of its aiming dive, hit the crest of a ridge, bounced three thousand yards and exploded amidst a belt of pines in a holocaust of ignited fuel and touched-off warheads.

The scene stamped itself indelibly on Polhill's mind: the great banners of purple flame leaping at the stars, the pine trees disintegrating in the all-consuming heat, the great billows of steam as rivers of molten fire bored through the snow. He shut his eyes. There, he thought, but for the grace of God go I.

By the time he opened his eyes—about three seconds later—the pyre of the night fighter was a mile behind them: a thing of the past, not to be thought of. All that had to be thought of was getting to Moscow.

They'd been driven to the north of their track, and they had to get back—quickly. For the eastern horizon now was faintly diffused with light from the homes and street lamps of the Soviet capital.

They cut back across the Kalinin–Moscow railway. The night fighters seemed to have vanished—probably, Polhill thought, we're too near the suburbs for them to fire. The ack-ack, too, was silent—unable, he guessed, to pick up the jinking course of the Bat.

They got a perfect final check for their map, resetting it for the last time as they passed over the intersection of two railway lines at the toe of a lake. Then they were on their

224

final approach, hurtling at zero feet over the Istra–Moscow railway.

There could be no weaving or jinking now: nothing but exact, dead-accurate flying in the seconds before they released their bomb.

They passed over their final check point, where railway and autobahn crossed.

"One minute to go." In the overheated air Polhill's voice was grating and strained.

Oakman's eyes flickered from his altimeter to the arc lamps of the autobahn, streaking past like sodiums in a continuous belt of gold. His hands were clenched tight around the control column. Sweat, salt and bitter, ran over his mouth.

"Thirty seconds to go. We're slap on. Hold her steady."

Away to their left a gun emplacement was firing blind into the night. The shells came nowhere near them.

Polhill's finger rested lightly on the bomb switch. His eyes were on his chronometer.

"Ten seconds . . . Hold her steady . . . Five. Four. Three. Nose up. One. Fire!"

The Bat jerked like a struck salmon as the weight of the bomb fell clear. Out of the corner of his eye Polhill saw the blast of flame as their self-propelled warhead shot off for Red Square—nothing could stop it now. He reached for the transmitter, already tuned in for him to pass back the vital message.

Then the aircraft was suddenly full of light. There was a blinding crack—a gasp of pain—a whistling clunking sound from the rear of their fuselage. And the Bat, caught in a sudden blast of gunfire, was flung half onto her back.

The release of the bomb, freeing them in an instant of both weight and drag, had jerked them high into the air. And the ack-ack gunners had spotted them. And hit them.

225

Oakman thought he was going to faint. Pain knifed through his right shoulder. But instinctively, with his left hand, he swung the control column over and forward, seeking to regain the safety that lay in the couple of hundred feet above the ground.

The Bat answered. Whatever else had been damaged, the controls were unimpaired. As they leveled off, the cut of the straps into Oakman's shoulder was unendurable. He heard, as if from far away, the noise of teeth grinding in agony; then, as the pressure faded, so did the noise, and he realized that the grinding teeth had been his. He blinked the sweat out of his eyes and peered at the ground ahead. The throttles were still wide open. He wanted them back. But he couldn't move his arm.

"Jim," he gasped, "pull back the throttles."

He couldn't hear himself speak. For a second he was terrified; he thought he'd been deafened by the blast; then he noticed that Polhill was switching over to the emergency intercom. So their radio had gone for a burton. The implications didn't at first sink in.

"Ken! Are you all right?" His navigator's voice came through on the emergency circuit.

"Can't move my arm. Pull back the throttles—just a bit."

Jim stretched over and inched back the levers. Their speed dropped, and the Bat became a little easier to handle.

"Can you keep a course, Ken?"

"Think so."

"Fine. Turn starboard a bit. Onto 320."

The Bat banked accurately enough and settled onto her new heading.

"Safety height's nine hundred. For quite a while. Now let's have a look at your arm."

Polhill unfastened his straps. He had a quick look at the

226

rear of the cockpit, checking damage; then he worked his way around to the back of Oakman's seat. They had been hit amidships. A dozen feet farther aft and their tail plane would have been severed; a dozen feet farther forward and the pair of them would have been colandered like sieves. They had been lucky. But a burst of splinters had sliced through the plates of Oakman's back rest, and one of them had lodged in his shoulder; not deeply enough to be dangerous, but far enough into the muscle to make his right arm virtually useless.

"There's not much bleeding," Polhill said. "Reckon you'd better be left as you are."

Oakman nodded. So long as he kept still and used only his left arm, he didn't feel too bad. He noticed Polhill tinkering about with the special transmitter which had been set up in the rear cockpit, beside the Doppler. He moistened his lips. "Is it badly damaged?"

"Yes."

"Can you fix it?"

"Not a hope."

Fear took root inside him. The fear spread, quickly, like a virulent poison, until his whole body ached with a numb, incredulous disbelief. "Did you get it back?" he whispered. "The message?"

"No."

No, he thought. Just like that. A wave of fury swept over him—blind, impotent fury. He felt like slamming the Bat into the steppe, putting an end to the whole futile affair. For he saw how it was. Unless they could pass back news of what they'd done, they might just as well never have done it. For the Russians weren't going to tell the world what had happened, were they? *They* weren't going to broadcast the news that the West, at the eleventh hour, had met their challenge; had proved by the landing of a reply that they still had a real deterrent.

So for all the good we've done, he thought, we might as well have been propping up the Farnborough bar.

It was ironic, wasn't it? The last cruel twist of fate. The stumbling block that no one could have foreseen or made provision for—that they should have got through, against all the odds, and then not been able to let the world know.

"Look out, Ken! We're low."

Polhill's warning got through to him. He corrected automatically, but sloppily, without interest. "What the hell does it matter?"

"Stop that." Polhill's voice was sharp. "We've still got a chance."

"A chance! A chance of what?"

"If the trawler's there, *she'll* get the message back."

That, he had to admit, was true. But he could see little hope of the trawler's keeping the rendezvous. "If she wasn't there on the way in," he muttered, "she won't be there on the way out."

"She might be. Pull yourself together. Have some guts."

Oakman was resentful, but the gibe got home. "All very well for you," he muttered. "You've two arms."

"Sorry, Ken. But don't give up. I'll help you."

The next twenty minutes were like a canto from Dante's Inferno, from one of the lower circles, full of weariness, disillusion and pain. For they now had all the anxieties and dangers of the flight in, without the certainty of achieving something worthwhile if they got to the end of it. They had to keep low. They had to keep an accurate course. And they had to avoid the Russian defenses—now thoroughly alerted. They were fired at twice. On the first occasion, the shell bursts came nowhere near; but on the second they flew slap over the town of Demyansk, and for perhaps ten seconds guns were opening up all around them. But they weren't hit. They kept heading northwest. Back to the Baltic.

They flew at just under the speed of sound, at Mach .9—fast enough to be a difficult target; slow enough to cut their consumption of kerosene. But no matter how economically they flew, their kerosene drained away inexorably, at a speed which appalled them. And long before they came to the coastal plain, they were drawing on their emergency tank, a mere hundred gallons—enough, at the most, for fifteen minutes' flying.

Oakman found he could manage to control the plane well enough with his left hand so long as Polhill, when the need arose, leaned over and adjusted the throttles and trim tabs. And they went limping west. Their saving grace was that they didn't have time to think of anything but the immediate problem of flying the plane.

When they were forty miles short of the coast, Oakman switched in the beacon. But the little green light was lifeless.

They knew then that the end was very near.

Soon they had fuel for only five minutes' flying. And their thoughts were of the sort that could no longer be dammed back.

They had just caught sight of the sea, right on their port bow—dark, nearly frozen and singularly uninviting—when the light at the base of their left/right indicator flashed suddenly green. A second later the indicator needle hoisted itself vertical, oscillated for a moment, then steadied to the right. They stared at it, as if at a vision. For a second they couldn't believe it. Then Polhill, frantically, began to work out a course.

"Twelve degrees to starboard, Ken. We're going to make it!"

Oakman shot out of the semi-coma he'd been sunk in for the last few minutes. "Range?"

"About twenty-five miles." Polhill switched on their emergency receiver, which worked independently of the main radio and which enabled the trawler to speak to him, but not—alas—him to speak to the trawler. And Christabel's voice, unexpectedly clear, flooded into the cockpit. She was reading off their course-to-close and range, parrotlike, like a weather recorder.

"Mockingbird O for Orange, turn four degrees to port and steer 340 magnetic: your range twenty-one miles . . . Steer 340 magnetic—steady—your range nineteen miles . . . Steer 340 magnetic—steady—your range seventeen miles . . ." Then, unexpectedly, "Oh, Ken, thank God you're going to make it . . . Steer 340 magnetic—steady—your range fifteen miles . . ."

Their fuel gauges were reading zero, and their port jet was losing power as it sucked in the last few drops of kerosene. But even, Polhill thought, if the jets *do* pack up, we've got enough flying speed to carry us a dozen miles. He ought, he knew, to be thanking God that after all their vicissitudes, the message which meant so much to so many would get through; but all he could think of was the wonderful longed-for moment of his reunion with Jennifer, and Robert, Nicola and Anne.

Then a sudden fear welled up in him. Maybe Ken couldn't eject; maybe his shoulder was too badly hurt for him to pull down the lever.

The same fear, a few seconds earlier, had swept over Kenneth Oakman. He'd experimented, reaching back with his injured arm and groping desperately for the ejector mechanism. And at last, after much effort and no little pain, his fingers had closed around it. He'd been too relieved at first to notice the lever was loose and several inches lower than usual. But as his fingers slid off the protruding bar and it moved, he realized something was wrong. The lever ought to be rigid, unyielding to anything short of a good strong pull, not threatening to come adrift in his hand. He unbuckled his safety harness. As Polhill leaned forward to check the instruments, he squirmed around and peered at the mechanism at the back of his seat.

It was shattered. Shattered beyond repair, by the splinters lodged deep in his back rest.

So he couldn't eject.

Things were going too fast for him. Five minutes ago he'd been resigned to dying; then he'd been reprieved; and now, it seemed, he was back to dying again. He realized Polhill was staring at him.

"Ken! Can you reach the lever?"

"Yes," he said. "I can reach it."

He was too played out to go on fighting. Hope had proved false too often; it no longer moved him. He'd given up. All he was waiting for now was for his navigator to eject; then he could close his eyes, surrender thankfully to the mounting waves of pain and let the Bat roll slowly onto her back and into the sea. But I can't close my eyes, he thought, till Jim's ejected.

They climbed to four hundred feet, their ejection height. They throttled back to two hundred and fifty knots, their ejection speed.

And Christabel's voice kept coming through: "Steer 340—steady—your range six miles . . ."

"You first, Jim. When we're two miles short."

"No, you. With your arm."

For God's sake! he thought. He saw what was going to happen. If his navigator realized he couldn't eject, he'd have heroic ideas about staying with him. By the time they'd argued it out, they'd be over and past the trawler; neither

231

of them would be picked up, and the message would never get through.

"You first." His voice was cold. "And that's an order. Eject now."

"Say, Ken, with your arm—"

"Shut up. I'm captain here and you'll bloody well obey an order. Eject."

Polhill stared at him, moistening his lips. For a second Ken thought he was going. Then his eyes focused on the drooping lever of the ejector.

"God Almighty, Ken . . ."

"Steer 340 magnetic." Christabel's voice was so loud she might have been with them in the cockpit. "Your range one and a half miles. Eject."

He did what he did not because he who all his life had been secretly afraid was made suddenly brave. But the waste and the pity and the pointlessness of it all appalled him. I've got to die, he thought. That's certain. But I'm damned if Jim's going to die as well. He stood up. He leaned over. And before Polhill realized what he was doing he had hauled down on the navigator's ejector lever.

He heard the slide of metal on well-oiled metal and the click of the securing pin as the mechanism locked home. He knew he hadn't a hope of throwing himself clear before Polhill's seat shot up and into him at over a hundred miles an hour. In less than a second, he thought, I'm going to die.

Time, in that last fraction of a second, had no meaning. Aren't I supposed, he thought, to start seeing my life in microcosm? To relive all the moments that have mattered most? But his mind refused to accept the fact that he was going to die, and his thoughts were not of the past but of the future. His body didn't seem to belong to him; there was a weightlessness to it, as if, it seemed to him, he were flying through air. His arms clutched Polhill tightly. We

232

must have ejected, he thought, and somehow I'm still hanging on to him, parachuting down and down and down. There was a taste of salt in his mouth. So we've hit the sea, he thought, and it seemed to him that the dinghy was inflating around them, and everything was warm and soft and comforting. So I'm not, he thought, going to die after all. Then the dinghy turned somehow into a bed, and on the bed with him was Christabel, and she was taking his head very gently between her hands and laying it on her breast. "Oh, Ken," she was saying, "I understand everything now. You don't have to put on an act any more. I know you're often afraid, and that what you're afraid of most is showing your fear; but I understand you and love you for what you are, not for the part you've made yourself play." And he was filled suddenly with a great peace. So this is happiness, he thought; this is what I've been missing all these years.

Then the ejector seat smashed into him at two hundred feet a second.

20

The *Ladoga Star* stood north from the Neugrund. We must hide, Carl Ekolf thought. Other gunboats will have seen the explosion, and they'll come to investigate.

But to hide was easier said than done.

There was only one hope. Northeast of the Neugrund a chain of reefs and sand bars reached out into the Baltic: a race of water too troubled for fishermen, in normal circumstances, to risk their boats in. But the reefs and sand bars—if only the *Ladoga Star* could live in them—would make it difficult for Russian radar to pick them up and Russian gunboats to follow. So they headed for the shallows.

As they stood north, Carl Ekolf watched the weather. It, too, he thought, could be an ally. For behind the cold front now passing over them, banks of mist were beginning to roll down from the north. The mist was thin and patchy as yet; but it would thicken, Carl knew, during the night. And it was like the reefs and the sand bars: it could either save them or damn them.

Soon the water ahead grew dark and choppy. Carl sent two men into the bow with plumb lines. He reduced speed. He looked at his watch.

"You transmit now," he said to Christabel. "But for a little time only. Unless the plane picks you up."

234

She nodded. She switched on first the radar and then the special coders. But there was no response. She wasn't altogether surprised—if the Bat *had* got through, she thought, it would have been a near miracle—but she could have wept with the pity of it. She waited five minutes, then switched on again; and again there was no response. By the time she got around to making the third attempt she had almost lost hope.

But this time, as if in answer to a last-minute prayer, their transmissions were reflected back—by an aircraft low in the east.

It *must* be the Bat, she thought; somehow, against all the odds, they've made it.

She realized she was trembling, and—to her fury—having to hang on to the bridge rail to stop herself fainting. Now pull yourself together, she thought; stop acting the Victorian miss with the vapors and get busy talking them in. She spoke breathlessly into the transmitter. "Mockingbird O for Orange, turn four degrees to port and steer 340° magnetic; your range twenty-one miles . . ." Oh, it's just like a fairy story, she thought; it's all coming right in the end. She passed the range and bearing of the aircraft to Carl, and lugged her transmitter onto the deck space aft of the hold—she had a good view from there of the sky astern. Now careful, Ken, she thought, with the ejection, and in five minutes we'll be together and Jim will be on his way back to Jennifer and we'll have saved the world from a nuclear war.

The *Ladoga Star* rolled uneasily beside the reef, her lights out, her engines idling, and little wisps of sea mist drifting across her bow.

"Waldi! Masa!" Carl's voice echoed down from the bridge. "Sling a scrambling net over the port quarter. And get bearings on the parachutes as they hit the sea."

235

They waited—tensely—straining their ears for the whine of jets and their eyes for the silhouette of the plane.

One of the fishermen saw it first. *"Tuolla se on."* He flung out an arm; and away on the horizon, glinting in the sporadic patches of moonlight, they saw the pinhead of silver. A moment later the fading whine of jets came to them softly out of the night.

She came straight at them, like a ghost plane out of the opalescent layers of mist. Her silhouette grew larger, darker, more clearly defined. "Now!" Christabel whispered. "Now!" And as if triggered off by her command a black bundle shot suddenly out of the nose of the plane. There was a muffled explosion, and she could follow—quite easily—the glow of the propelling cartridge as it soared in a great arc across the sky. The seat fell clear, and the parachute unfolded gracefully, almost overhead.

She waited for the second ejection.

But nothing happened.

"Quick!" she whispered.

The first parachute drifted into the sea and collapsed, only a few cables away, among the shallows and reefs of the Namsi. But of the second ejection there was no sign: no explosion, no upthrust of black from the cockpit, no glowing cartridge, no parachute. Nothing.

So one of them wasn't going to eject. She knew intuitively it was Ken.

She knew the facts about air crew ejection: that pilot and navigator had to eject pretty well simultaneously, because as soon as one of them ejected, the plane went out of control. So what happened next came as no surprise to her; it had, on the contrary, all the horrifying fascination of the inevitable.

For perhaps three or four seconds after the ejection the Bat held course. Her throttles were closed; one engine had cut and the other was idling, so she flew quite slowly. She

236

was almost directly overhead when she started to turn onto her side, like a tired, rudderless ship surrendering to the inevitable sea. She rolled over slowly at first, then with gathering momentum. She rolled right onto her back, and plummeted like a falling star into the sea.

She hit the water with a clap like an exploding bomb. Her wings were ripped off. Her fuselage disintegrated. And, as the last drops of kerosene in her tanks ignited, a circle of flame leaped out of the wreckage.

Christabel's microphone fell to the deck. She moaned. Her hands opened and closed. She tried to shut her eyes, but the flames had the compelling fascination of a nightmare come suddenly and terribly to life. She couldn't take her eyes off them.

The flames spread. They got larger and fiercer, till even from the deck of the trawler she could feel their heat. And it came to her in a moment of horror that she was reliving the dream she had dreamed six nights ago at Culdrose, and that somewhere among the flames was the body of Kenneth Oakman. She screamed. A great roaring, like the rush of a mighty wind, filled her head. She tried to claw her way over the deck rail and into the flames. But hands gripped her shoulders, holding her back. And then, through the roaring, she became aware of a voice that was saying, quietly and judicially, over and over again, "Those who play with fire must expect to be burned."

But it's not me who gets burned, she thought. It's other people: the Russians on the road to Lovisa, Iain Mackinnon, the crew of the gunboat, Ken. Oh, Christabel Barlow, she thought, what have you done? What has your meddling led to? You had your warning not to play with fire: that dream at Culdrose. But you had to go on, like a child striking matches in front of a gas stove. And because you wouldn't stop playing with fire, other people, all along the

237

line, have died in the flames you've triggered off. You told yourself it was all in a good cause; that you'd save the world and the man you loved. But what have you done? You've burned the man you love to death. There. In front of your eyes. The roaring in her head rose to a great crescendo. This can't be happening to me, she thought. I'm an ordinary, everyday girl who works on aircraft instruments; my world is a nice little niche in the affluent society, not being shot through the head and made to watch the man I love being burned to death. Oh, God, she thought, I'm not so very wicked, am I? What have I done to deserve this? The roaring stopped; everything became suddenly very quiet; and in the silence it came to her, in a moment of truth, that the aircraft instruments she was so proud of designing were the cause of it all: that everyone in her special world was tarred with the same brush, from the technicians who designed and built the planes and their instruments right down to the casual laborer who hedged and ditched the airfield perimeter. They were all Prometheans, players with fire, and the world she had thought so safe and affluent was in fact a world of touch paper, held to a powder keg. It was the last straw, this turning upside down of values she'd all her life taken for granted. I just can't stand any more, she thought. Then the voices started: sometimes her own voice, sometimes other people's. "You're very sure of what's right and wrong, aren't you?" "What's the water bug doing, Jim?" "When's my daddy coming home?" "I *promise* you, Jennifer, we'll get him back." "I think he's just plain scared." "I'll be with you in a second, Jamie." I wish I were a child again, she thought: at my mother's breast, when all the world was warm and soft and comforting. I wish the last week could be sponged away. And I could forget. Sleep and forget. Sleep and never wake up.

The voices stopped. The flames on the sea flickered and

died. Oh, Ken, she thought, where are you now? Her head felt numb, and her body curiously empty. In the bright white light of the arc lamps the deck of the *Ladoga Star* seemed to be undulating: slowly at first, then faster and faster. She shut her eyes. She felt herself falling. The deck swung up and hit her, and oblivion came like a benediction.

They had no time for fainting women—for the *Ladoga Star* was among the reefs of the Namsi. One of the fishermen hauled Christabel away from the scuppers and wedged her behind a fish crate, so there'd be no chance of her sliding over the side. Then the crew were having to call on all their skill to get alongside the parachute.

They edged up to it slowly, head into wind, between a hump-backed shoal and a wicked-looking reef whose jagged teeth showed only momentarily in the troughs of the waves.

When they were a couple of cables away, the parachute sank. But by this time they could see the dinghy quite clearly, bobbing about among the waves. There was only one figure in it, of course, and he was slumped across the rubber floor, taking little interest in their approach. Carl guessed he was either wounded or unconscious.

"Waldi! When we come 'longside give him a hand."

The *Ladoga Star* rolled uneasily. Carl rang for dead slow, and the trawler lost way, yawing awkwardly; one moment it looked as though she'd run the dinghy down, the next as if she'd swing wide of it. But Carl knew what he was doing. At the right moment their port quarter brushed the rubber gunwale. Waldi slithered aboard, and the dinghy was grabbed and secured to the scrambling nets.

It took them five minutes to get Polhill into the *Ladoga Star*.

He was only half conscious. For the ejection hadn't gone well.

He'd not been prepared for it, either mentally or physically. His anti-flash visor wasn't lowered, and his arms weren't tucked in. As a result, he was flung clear of the plane awkwardly, and his shoulder dislocated. His first reaction at finding himself soaring unexpectedly through the night sky had been one of shocked disbelief. Then the jerk of the parachute straps on his injured shoulder had made him faint.

He'd come to a couple of minutes later in his half-inflated dinghy to find himself being towed downwind by the collapsed parachute. Releasing the harness had brought him again to the no man's land of semi-consciousness, with every move of his arm sending red-hot needles of pain across his shoulder and back. But when Waldi came slithering into the dinghy, he fought the waves of pain down. He knew what had to be done.

"A transmitter!" he gasped. "Where's your transmitter?"

When he discovered Waldi spoke no English, he could have wept with frustration. So I can't faint yet, he thought—not till they get me aboard.

It didn't take long for Waldi to realize where the airman was hurt. He thought of trying to strap up his arm in the dinghy, but with the *Ladoga Star* yawing among the reefs it wasn't possible. So with the other fishermen helping, he hoisted Polhill across his shoulder and began to claw up the scrambling nets as carefully as he could. It wasn't an easy climb. Each time the trawler rolled, bumping them against the hull, he could hear the airman's teeth grinding together like stones in a mill. But at last Polhill was lowered onto the deck.

"Christabel," he whispered. "Where's the girl?"

They fetched Carl, the only one of the crew who spoke English.

To start with, Carl thought him delirious; his talk of

mockingbirds and nets just didn't make sense. Then he got it.

"Your radio was damaged? You must our radio use to pass your message?"

"Yes."

"Our radio is short-range. We cannot to England transmit."

Polhill shut his eyes. "Then transmit to Finland," he said faintly. "To someone you trust, who can pass the message on."

Carl nodded. "That I can do."

"I'll come with you." Polhill tried to struggle to his feet, but without much success. They wanted to carry him below, to see to his shoulder; but he insisted they take him to the radio room.

Carl Ekolf got him to write down the words "Mockingbird nested" in English. Then he sat down to transmit a signal to Lovisa, to be delivered immediately and in person to Juhani Kellala—"Personal from Carl," the signal read. "Most urgent. See that the message MOCKINGBIRD NESTED, SIGNED OAKMAN, is passed at once to the British Government."

As he heard the message transmitted, Polhill shut his eyes. At last, he thought, it's all over, and I don't need to fight any more. He surrendered thankfully to the waves of tiredness and pain now sweeping over him like great rollers after a storm. Then, as he was on the brink of unconsciousness and thinking of the moment of his longed-for reunion with Jennifer, a small niggling doubt lodged in his mind. The doubt grew. It refused to be dislodged.

For the captain of the trawler was repeating the message into his transmitter over and over again.

Polhill could guess why. At first he refused to think about it; it was so much easier simply to drift away into his com-

241

fortable world of semi-consciousness, where it didn't matter a tinker's curse whether the message was getting through or not. Then he remembered Oakman's death, and how much was at stake. Wincing, he tried to haul himself across to the transmitter.

"Let me try."

He could guess what had happened. The Russians had realized no message had been passed back, and they were now blocking every channel in a desperate effort to stop the news leaking out. But they couldn't, it seemed to Polhill, block all the frequencies all the time.

The transmitter crackled and moaned, like an old-fashioned crystal set. At last Lovisa acknowledged Ekolf's call and listened to it in comparative quiet, but a moment later they were driven off the air in a maelstrom of high-pitched shrieks, and no amount of tuning could bring them back.

So they had no means of telling for sure whether their signal had been understood.

Carl *thought* it had got through. He *thought* he'd heard the Lovisa operator repeat it correctly before he was jammed off the air. But he couldn't be sure.

For all that, he smiled reassuringly at the airman. "You can rest now," he said. "I have passed your message."

"Did it get through?"

"I think so."

"You think so! God in heaven, man! The fate of the world depends on it. You make damned sure it's got through!"

Now it had occurred to Carl that whenever he used his transmitter the Russians would be able to get a radio fix on the *Ladoga Star*. If he transmitted too long, too often, from the same spot, he'd have a swarm of gunboats about his ears. And this time, he knew, they wouldn't board his trawler—they'd sink her on sight. But he doubted if his

242

English was good enough to make the airman understand. "You rest now," he said. "I transmit again soon."

"You transmit again now!"

"The Russians"—Carl Ekolf spread his hands—"they board me once. Next time they sink me."

"You must risk it, man! Even if we *are* sunk, we *must* pass on the message."

Carl pursed his lips. He tried to explain that it was no good transmitting blindly on a frequency that was jammed; that it was best to wait, then try later from another position. But Polhill was in no mood to listen. Pain, exhaustion and shock had warped his judgment and blinded him to every need but one. Only, it seemed to him, if they got back the message would all the terrible things that had happened in the last seven days make sense.

"If you won't go on transmitting," he muttered, "I will." And he began to haul himself, slowly and painfully, toward the radio.

"Skipper!" A frightened shout from the bridge and a seaman came clattering down the companionway. "Reefs dead ahead!"

It was no time, Carl Ekolf decided, for half measures. He nodded at Polhill. "Take him to my cabin," he said. "See to his shoulder. But if he makes trouble lock him in."

As he scrambled on deck he could hear the hiss of waves creaming over the reefs on the Namsi.

Polhill felt physically sick. Anxiety, frustration and pain blinded him to every need but one. He tried to claw his way to the transmitter, pushing the fishermen aside. They did their best to be gentle with him. But when he made a grab for the switch, one of them knocked up his arm. With the inevitable result. He fainted.

They lowered him onto a stretcher and took him below. They laid him on Carl Ekolf's bunk. They stripped off his

243

overalls and immersion suit, and reset his shoulder. Then Waldi gave him a shot of morphia. They had just made him warm and comfortable when another fisherman lurched through the doorway, carrying the girl. She was still unconscious.

They were none too sure what to do with her. Waldi—who was the expert on first aid—listened to her breathing; it seemed normal. He looked at the splinter furrow across her scalp, and it seemed too shallow to be dangerous. Yet she was still unconscious. They bathed her face, but she showed no sign of coming around.

"Head wounds are strange," Waldi said judicially. "We must keep her warm and still."

So they made up a bed on the cabin deck, loosened her clothes and wrapped her in blankets. And by the time they'd finished, Carl Ekolf's cabin looked like the ward of a hospital. They wondered whether one of them ought to stay in the cabin; but decided, after a brief discussion, they were likely to be of more use on deck. So they left them, unconscious, side by side: the two strangers who had brought in their train such sudden and terrible violence.

The *Ladoga Star* hugged the shallows.

With mist rolling down from the north, the lightships out of commission and Russian gunboats patrolling the sea lanes, it was a night for strong nerves and first-class seamanship. They wouldn't have survived an hour if it hadn't been for Carl.

As a young man, before the Russo-Finnish War, Carl Ekolf had often come crayfishing among the reefs of the Namsi and Kosaya. Few fishermen, either side of the Baltic, knew the area better. And his knowledge was tested now as never before. Twice in the next couple of hours the *Ladoga Star* grounded (the second time they had to lighten her by

244

jettisoning part of their catch); once she missed an under-water reef by a matter of feet; and once only a single out-crop of rock stood between her and a searching gunboat. But she survived. As the hours passed she gradually inched her way north. And whenever Russian jamming eased off, Carl broadcast to Lovisa.

And it seemed to him unbelievable that one of his signals shouldn't be picked up.

Then, in the small hours of the morning, the gunboats suddenly disappeared from their radar screen. Either, Carl thought, they've lost track of us, or else the search has been called off. By 3 A.M., the *Ladoga Star* was clear of the shallows and heading fast through the mist for Finland. Maybe, Carl thought, our message has got through, and the Russians know it and realize they've nothing to gain by going on with their search.

About an hour after they gained the open sea, Waldi came up to the bridge. "The airman is conscious," he said. "I think he wants you."

"And the girl? Is she conscious too?"

Jim Polhill came to with a splitting headache, a nasty taste in his mouth and the feeling that something urgent had to be done at once. He couldn't for a moment think what the something was. Then he remembered. The message.

He hammered on the bulkhead.

The first fisherman to come could speak no English; but the second he recognized as the trawler's skipper.

Carl stayed with Polhill for the better part of an hour. In his halting English he told him everything: from the moment the *Ladoga Star* had cast off, almost twenty-four hours ago, from the quay at Valkom, right down to the last signal they'd tried to transmit, only a few minutes earlier, to Kallela's head office in Lovisa. And this time Polhill listened. And as he listened, he soon came to realize that everything humanly possible was being done to get the message through, and that all he could do was wait and hope: wait and hope and pray. It wasn't easy to lie inactive when so much hung in the balance. But there was nothing else he could do.

They drank mugs of hot, sweet tea brought up from the galley. They discussed the odds on their signal getting through, the odds on Kallela's passing it to the British Government in time and why the girl should still be unconscious when there seemed little physically the matter with her. Then a fisherman shouted down from the bridge that Carl was wanted on deck to see them through the inshore shallows.

Carl Ekolf got to his feet. "In maybe three hours," he said, "we land. Till then you can nothing do." And he left Polhill with his thoughts.

About ten minutes later Christabel opened her eyes.

She opened them quite suddenly and very wide. She blinked slowly, several times; then she put out a hand and ran her fingers uncertainly over the deck plates. She doesn't realize yet, Polhill thought, where she is. But even as he watched, memory came back; and her face crumpled into lines of pain.

"Christabel!" he said.

She jerked. She stared at him, and for a second her face was alive with hope. Then, when she realized the figure on the bunk was Polhill and not Oakman, she started to weep. She made no noise; the tears simply welled out in a silent uncontrollable flood, and they went on and on.

Polhill levered himself awkwardly to the deck. He knelt beside her and laid her head on his shoulder. "Don't cry, Christabel. It's all over now."

"He's dead, isn't he?" Her voice was without hope; she was simply registering a fact.

"Yes," he said.

"I wanted to help him," she whispered. "But I didn't help him, I killed him."

"No," he said gently. "You must never think of it like that. You did help us. You did everything you possibly could. It's not *your* fault Ken didn't get back." And he went on to tell her about the ejection: how Oakman had deliberately leaned over and pulled his (Polhill's) ejector lever.

She didn't get it. "But why, Jim? Why couldn't you both eject?"

He explained that the mechanism at the back of the pilot's seat had been shattered. "You see," he went on, "Ken was afraid I'd stay with him; that we'd both be killed, and the message would never get back."

She stared at him. "But surely by then you'd *got* the message back?"

"No. Our radio was hit."

She shut her eyes. She saw the way things were. "So it isn't all over at all."

"My dear, Carl's been transmitting the message 'Mockingbird nested' solidly for the last three or four hours. It's bound to have got through."

In spite of his efforts to reassure her, she sensed his uncertainty. "But you aren't certain it's got through. You can't be!"

"Not," he said slowly, "a hundred per cent certain. But I *am* certain of one thing: there's nothing more we can do."

There was a long silence; then he realized she was weeping again.

"Christabel," he said gently, "try to see things in proportion. Ken's dead. But millions of other people are going to live."

"But I don't know the millions of other people. I don't care about them. And anyhow, if the message hasn't got back they *won't* live."

There wasn't anything he could say to that.

Outside, the mist grew gradually thinner and paler. Soon it was the false dawn: those few minutes before sunrise when the world is especially still and quiet.

He shifted the weight of Christabel's head off his shoulder. "Jim!" Her eyes were suddenly anxious. "You're hurt!"

"Not badly."

She scrambled to her feet. "What a beast I am. Leaning on a shoulder that's hurt." She made him lie down while she inspected Waldi's bandages with a critical eye.

"Your arm," she said, "ought to be in a sling."

He didn't try to dissuade her as she hammered on the bulkhead for more bandages, fussed over him like a novitiate nurse and finally set his arm, quite professionally, in a sling. Anything, it seemed to him, which occupied their minds was a blessing.

But when her Florence Nightingale act was over, her thoughts soon turned again to that which mattered most. "You know," she said, "I can't think straight yet. All I can think of is Ken. But I suppose in time I'll see it's all been worthwhile, if only we *have* stopped a war; if only the message *has* got back."

He couldn't quarrel with that. It was the way he saw things himself. It was the uncertainty that racked them— the not knowing whether all they'd been through had been in vain.

Time passed slowly.

The *Ladoga Star* had less movement on her now; probably, Polhill thought, because we're coming into the shelter of land. He heard the tinkle of the engine-room bell as Ekolf rang for an alteration of speed; he heard the thud of sea boots on the deck above and the thousand and one little sounds of a ship at sea—the pulse of engines, the muted hiss of the bow wave and a host of small complaining noises from bulkheads and deck plates.

Then he heard something else: an unexpected burst of music, followed by the sound of excited voices and running.

A second later the door burst open, and Waldi was jabbering excitedly in Finnish. *"Tule nopeasti radiohyttiin!"* He grabbed Polhill by the hand.

They understood the one word: *radio*. They scrambled after him.

There was a good deal of atmospherics from the *Ladoga Star's* receiver, for the volume had been thumbed up to maximum; but the interference had faded now to an occasional crackle.

"It is your BBC," Carl shouted from the bridge.

They waited tensely, in an agony of hope.

Faintly over the radio came the sound of church bells. They looked at each other. Surely the BBC European network didn't usually go in for church bells?

The bells stopped. There was a moment of silence. Then the announcer's voice, on the surface impersonal and matter-of-fact, yet infused with a pent-up thankfulness and joy too heartfelt to be altogether suppressed:

"To the people of the free world, good news! Last night the Royal Air Force, as challenged, landed their reply to the Russian ultimatum in the center of Red Square, Moscow. The reply was landed by a secret British weapon, capable of great accuracy and able to penetrate *underneath* the Soviet anti-missile defenses. Moscow Radio has already admitted a reply has been landed, and negotiations between the two governments are now under way.

"This demonstration of the West's strength has been greeted with joy and relief throughout the free world. At the end of this program we shall be bringing you on-the-spot reactions from Washington, Paris, Bonn and other capitals . . ."

The announcer went on to speak of tentative arrangements, sponsored by nations of the Afro-Asian bloc, for a disarmament conference in New Delhi.

So it had been done.

The sword of Damocles was back, at least for the time being, in its sheath.

Tension ebbed out of her, physically and mentally, as though a load had been suddenly lifted from both her body and mind. She hadn't realized just how overpowering the load had been until it was gone. And now that it was gone she felt, quite literally, reborn.

And it must be the same for everyone, she thought, in every country, all over the world. Mothers like Jennifer Polhill won't be weeping this morning as they feed their children; women like Mrs. Harley will be coming home; tycoons will be emerging like beetles out of their fall-out shelters; the world has had a reprieve. God grant, she thought, we put it to good use.

She walked across to the deck rail.

The sun was shining now, cutting great swaths of light across the water and laying bare patches of cobalt sky in one of which Venus the morning star still glinted, as pale as a Christmas rose. After a while she realized that Polhill was standing beside her. For a moment she was touched with sadness—if only it had been Ken . . . Oh, Ken, she thought, I wasn't much help, was I? I scotched our love before it could flower. Wherever you are, forgive me . . . But even as tears were pricking the back of her eyes, she knew instinctively that her sadness was transient, was like a melody played in a minor key. For what *I* feel just isn't important, she told herself. What does one broken heart matter when the world we know and love has been saved?

For she could see how things were. A low-level bomber was no sort of permanent answer to the problems facing East and West—apart from anything else, Bats in a few years would be as dead as the dodo—but at the moment of crisis, when more ambitious weapons had failed, they'd plugged a gap; and plugged it in the most effective practical manner. The question now was how to use the breathing space that the Bat had won them.

"Jim"—she turned to him suddenly—"what are you going to do when we get back home?"

"Go on flying Bats, I guess."

"And?"

"And hope our technicians get movin' and close the missile gap."

"Hmmm! I suppose that's one answer."

"Can you think of a better?"

"We could try lying down in Trafalgar Square."

He was neither surprised, shocked nor patronizing. "That's a thing, Christabel, each individual must work out for himself."

"But it's not the answer for you?"

"No. I thought about it. But it's not for me."

She stood by the deck rail, staring at the great pathways of light carved out of the sea. I wonder, she thought, what the answer is. Ken didn't know, and I don't know, but I've an idea Jim Polhill knows. And it seemed to her somehow fitting that at the end of all the violence, terror and death of the last seven days, a man as good and sane as Major Polhill should have survived.

"*Siirtykaa maikin keulasta oikealta puoleta!*" There was a sudden shout from the bridge. "Land on the starboard bow."

At first she could see nothing; then the mist shifted a little and she could make out, quite distinctly, a tree-capped headland, bathed in light: Finland.

Slowly a sense of peace stole over her. The days of doubt and fear were over at last. The night of the mockingbird had ended. And life went on. That was what mattered most. Life went on.

She turned to Polhill. "Jim!"

"Hmmm?"

"D'you think we'll have time to shop in Helsinki?"

"I reckon so. Why?"

" 'Why,' you thoughtless man! So we can buy your children some presents, of course."

"Yes," he said slowly. "There's some point, isn't there, in buying them presents now."